Monsters in My Mind

Ada Hoffmann

An imprint of Autonomous Press.

Weird Books for Weird People

Autonomous Press is an independent publisher focusing on works about neurodivergence, queerness, and the various ways they can intersect with each other and with other aspects of identity and lived experience. We are a partnership including writers, poets, artists, musicians, community scholars, and professors. Each partner takes on a share of the work of managing the press and production, and all of our workers are co-owners.

ISBN: 978-1-945955-08-2

Cover art by Chris Henry.

Contents

You Have to Follow the Rules 1
Self-Portrait as Bilbo Baggins 10
And All the Fathomless Crowds 12
Mama's Sword 24
Hippocamp 36
Moon Laws, Dream Laws 37
Memo From Neverland 48
Goblin Love Song 49
Atavist 50
Lady Blue and the Lampreys 51
A Certain Kind of Spider 65
The Siren of Mayberry Crescent 66
Evianna Talirr Builds a Portal on Commission 70
The Mother of All Squid Builds a Library 72
Turning to Stone 75
Crocodile Tears 77
The Self-Rescuing Princess 78
The Dragon-Ship 80
The Screech Owl Also Shall Rest There
    (written with Jacqueline Flay) 81
Taylan 101
Lament for a Faithless Prince 102
Ekpyrotic Theory 104
Feasting Alone 105
Synchronicity 108
How My Best Friend Rania Crashed a Party
    and Saved the World 109
The Parable of the Supervillain 129
The Company of Heaven 131
Abominable Snowman 140
Nightmare I 141
Ribbons 142
Blue Fever 143
The Pyromancer 151

The Mermaid at Sea World   153
Finding Shadow   154
An Operatic Tour of New Jersey, With Raptors   155
Under the Clear Bright Waters   162
Space Pops   172
Zori Server   173
Baku   181
Sage and Coco   182
Centipede Girl   190
The Changeling's Escape   194
What Great Darkness   195
Daphne Without Apollo   203
Miss Sprocket Tinkers   204
The Tooth Fairy Throws In the Towel   216
The Wives of Miu Fum   219
A Toast to the Hero Upon Her Defeat of
     the Wyrm of L'Incertain   220
The Chartreuse Monster   222

You Have to Follow the Rules

Two hours into Annalee's first convention, she started to notice things Mommy did not.

Of course, Mommy's noticing powers weren't very good. She'd said and said that the convention would have Star Wars, fairies, space captains, even a room the color of deep space where projected stars whooshed past, where Annalee could lie on her tummy and pretend to zoom through hyperspace. She'd said and said that Annalee could make friends, as if that was more exciting than a space-room. But she hadn't mentioned that the place would be *full* of people Mommy called friends — so thick with them that every step Annalee took, one almost hit her.

She had marched proudly into the building in her stormtrooper uniform, the Imperial March playing in her head. But after the long, long lines, the crowds, and the "TECHNICAL DIFFICULTIES" sign on the space-room, all Annalee could hear was noise. She covered her ears with her hands.

"Don't do that," said Mommy, peeling them off. "If we want to have quiet time, we use our words. Besides, you wanted to see the Stormtroopers Panel, and we're almost there."

When Mommy said "you wanted" she meant she'd said it would be exciting and Annalee had nodded or said "yes." Really it was Mommy who wanted to go to every panel, like a cargo ship visiting all the planets in the galaxy. Annalee pretended every room was a spaceport bar with an alien band playing, to explain the noise. There were lots of actors that she recognized, but they didn't act like the space captains they played on TV, even though *everybody* in the building was here to dress up and act like space captains. That was the whole point.

So the things Mommy could not see made as much sense as anything else.

First there were the doors in places doors didn't belong, like way up above Mommy's head. There was even a lying-down door in the floor. All the doors said, "DO NOT ENTER."

"Mommy," said Annalee, "why did they put a door in the floor?"

"Don't be silly," said Mommy. "I don't see a door in the floor."

The next panel was just vampires. None of the vampires had spaceships or even fairy wings. Annalee's feet got bored and drummed on the floor.

She turned her head to try to distract her feet. The wall at the side of the room had gone all clear like a mirror. The panel room was thick with people, but its reflection was thin. Everybody in the reflection had space to swing their arms. Everyone was a fairy or a space captain, with trailing flowers and white pupilless eyes. Half of them were children. Bad children, too — rocking, scratching, staring into space, or biting their nails, things Mommy told Annalee never to do. But when the people up front made a joke, they all laughed, soundlessly, even the ones who weren't looking.

"Mommy," said Annalee, "why did they make the wall a mirror?"

"I don't see any mirrors," said Mommy, straightening Annalee's stormtrooper helmet. "Are you playing a pretending game?"

Annalee shook her head.

When she saw the girl in the Jedi cloak, with the trailing flowers in her topknotted hair and the white pupilless eyes, she didn't tell Mommy.

Annalee liked the Jedi girl. She spotted her everywhere, sometimes on the other side of the mirror wall, but more often on Annalee's side, a few rows down, laughing at the same puns Annalee liked. At a Lego contest in the evening, the Jedi girl stood next to Annalee and worked quietly. Annalee built a TIE fighter, and so did the Jedi girl, only hers was an interceptor with pointy wings. When Annalee glanced at the interceptor, the Jedi girl glanced back. Annalee didn't often notice such things, but when the Jedi girl looked at her, she wanted to smile.

"You were so quiet and good," said Mommy after the Lego contest. "The whole time. I'm proud of you. I know places like this can be hard."

"I liked the Jedi girl," said Annalee.

Mommy's face made a great big smile. "You talked to a girl?"

"Not exactly."

"But there was a girl? You're making friends already?"

"I guess," said Annalee. "We didn't talk, but I liked her."

"Oh, Annalee, I'm so happy you found someone you like. Why don't you go up to her and introduce yourself?"

Annalee squared her shoulders. "Don't want to."

Mommy sighed, and her voice went soft like a Wampa's pelt. "People here aren't like the people at school, Annalee. They aren't going to hit you or call you names because you talked too long about Star Wars. If she's dressed as a Jedi, she probably likes it as much as you do. Please try."

Annalee just shrugged.

She didn't feel icky or bad when she thought about talking to the Jedi girl. But the Jedi girl had been fine just making TIE fighters, not talking, and besides, she wasn't here anymore. The building was already full of too many introductions. Earlier in the day, a man in a Starfleet uniform had swooped right down and scared her.

"Aren't you just the cutest little stormtrooper!" he said, tapping her on the helmet and making her wince. "What's your name?"

Annalee flapped her arms, warding him off. "I don't like you."

"Oh, come on," said the man, tapping her on the helmet again. "That's not a name."

Annabel ran away. Mommy had to chase her down to stop her from getting lost.

"What do you think you're doing?" said Mommy, huffing and puffing.

"Don't want to," said Annalee. She hadn't liked the man coming so close. It gave her creepy feelings, like being in a trash compactor and almost-crushed. "I didn't like him."

Mommy sighed. "I know you don't like strangers, Annalee, but this is a convention. People come here to make friends. He couldn't have known you don't like being touched."

"I told him," said Annalee. "I told him I didn't like him."

"But that's not what you say when someone is trying to make friends," said Mommy. "It's not polite. When someone introduces yourself, you say, 'Hi, my name is Annalee, what's yours?' That's the rule for introductions."

"He shouldn't have touched my helmet," said Annalee.

"Maybe he didn't know that," said Mommy. "You didn't ask him politely to stop, did you? Maybe he has Asperger Syndrome, like you, and he doesn't know how to behave around people. Now, come on. We're late for Time Machine Improv."

Annalee did not like Time Machine Improv. She couldn't tell where any of the jokes were, and the audience kept laughing for no reason. There wasn't even a single pun.

Mommy laughed so much that she had to get in a big line to try it herself, leaving Annalee in her seat. On the chair to the other side of where Mommy had been sat the Jedi girl. Annalee stared at her, wondering how long she'd been there, invisible.

The Jedi girl took a paper and pencil from the folds of her robe and scribbled something. Then she folded the paper and handed it to Annalee, along with the pencil, being careful not to come too close.

The rules are different where I come from, said the paper, *Where I come from, no one touches your helmet unless you tell them it's okay.*

Annalee blinked, then picked up the pencil.

Where do you come from?

She handed it back.

I come from just past the wall. It's always a convention there, but a good convention, not like this one. Where I come from, you can rock or cover your ears or run away from people and no one will tell you that you're bad.

Annalee looked around. There was a door below the stage, and another one in the ceiling. They all still said "DO NOT ENTER."

Do you come from past those doors? Annalee wrote. She hoped that the Jedi girl did. That it was another world, like fairyland or Coruscant. *The ones grown-ups don't see?*

I do. Would you like to visit?

I can't. They all say "DO NOT ENTER."

Yes. That's to let us know who we can trust. If you go through a door when the door says you shouldn't go through, then we know you won't follow the other rules, even when we spell them all out. But there are other doors.

Annalee chewed her lip. She wasn't supposed to go places without Mommy. But going to another world was different, maybe. Lots of people in stories went to fairyland without their mommies. Even Anakin Skywalker, who was Annalee's favourite because their names were so close together.

And you have Star Wars there?

Of course.

Can Mommy come too?

If you like. It's dangerous for grown-ups. Grown-ups think their rules are right and ours are wrong.

But where I come from, you HAVE to follow our rules.

Annalee took the paper and hurriedly scribbled.

Tell me your rules.

"What *is* this?" said Mommy, staring at the paper.

"The Jedi girl gave it to me."

"Oh! So you two are talking now? I'm so proud of you! What's her name?"

Annalee hesitated.

Mommy sighed. "Well, I guess we have to take this one step at a time. I'm glad you're starting to get along. So you and she are playing a game about rules? It must be an interesting game."

"I don't know," said Annalee.

She remembered looking through the mirror-wall and seeing everyone rocking and squirming. She did not think this was just a game.

RULES, said the paper in Mommy's hand.

Do not go through the doors that say "DO NOT ENTER." There is another door on the top floor

that doesn't say it. Ask permission to that one before you touch it. You can tell who lives here by their eyes. Most

of them like to speak with notes or signs. Don't speak to them out loud unless they tell you it's okay.

Ask permission for everything. Stay in your own space. If you stay in your own space, you can do

whatever you like; there is no wrong way to stand, or sit, or look at someone's face. Remember that when you

talk to others. Don't tell them they are wrong.

"I don't understand this game," said Mommy. "I don't see any doors around here that say 'DO NOT ENTER.'"

Then she looked up from the paper and stared all around.

"Oh," she said weakly. "I see them now."

Then she took hold of Annalee's wrist and started walking very, very quickly.

Annalee had to tell Mommy twice not to go for the "DO NOT ENTER" doors. Mommy kept veering towards them.

"You can't do that one," said Annalee. "That's against the rules."

"Annalee," said Mommy, "do you remember what 'scared' means? I'm scared. These doors weren't here a minute ago and doors aren't supposed to behave this way and I just want to see if I'm hallucinating or not. Why can't I just peek through for a second? Who would it hurt?"

"The door you can use is on this floor," she reminded Mommy. Mommy's noticing powers were even worse than Annalee thought, if she didn't remember they'd already gone up all the escalators.

Mommy's voice rose very high. "Yes, but I can't *find* it."

When Mommy found the unmarked door, she squeezed Annalee's wrist so hard Annalee thought her hand would come off, like Luke Skywalker's, and she'd need a new one. The door was hidden behind a row of tables, and it stood tilted over in the wall. Mommy ran for it.

"No, wait," said Annalee as she was dragged along. "You have to ask it permission first."

Mommy breathed hard. "Honey, that doesn't even make sense. Doors don't talk. These rules are just pretend, don't you see?"

Annalee tried as hard as she could to remember all the polite words Mommy had taught her.

"Door," she said, "may we please go through?"

The door opened.

"Thank you," said Annalee, because Mommy had taught her that, too.

The two of them hurried through.

The other side of the door looked just like the other side of a mirror. The carpets and walls were the same color; the big schedule on the wall had the same logo at the top, even though the writing on it was different; there were tables in the same places and stacks of piled-up paintings on them. But it was quiet, like in Annalee's room when she closed the door and couldn't hear Mommy's television anymore. And there was room to move around without crashing into anyone. Bad children just like Annalee wandered around on their own. They flapped their arms like chickens and spun in circles. Their eyes were blank white, without pupils.

Annalee suddenly wanted to hide in this room all the rest of the convention and not come out.

"Oh, Annalee," said Mommy. "This isn't a nice place."

The quiet and Mommy's disapproval were like both sides of the trash compactor again. Annalee didn't know how to get safely between them, how to explain that she liked it here. That it was wonderful. She knew Mommy was just about to pull her back out, and there was nothing she could do.

But Mommy didn't do that right away. She swallowed hard and said, "Well. We're here. We may as well look around. Maybe we can find the Jedi girl you were talking to. Is she here?"

Mommy walked in very quick circles until she saw a girl in a Jedi cloak. She wasn't the right girl: her hair was wrong, short and blonde like Tinkerbell. The real Jedi girl had dark hair in a topknot with flowers coming out, but Annalee couldn't see any topknots in the room, however fast she turned her head.

"There she is," said Mommy. "Stop shaking your head like that, Annalee. We found her. Now, I promise, if you two have been playing together and making up this whole game, that means she likes you. She's not going to hit you or call you names, and she's not going to mind if you tell her who you are. And that's how you can get to be friends. Please try it. For me."

"But the rules say—"

"Stop," said Mommy. "Stop. I don't want to hear about your rules. Do you understand? There is a whole world full of rules already, like 'don't insult people and run away from them,' and 'don't terrify your own mother half to death,' and you aren't following *those* ones. Why should you get to make your own? I am trying to help you learn and make friends, and this is just a thing that you have to learn. I'll show you."

"But—"

And Mommy marched right up into the pixie-girl's face.

"Hi," said Mommy. "I'm Annalee's mommy. I hear you two have been playing with Legos together. What's your name?"

Everything fell silent.

Jedi Tinkerbell stared up at Mommy with her blank eyes. There was a horrible flash, like a too-bright spotlight, and when the spots got out from in front of Annalee's eyes, Mommy was gone.

Jedi Tinkerbell walked away.

Annalee lay down in the floor and held her head in her hands.

She knew what Mommy would say if she saw her. *You can't curl up on the floor like that. It will make everybody worry about you. Come on, honey, get up.* But Mommy wasn't here.

Mommy wasn't here. Maybe the mirror people had killed her. Maybe they had frozen her in carbonite or sent her to another dimension. Mommy had broken the rules and Mommy wasn't here.

Annalee did not want to break the rules.

She closed her eyes and thought about rules. Maybe, she thought, just maybe she *wasn't* breaking the rules here, even though she had come in with the wrong mommy and then lain down on the floor and made everybody worry. Maybe everybody wasn't worrying. It was still quiet, and no one had touched her or yelled at her or even asked what was wrong. It was like having quiet time in her own room with her Star Wars blanket pulled up over her head. She could lie here as long as she liked, and it wouldn't hurt anybody.

So she lay there and breathed deep, until she had enough breaths in her to open her eyes and look up, and there was a slip of paper on the floor by her face.

We have a room here that's all dark, said the paper, *with stars on the walls. Want to see?*

For a minute Annalee wanted to scream. She wanted to say, *No! Not until you tell me what happened to Mommy!*

But she did want to see the room with the stars on the walls.

And maybe this was how things went in fairyland. Maybe when you went to another world to be a Jedi, you *had* to leave your mommy behind. Like Anakin Skywalker. He had been brave, and so would Annalee.

She took the paper and started to write.

The Jedi girl spoke only in notes, but Annalee didn't mind. They both lay on their tummies in the dark room and whooshed through hyperspace, stars flashing and streaking all around them. Annalee was sure that she was travelling millions of miles, leaving Earth and the Milky Way behind.

Finally they came out, and the Jedi girl hesitated extra long before scribbling another note.

You could stay here forever if you liked. It would be all Lego and dark rooms and Star Wars all the time. As long as you followed the rules, nobody would bother you.

Nobody would tell you that the way you do things in your own space is wrong. You could get white eyes like us and forget Mommy and be happy as long as you wanted.

Annalee chewed her lip.

This place's rules were better than Mommy's rules, and its space-room was better, too. Everything about it was better, except that Mommy couldn't live here.

And Annalee couldn't leave Mommy behind. Not forever, when Mommy might be in trouble or hurt or worried to death. Mommy had been bad, but only by-accident bad, only because she got so worried about Annalee having friends. Not bad like a Sith lord. Not hurting the mirror people on purpose.

No, she wrote, *I have to go and find her. But I'd like to come back some day.*

Then I'll teach you, said the Jedi girl. *There are doors to places like this everywhere. You just have to learn how to see them.*

Mommy was standing at the comics table leafing through a book. Annalee ran to her so fast that she crashed into her legs.

"Oof," said Mommy. "Hi, you. Watch where you're going."

"I'm here, I'm here!" Annalee shouted, wrapping her arms around Mommy. "I'm here!"

"Well, you're very excited about something," said Mommy.

She didn't yell at Annalee for going missing, or for leading her into the mirror world, or for not coming right back. It was like Annalee had just run to the bathroom for a minute.

She'd been mind-tricked, Annalee realized. She didn't remember any of it.

Annalee and Mommy went home with a bag of books so huge that Annalee had to walk funny with her arms wrapped around it. In the car, she pressed her nose to the glass and saw doors laid down in the middle of the street. At a funny angle in the outside of a building, or in the bark of trees.

Some of the doors said "DO NOT ENTER." Some of them didn't.

Every once in a while, in Annalee's reflection, she thought she saw the Jedi girl. Glancing at her. Then glancing away. Always leaving just enough space.

I have a friend, Annalee thought to herself. Then, smiling wider, *I have a world.*

Self-Portrait as Bilbo Baggins

I am barefoot, eight, and buried in ten thousand teddy bears
while you read to me. I pick them up in twos and threes,
match them to the nonsense names of dwarves.
I march them all around your room
in our little hole in the ground.

I pile the pillows up to make a mountain. Inside
hides a white bear half my size.
I can't cram in all the dwarves
for their dashing around, the theft,
the secret doors. I arrange
and rearrange, undaunted.
You tell my mother later,
"I don't know if she was listening,
but she had a good time."
Over casserole you explain
that hobbits are three feet tall, like me.
I want to stay this size forever.

Later, your *Lord of the Rings* waits on onionskin,
marked by a ribbon. I am nine now, and practical.
You are the hairy-toed audiobook playing,
entertainment while I clean my room,
until it bores me. You have the patience of meadows
but this is an awfully long book,
and there are things to do.
Pictures to draw.

Maybe you already see it,
how thirteen will break me, how even eleven

will grind. Maybe you are a wizard. You're too wise
to call me ungrateful, but maybe you see
how I'm growing too slow and too fast, both at once,
like a lopsided spider. And you are growing
sick.

There will be screaming between these walls
when the poison in your veins and mine
finds its voice. There will be creatures,
veiled in shadow, who ride in through the cracks,
whispering,
Shire.

I know none of this. I have not longed to be invisible.
I have not yet known the hates and needs
that make men wraiths. I am eleventy-one and three feet tall,
and not even I understand
what I have got in my pocket.

And All the Fathomless Crowds

Queen's University
Department of Survival
SURV 110
Final Examination
April 21, 2031
Professor Lita Yao

Name: Sandra Chakarvarthi
Student Number: 1715-5730

Written Component, Part 1

Q. When is it advisable to use deadly force against a Non-Mind?

A. When you are threatened, and not before. Attempting to exterminate Non-Minds on sight is a sign of Romero Disorder. In the days immediately after 12/12, many human survivors developed this disorder. The sheer number of Non-Minds overwhelmed them, and each human died of exhaustion mid-rampage — if the Non-Minds didn't get them first. Arguably, Romero Disorder itself is a form of Mindlessness.

Practical Component, Part 1

Five hours, forty minutes, and fifty-eight seconds to go.

Your first destination is City Hall, and you've picked a lakeside route because that's what gets you top marks: Professor Yao needs to know you can deal with any terrain. There are plenty of creatures on land who cannot enter running water. But there are creatures in the water as well. You split the difference and jog along the wave-lapped rocks, past the Time Statue, which was once a pair of simple metal blocks but nowadays dances to its own irregular ticking sounds, half-melted. Sunlight glints off the water, drawing your eye to the storklike walk of the windmills on the other side.

First lesson: Apart from the insides of Certified Homes, everything is alive.

Confidence is more important than speed. You can't look like you're fleeing. So you jog along, not too fast, and fix the thought deep in your centre. *I am safe in this place. I refuse to be afraid.*

It's not like you haven't walked this route before. Even walking from your residence to the classroom is a form of practice. All year you've gathered your friends on assignments and walked all around the city: visiting shut-ins in their Certified Homes, harvesting resources from emergency stores, gaping at the beauty of the lake and the old buildings. But alone, with the clock ticking and your grades at stake, the trip gives you jitters.

I refuse to be afraid.

A tentacle of pure water rises out of the waves and gestures to you. You wave back, but don't look at it long. Be polite, says the rule, but don't get them too interested. The tentacle dissolves back into the lake.

A few blocks on, a small crowd of Purples emerges from City Park. You see Purples at least once a week around campus: violet-skinned, young and beautiful, except for the matted, paint-colored hair. You wrote your ANTH 101 midterm essay on Purples, on how they retain just enough Mind to ape human sociality. They crawl out from the trees, howling and hooting and slapping their jackets on the ground. One calls to you.

"Oil Thigh na Banrighinn!" It's the only thing Purples ever say.

It's a crapshoot with Purples. You can ignore them and risk their ire. Or you can interact — even a little — and risk being swarmed.

I refuse to be afraid.

"A'Banrighinn!" you call back, grinning jauntily. Not breaking stride. Making it clear you're on your way someplace else.

The Purples cheer, and the rhythmic *thunk* of jackets slapping on the ground follows you all the way to the harbourfront, where twist-sailed boats mutter unintelligibly to each other. When the sound dies away, you glance over your shoulder: they aren't following. Not a threat.

You look forwards again and there's a dead woman standing there.

You freeze. You stare. You've heard of zombies before, but never seen one up close. She's not pretty like Purples, not ethereal like the tentacle. She's foul-smelling and swollen and bluish, with a rigor-mortis smile. Bits of her have come off or rotted away: you can see the bones of her knuckles.

You've seen other disgusting things since you came of age and left your

Certified Home. The disgust by itself would not stop you. You stop because you know those eyes. You know the red sari she wore to your sending-off, which the robots dressed her in again before they lowered her body into the earth.

You're suddenly not thinking of the exam rules at all.

You open your mouth:

"Mom?"

Written Component, Part 2

Q. Briefly list the major known causes of Non-Mundane Events, including the creation and control of Non-Minds, and explain the implications for the Minded.

A. 1. The mental energy of the Minded. (Fear, faith, desire, and other strong emotions, as well as deliberate spellcasting.)

2. The pseudo-mental energy of Non-Minds. (Different from Minded. Poorly understood.)

3. Ordinary physical processes working with Non-Mundane sources. (E.g. Infection with Non-Mundane viruses; operation of Non-Mundane mechanics and circuitry; Non-Minds reproducing sexually.)

4. Divine intervention (rare)

In special cases the Minded have some control over 3, but in a normal situation, 1 is the only way we can hope to have a say. This is why any Minded venturing out of their Certified Home must learn to control their mental energy above all else.

Practical Component, Part 2

Your mother's corpse follows you into City Hall. You haven't been able to make her speak. After the third inarticulate groan you started to ignore her. You can't get too fascinated with the Non-Minded, even if they look like your mother. Maybe especially if they look like your mother.

City Hall is a big limestone building, domed and pillared. When you were too little to leave your Certified Home, your mother showed you a picture and told you they used to administrate all of Upper and Lower Canada from here. You misunderstood at first. She had to explain that this was long before she came to Canada, long before her own parents were born. By 12/12 the place was mostly a tourist attraction.

She had to explain five times what a tourist attraction was.

"And," she whispered sometimes, "not everything was Mundane, even then. There was always a little magic. But it was different. Hidden."

The next page of your exam lies neatly on the front steps. When you've answered the question, your next destination blooms on the paper. *The altar at St. Mary's.*

You goggle at the page. The church district is the second-worst part of the city. Worst are the prisons, of course, but no sane professor would send you there in your first year. A sane professor wouldn't send you to the churches either. In a place like that, belief metastasizes.

But that's what the page says. That's what you have to do.

You rise to your feet and march down the steps. Worrying will only waste time. You breathe deeply. You stay in your centre. *I refuse to be afraid.*

Your mother's corpse trails after you. Groans again.

"Go away, Mom," you say through your teeth. She shambles along in your wake, undeterred.

Almost everything is dangerous when provoked, even your mother. You think of the question on Romero Disorder. You wonder if she will attack you later, if Professor Yao will grade you on whether you made the transition to combat at the right moment. *Am I going to have to kill my mother?*

Then you close your mind on the question. Thinking it might make it happen. You do times tables. You recite poetry. You breathe deep.

You detour around the hospital, which is the third-worst part of the city, and venture into the bowels of the church district. Your mother has shown you pictures of how it looked before 12/12 — like normal buildings, lined up along the street and neatly separate, their steeples and stained glass the only hint of magic. You've never seen a church in real life that still looks that way. They're overgrown and bulbous, intersecting at odd angles and growing knots around the connections. Between Sydenham Street United and First Baptist there's a place where needlelike stones wave in a slow-motion battle, the remnants of sectarian disagreements no one remembers anymore.

The street itself grows over with Gothic arches until you can't see sunlight. You've never gone this deep into the church district. You don't know what church this stretch of the road belongs to this week, but it's candlelit and lined with icons: St. Francis and the Animals, St. George and the Bulldozer, the Warrior Angel of the Three-Headed Sharks.

Your mother trails behind you, staring into space. You wish she would go away.

There's a rumbling sound.

You think they're Minded for a second. Pilgrims. There are religious people crazy enough to try to live in these places. The creatures creeping out of the walls look almost like humans. Broad, clean faces, smiling, in the whole range of human colours, not purple, not gray and rotting like your mother. Covered in robes: white, blue, and burgundy.

But they lurch while they walk. They hum dully together in the ghost of a hymn.

Pergolesi's *Stabat Mater*. The Non-Minds have a sense of irony.

And they are coming right for you, their fingers outstretched in claw shapes.

You're outnumbered. You don't know how powerful they are. You should run or call the emergency robots. But you *have* to get to the next question. You're so close. You can see the arched nave of St. Mary's just past them. And you don't know any other way in.

You are too tempted.

You know how to jump and how to balance; you did gymnastics for years in your Certified Home. You can stand on the railing and run past them. It's ambitious, but you can do it. *I refuse to be afraid.*

You hop up onto the railing with ease.

The closest Non-Mind grabs your shin and pulls you back down.

In an instant they're all over you. Heavy robes and grabbing, tearing fingers. You roll to your feet and punch out at them blindly. In American schools the students have guns for this, but Professor Yao doesn't allow them. They make you arrogant and a lot of the interesting Non-Minds are immune to bullets anyway. So it's back to your punches, blocks, kicks and throws.

You get one in the nose, one in the neck, and they stagger backwards. You trip another one behind you. A jab from your elbow and a fourth goes down. But every time you hit one, two more grab you.

There are too many. They're coming too fast.

You punch out again, but your arm doesn't even fully extend before a

group of three Non-Minds grab it away. You panic. Try to peel them off with
your other hand but they trap that one, too.

You fall. The floor hits your shoulder and they're on you. Their mouths
gape open, the ghost of the Stabat Mater still echoing in the air. Blunt teeth
close on your shoulder.

Then there is a roar.

Your mother plows into the fray, tossing Non-Minds aside like Styrofoam.
Her half-rotted fingernails tear their flesh. A hand lets go of you, then another,
and you leap to your feet. Adrenaline surges through you. You punch and kick
and shout alongside her, but it's her they run away from.

And run away they do. Until the arched-over street is empty again and
you're catching your breath in silence.

Your mother has no breath to catch.

You don't know if you just failed your exam. You don't know if it's safe to
touch your mother. But oh, God. It's your mother. She's saved your life.

You wrap her in a bear hug the way you used to when she was alive. She
smells horrible, like meat left out on the counter too long, and you don't care.

Written Component, Part 3

Q. What would you have done in that fight if your mother had not been
there?

A. Did I just fail? Did I fail because I got in a fight? It wasn't Romero
Disorder. They actually attacked me. Did I fail because I fought instead of
running away? Did I fail because I didn't beat them on my own?

Q. What would you have done if your mother had not been there?

A. Did I fail?

Q. What would you have done if your mother had not been there?

A. You're not even going to tell me if I failed, are you?

I might have waded in anyway, but that would have been really stupid. It's
important to know when you're outnumbered. What I *should* have done is run
away. If there was no suitable escape route, I should have called 911. Emergency
robots are not a sure thing, but if they get there in time, you'll probably survive.
That is what I should — would have done. Avoided the confrontation.

No human can win against everything. Knowing when to back off is as
important as knowing how to fight. And so is knowing who to turn to for help.

Practical Component, Part 3

Fort Henry Hill. A cakewalk compared to the churches.

You were scared of the Hill when you first came to Queen's. The squat fortress on top was paced by uniformed Non-Minds and cannons that rolled along of their own volition. Every so often a thundering boom echoed from the ramparts. You pictured it worse than the churches or even the prisons, a place infected with the brutality of war. Professor Yao had to explain to you that the war was over long before 12/12.

The Non-Minds here are friendly, as Non-Minds go.

You stride up the hill, one hand held in your mother's, keeping an eye on the cannons. Showing fear is not recommended here. Neither is excessive speed, furtiveness, belligerence, or the carrying of weapons. They're friendly, but you don't want to get them excited.

"Left! Right! Left!" barks a small group of Non-Minds marching past you, ramrod-straight in bright red. It's like the Oil Thigh: the only thing they can say.

The swing bridge holds as you creep across the protective ditch. The Non-Minds have left the front gates open. Easy. The interior is an ancient limestone courtyard, gray and stately.

You try to catch your mother's eye in triumph. Which is when you notice the flesh sloughing off her face.

She was rotting before. But the blood of the Non-Minds at the church has done something. Acidic, maybe. She's coming apart where it splashed her. No one's skin should peel off like that, even if they're dead already.

You bite down the panic. Panicking will attract all the fear-seeking Non-Minds for miles. But you're already walking faster, aiming for the Lower Fort. Maybe they'll have something. A washbasin. Water.

What if they don't have water? The lake is close by. You can take your mother there. If running water doesn't drive zombies off. If the sharks and tentacle-things don't get you.

If water can get the blood off at all.

You duck into one of the fort's corridors. They're narrow and short, and torchlight creeps across them. There will be a washbasin in here somewhere. Or at least the next page of your exam. But it may be too late.

Written Component, Part 4

Q. Tell me about your mother.

A. What does this have to do with the course?

Q. Tell me about your mother.

A. She's dying.

Q. Tell me about your mother.

A. Is this part of the exam? Did you bring her here somehow? A spell?

Q. Tell me about your mother.

A. You have to be sure I can control my energy. So you purposely give me something that will make my HEAD EXPLODE. To see if I can control THAT. Is that how things are?

Q. Tell me about your mother.

A. No.

Q. Tell me about your mother.

A. She came to Queen's from India two years before 12/12. For graduate school. She was studying chemistry. She was home with morning sickness when it happened. She still wasn't sure if she was really pregnant or if it was stress and bad food. The other two RAs in her lab got eaten when the hydrochloric acid came to life. My father died a few days later.

She survived. Flying home was out of the question. So was giving up. Even without her parents, without my father, she knew she had to make a life for me.

She learned VAL3 and OpenRDK so she could help program the emergency robots. She designed some of the first Certified Homes and did some of the first mapmaking on the post-12/12 city and its hazards. She took me to see the local shut-ins, and she said, "That's no life. It's good we have these homes. You can't imagine life without them. But when you grow up you have to go further, or what's the point? You're my strong, smart, brave little girl. You can go wherever you like, if you are prepared."

I went to school because of her. She was so proud of me. She made me stay in residence, even though she lived in town, just so I'd know what it was like to live without her. She came by every weekend with curry. Everything she did was for me.

By Thanksgiving, something had started growing in her lungs.

I watched her die. I watched the robots put her body in the ground. And now, you bastard professor, you're making me do it again.

Practical Component, Part 4

You stop writing. Writing is making you angry. Anger will attract Non-Minds full of rage, and you can't afford that now. You go into your centre. Breathe deep.

Fort Henry has hot and cold running water, it turns out, but no amount of washing will get the blood out of your mother's skin. The flesh is coming off her arms altogether now, exposing bone.

You want to ask if it hurts. You're afraid to ask. She groans, long and loud, again and again, but you don't know if that's because it hurts, or because that's the sound zombies make.

Back to campus, says the latest page of the exam, *by way of Aberdeen Street.*

You slip out of your centre for a moment. You want to tell Professor Yao you don't care where she wants you. You don't care about this stupid exam anymore. But that's an angry thought. You have to let it go.

Aberdeen Street is the densest haunt of the Purples. It's literally crawling with them. And that makes sense, if you think about it calmly: Professor Yao wants you to walk through the Non-Minds' nest, staying in your centre, even though your mother is coming apart. If you can do that and live, you can go anywhere.

"Would you like to stay here?" you ask your mother. "Would that help?" You don't want to drag her across town in the shape she's in. Walking might make it worse.

She gives you a piteous look. The skin around her eyes is rotting and sloughing off, but you can still see pain in them. Pain and terror.

You don't know if that's a yes or no to your question.

You look away.

"Do whatever hurts less," you say. "Please. I'll be all right." And you start to walk.

Your mother shuffles slowly behind you.

You barely see the roads go by as you walk. Your feet are already aching, but you don't care. All your energy goes to putting one foot in front of the other. Keeping your breathing going. Keeping your emotions at bay. Not looking over your shoulder.

It's only when Aberdeen Street looms up in right in front of you that you work out what's wrong.

The street is there — sort of. The close-set red-brick houses. The thick groups of Purples lounging in nests, tossing garbage around, climbing through the windows or slapping their jackets. But something *else* is there. It's not just a nest for Purples today: the bulldozers have moved in, bringing a maze of scaffolding and temporary wire fences with them.

These things roam the outskirts of campus. Digging up roads and putting them back. Smashing old, living buildings and assembling new ones. Something hovers around the university that is insatiable, that cannot stop building, and the bulldozers are its midwives.

You almost fall back and detour. But Professor Yao is too good to send you here by mistake. She has a virtual map keeping track of the bulldozers' migrations. She wouldn't have sent you to them unless she wanted you to face them.

Still, you falter. You risk a look over your shoulder.

Your mother has come entirely apart. Barely more than a skeleton now, dusted with clumps of black hair, fragments of the red sari.

You squeeze your eyes shut.

"Go back," you whisper. "Please."

She gives you the same pain-and-terror look with those empty sockets. You never studied how zombies are made, what spells are used. Maybe she can't go back. Maybe the same force that brought her to life keeps her cloven to you.

Your hands are shaking. You breathe as deep as you can. You have to fight your way to the centre now.

You walk forward.

The bulldozers rumble and roll of their own accord, chattering to each other every so often with piercing beeps. You walk into their midst, into the wire-fence maze.

Your presence makes them pause. It turns the Purples' heads. They stare at you. Murmur to each other. A few shift like they're thinking of getting up.

You fight down panic. You're not quite in your centre. You're radiating too much emotion and they're noticing you too fast.

What did Professor Yao tell you to do in a situation like this? Better meditation? A detour? You can't remember. You hardly care. It's hard enough to put one foot in front of the other, let alone think of other options.

You put one foot in front of the other for a while. And then the maze comes to a dead end.

You pause. Try to retrace your steps. But looking carefully, there is no way forward. There's a wire fence here stretched all the way across the street. No opening. No gate. You're stuck.

You waver.

And then, before you can stop her, the skeleton of your mother leaps up and begins to climb the fence.

You rush after her. You're not the best climber. But you're suddenly frantic to reach her. Little slivers of bone are clattering to the ground now as she hooks her fingers into the links. "No," you whisper. "No, no, no!" But she climbs faster than you. You're up at the top of the fence, nearly at her, before you can think straight. She wobbles. You reach out to steady her.

Before your fingertips reach her, she falls forward.

You leap. It's only eight feet down from the top of the fence to the other side. Not enough to do more than jar you, with your gymnast's sense for landings. But where your mother hits the ground there's suddenly nothing but red fabric and broken fragments of bone, rolling outwards in all directions.

You land on your hands and knees. You stare at the red fabric in disbelief. You scrabble at it, like you can put her back together again.

Where is your centre? You can't find it. You can't even imagine where it would be. All you can do is crouch on the ground, staring, shivering.

The Purples, in your peripheral vision, are all crawling towards you.

Fine. You have no centre. You can't even bring yourself to get up. You don't care. So the Purples will take you. There are too many of them to fight, and not enough time for the emergency robots to get here. There's nothing you can do. You can refuse to be afraid. You can't refuse to grieve.

You hunch down and wait for them. A violet hand, surprisingly warm, grips your shoulder.

"Oil Thigh na Banrighinn," murmurs the Purple. As though it's sad.

"A'Banrighinn," echo the others. And there's a slow, rhythmic *thunk* of jackets on the ground.

Not an attack. A dirge. They are mourning with you.

You bury your face in the Purple's shoulder and weep.

Written Component, Part 5

Q. Do you think you have passed your exam?
A. I think I have survived.
I think Non-Mind is the wrong name for them.
They're not safe. Their minds are not like our minds.
But sometimes they are just close enough.

Mama's Sword

Mama came back from her last mission different. Stooping and stumbling, like her knotted limbs were too heavy to bear. The sword she'd always groomed like a second daughter dragged carelessly through the dirt behind her. And her eyes — something about them. The shape. Like someone had taken them out and put new ones in, and hadn't quite got it right.

Mama came back from her last mission alone.

Daddy ran out to greet her so fast he scared the chickens. They flapped and ducked their heads, avoiding the dirt kicked up by his heels. He stopped right in front of her, and they stared at each other a moment, then embraced so hard she lost her footing. Just sagged against him like she'd died.

I was seventeen. I was old enough to know what it meant when a woman came back alone and stumbling. Battle was a routine for Mama: every six months she strapped on her sword and armor, and rode off in a confusion of gleaming strangers. It never seemed to matter to her where she went — a faraway war, an ancient tomb, an unexplored valley. All she wanted was the glory. When Mama came home the strangers came with her, and so did more money than was really seemly. When Mama came home it was time for feasts and long adventure stories. She gave most of the treasure away, but with the portion she kept, our house became the biggest in the village, with a herd of almost a hundred cows and enough shade trees to smother the world.

I knew as soon as I saw her that there would be no more feasts.

I wavered there on the doorstep. Daddy turned and half-carried Mama inside, storming past me without even looking up.

"Mama..." I said, feeling uncertain. I was at an age where I didn't know what to think about Mama. I had always wanted to be like her, tall and broad and strong, with stories of daring deeds and glorious battle rolling off my tongue. But I was no longer small enough to traipse after her wanting to be picked up and have my hair brushed. I had been sneaking off to see boys after school, sometimes for kissing, sometimes for sparring and knocking them across the road with my blunted practice sword. I was the equal of any young woman or man in the village: they learned swords a little, in case their neighbor or another village needed rescuing, but I had always set my sights higher. I wanted to be Mama's equal. I didn't understand why I also wanted to hang off her waist like a child.

She mustered the energy to glance up at me, her face drained of everything but exhaustion. She weakly held out a hand. Whispered my name. "Kejiu..."

But that was the first time I looked in her eyes. Their wrongness. The way they had changed. Fear gripped me suddenly, and I backed away and fled to my room.

I sat on my bed under the mosquito netting, gripped my pillow in my arms, and lay my ear against the wall. We were rich enough to have metal pipes in the walls bringing water all the way into our home from the well, in case we should need to lie in a bath in private or boil soup. Sound carried very strongly.

"Tell me what happened," Daddy murmured in some other room. "Please. Tell me what killed them."

"Oh, love," Mama keened. "Oh, gods. We didn't mean to."

"What? What did you not mean?"

Mama's voice dropped to a whisper.

"We went Outside."

When I was little, I used to pore over maps trying to find all the places Mama had been. The village schoolteacher, Sounin, had an atlas of the whole world, and I would turn the yellowed pages, pointing. *There,* that is the land where Mama rescued the kidnapped prince. *There,* that is the land where a beast like a miles-long crocodile guarded treasure. It was a source of endless frustration to Teacher Sounin, who wanted to teach me those nations' flags and the names of their kings and queens, not what my mama had happened to do there.

When I was old enough to speak to the strangers at Mama's feasts, some of them gave me maps of other worlds. Auntie Ayu—Mama called them all my aunties and uncles—gave me a map of an inside-out world, with ground overhead in place of a sun. She said, *there* is where we fought the hordes whose very flesh was steel. Uncle Paca, who was thin and wore a healer's robe, gave me a map of a world made of islands, none bigger on the map than the print of my young thumb. He said, *there* is where Auntie Kartika came from, and where she brought us together in the first place. Do you think we are all from this world?

None of them told me about Outside.

I heard the name Outside when I was fourteen, shouted at me by a rude boy who was angry because I wouldn't sneak behind the butcher shop with him.

"You think you can do anything you like," he said, "because your Mama's so great? Even your Mama can't do anything she likes."

"My Mama can do anything and go anywhere," I shouted back. "My Mama's even been to the realm of the gods!"

"Ha!" said the boy. "But has she ever been Outside?"

"There, too!" I shouted, because I could not bear the thought of losing an argument to this boy. "My Mama's been everywhere!" But the boy clutched his sides and laughed as if this was the most foolish thing anyone could say.

Later I asked Teacher Sounin about Outside.

"Never you mind," said Teacher Sounin.

"I want to know about Outside," I said. "I'll find it in books myself if you don't tell me."

Teacher Sounin gave me an unaccountably sharp look, though she was normally a great proponent of looking things up in books.

"Past this world," she said, "there are other worlds."

"I know that," I said. "My Mama has been to them."

"Past the other worlds, there is the realm of the gods, wrapped around them all like a blanket."

"I know that. My Mama has been there too."

Teacher Sounin sighed and pinched the bridge of her wide nose. "Past the realm of the gods, Kejiu, is Outside. And you must not ask about Outside. It is not fit for mortals. It is not fit even for gods. If you read too much about Outside, if you so much as think a little too long and hard about Outside, your mind will break in ways no doctor can fix. Now go say your prayers and never ask about this again."

But I was a stubborn girl, and I was tired of Teacher Sounin with her provincial little one-world maps and her lessons bare of adventure. The next time Mama came home, at the feast, I asked Auntie Houngba—the fattest and most fearless of the company, the one who thumped and drummed on the table, nearly breaking it, and told jokes not meant for fourteen-year-old ears. I cornered her outside of the house, on her way back from relieving herself, so that no one else would overhear.

"Auntie," I said, "most respected Auntie, will you tell me about Outside?"

Auntie Houngba hooted and slapped her thighs. "Who's been telling you about Outside, girl? Who's put that thought into your head?"

"No one, Auntie," I said, but she looked at me with such alarm for a moment that I revised my statement. "I mean... Just a boy. I was curious."

"Just a *boy*, hmm," said Auntie Houngba, looking me up and down. "A pretty one? One you'd like to drag home when your mama's not around?"

"*No,* "I said. "A rude boy. I hate him. He said Mama was no good because she'd never been Outside. That's why I wanted to know."

"Aah," said Auntie Houngba. She crossed her meaty arms and frowned, and I was glad at least that she believed me. "Well, then I'll tell you this. Any boy who would say a thing like that is too stupid to walk on his own feet. No one goes Outside. Even the gods don't."

"That's what Teacher Sounin said. But if no one goes there, how do we know it is there at all?"

Auntie Houngba lowered her voice, and in the twilight, she no longer looked big and loud and full of jokes. She looked frightened.

"Because sometimes things come *inside.* Not in my time, mind you. But my own mama, when she was a girl your age, something came *inside* to the country in the north. A whole lot of somethings. Armies marched from all over the world to drive them back Out. They won. But they came back changed, every one of them. My mama saw things. Tentacles instead of legs. Mouths at the tips of their fingers. And stark raving mad, more often than not. You wonder why no one goes Outside? That's why. You're a growing girl; run back inside and eat your fill. And pray you never find out more."

When Mama came home from her last mission, I sat in my room until dinnertime, pretending to study.

"How are you alive?" I heard Daddy say through the walls. "How do you even have all your limbs, how are you still talking to me, if that's where you went?"

"There was a healer. I..." Mama sounded as though simply making sounds exhausted her. "I think I was worse when I came out. But I don't remember. I hardly remember anything. I try and it's all a jumble. I came out, and I was the only one left, and nothing made sense, and there was a healer. And then... Then I walked a long way. I think I walked here. Did I walk here?"

"What happened to your eyes?" said Daddy.

"Taken out and back in." That answer came out quickly. "That happens Outside. That's the least of your problems."

They talked a long time, mostly things I didn't care about. Mostly Daddy talking on and on about how much he loved her, wherever she'd been, whatever had happened to her. He sounded like he was trying to convince himself. He sounded like he was crying.

"Get some rest," he said at last, and then they were quiet and I didn't have anything else to listen to, apart from the buzzing of crickets and lowing of cows outside. I couldn't think of anything except Mama, Outside, all my aunties and uncles. And her eyes. I could still see those new eyes looking for me.

The eyes gave me a strange, sick hope. I thought Daddy had been too quick to listen when Mama explained about them. Maybe the eyes were a clue. Maybe this wasn't really Mama. Maybe a wizard or a demon had taken her shape in order to hurt us. I knew there were mortals who could do such things; there were demons who specialized in it. Maybe my real Mama had drawn the wrong kind of attention, and now here was her double, sent to destroy the people she loved most.

At dinnertime the smell came in of Daddy making stew in the big pot outside, and I edged my way through the house. Mama — if she was Mama — was sitting in the front room, at the table, drawing.

"I thought you were going to rest," I said.

"Couldn't rest. Can't remember."

You're not really Mama, I wanted to say, but the words wouldn't come out. What if I was wrong?

"What are you drawing?" I said instead.

She didn't answer at first. I peered impatiently over her shoulder. She was drawing something like a disembodied hand, thick and calloused, but wrong. Too many fingers — some on the end of the wrist, where it should have joined with an arm. Too few joints on some. Too many on others. A single eye, placed carelessly between a pair of knuckles, wide as if terrified.

Mama murmured almost too softly for me to hear. Like she was talking to herself. "That," she said, "was Auntie Houngba."

Daddy spent so much time with the new Mama that he wouldn't deal with the boys who kept the cows. They were good boys for the most part, not the kind who would hurt the cows or forget to feed them, but Daddy wouldn't even have noticed if they did, and I hated being in there with him. So I went out to supervise the boys while he whined and embraced Mama and told her it was okay, she was safe now. Mama mostly stared into space and sometimes drew things that made less sense than the hand. I stopped asking what they were supposed to be.

When Daddy got done talking to Mama, he went to ask the village doctor what he could do. It was a foolish thing to ask, and he must have known it. I'd heard that much even from Teacher Sounin: doctors can't fix you when you've been Outside. Even the healer Mama talked about, if there'd been a healer, could only do so much.

The boys were only a few years older than me, and not old enough to know how to suppress their curiosity.

"I heard they took out her eyes," said Pentu, the older boy, while he poured new water into the drinking trough. "While she was Outside. And put a different set back in. Is that true?"

"It's none of your business," I said. "That's what it is."

The other boy swatted away a few horseflies with a stick. "She dangerous? She going to start running around here with that sword of hers?"

"I don't know."

The second I said it I regretted it. Of course she wouldn't. Mama would never. Not even crazy. She'd always been so firm with me around the sword. Never even let me touch it. Gave me a thousand lectures before I even got my first wooden practice sword. They weren't toys. They were for justice. For righting wrongs. Protecting the weak.

But I wasn't sure this was really Mama.

I wondered whether to say that to the boys.

Just then there was a horrible shrieking sound in the distance. Near the edge of the village, from the sound of it. I dropped the stick I was holding and ran. The houses out there belonged to Pajo's family and old Yajile and his sons, and they had nothing to shriek about.

Of course, there are about two dozen houses between our house and Pajo's house. I run fast, but by the time I got there, a small crowd had already gathered, and more were coming. Kimile, Pajo's wife, was out front on the rickety steps, breathing hard and shaking slightly, but unharmed.

"I got it," she said. "I got it. It's all right. It's dead. I got it." She held up a heavy boot with something stuck to the bottom.

"A beetle?" I asked. It was the first thing I could think of that size. A stupid thing to suggest, though. Pale little Auntie Yaglithy had shrieked like that once at her first feast, when a beetle crawled up her pant leg. But no one who lived here bothered being frightened by those things, even the ones that were the size of Mama's fist.

"I don't know what it was," said Kimile. "But it wasn't a beetle. I don't know why it scared me so much—it just didn't look like anything at all. It had these tentacles, and these eyes..."

I gulped down sudden fear and pushed through the crowd, kneeling down to look at the squashed form on the boot. It was true, from what I could see. Tentacles. And a jointed body that didn't quite look like anything—not a bug, not a worm, not a crab or lizard. The only thing it looked like was one of Mama's drawings. Like it had come from Outside.

Like it had followed her here.

Daddy wasn't in the front room. Even the boys had gone to see Kimile. I didn't waste time checking if the cows were okay. I stormed inside and snatched up one of Mama's blank papers.

Mama stared at me, silent fear in her eyes, while I roughly sketched out the outline of the thing on Kimile's boot. I was no good with a pencil, not even passable with it like Mama, but it was close enough to recognize.

"This, Mama," I said as I drew. "This thing followed you home, right to the village, and Kimile stepped on it. Do you see?" And I pushed the finished drawing to her place at the table.

Mama screamed.

I had never heard Mama scream before. It startled me more than anything. I wanted to chide her. My real mama was brave and witty. Anyway she'd been drawing the same things I had, and she hadn't screamed at those ones.

Except she'd had control over those ones. They hadn't been harbingers of real creatures, remembered or not, coming after her.

Mama kept screaming and I stood transfixed. She drew huge, gulping breaths only to begin screaming again. She thumped her hands on the table, not like Auntie Houngba when she got excited, but like the table was attacking her. "Wrong! Wrong! *Wrong!*"

Daddy rushed in just then, back empty-handed from the doctor, and stared at both of us. "Kejiu, what did you *do?*"

I opened my mouth and shut it. I didn't know the word for what I had done.

"Wrong!" Mama screamed. "Wrong!"

She picked up the table and threw it down on its side, scattering pages everywhere.

Daddy turned to me with wide eyes. "Kejiu. Get outside."

And I ran.

When Mama finally stopped screaming, Daddy carried her curled-up shaking body to bed, then came out and gave me the longest lecture I had ever heard. I tried to say, *but at Pajo's house there was a creature —* and he shushed me and sent me to bed without dinner, even though I was much too old for that.

I avoided them both after that for two whole days. Went to school. Practiced with my wooden sword. Helped with the cows. Ate dinner at friends' houses, then crawled to my room late, too tired to say goodnight.

I couldn't sleep much.

On the second night Mama woke up screaming. I didn't have to put my head to the wall to hear it loud and clear. It didn't last as long as the one before. Daddy hushed her, sang to her, told her she was safe now and he loved her.

Me, I didn't think anybody was safe. Not with creatures around like the one Kimile stepped on. Not with this evil woman pretending to be my mama.

I started practicing with my wooden sword extra hard. Throwing boys all the way across the road on purpose.

Daddy cornered me once in a while to tell me things. That the doctor had said there was nothing he could do. That Mama missed me. On the third day, he dragged me to the front room with him and Mama to eat breakfast, despite my protests. We huddled there silently and sullen, apart from the noises of eating and the cows outside.

There was a knock at the door.

Daddy and I both rose to get it. Elder Degu stood at the door: the oldest man in the village, stooped and serious, his bright robe trailing on the dusty ground.

"Peace on this house," he said.

"Thank you," Daddy said, which was not the correct response to the greeting at all. Daddy stood up extra straight, the way I did sometimes when I thought I was in trouble, and he didn't invite the elder in.

"And peace to you," said the elder. "My son, I have no wish to bring you bad news at my age. But you must be the first to know. Another creature came in the night. Bigger than the last."

Daddy stood transfixed. They were both speaking too quietly for Mama, at the back of the room, to pick up their words.

"I must come in, my son. Or your wife must come out. She must speak with the council of elders on this matter."

"My wife is ill, elder. You know my duty to her. Surely you wouldn't ask..."

Daddy could argue a long time if he wanted to. Maybe he could actually argue the elder away. I knew it wasn't my place to speak to either of them just now. Instead I crept back to Mama's side, full of rage.

"It's your fault," I whispered. I wondered if she was going to start screaming again. Part of me didn't care. Maybe it would stop Daddy from arguing if she started screaming again. "You led them here."

"I did not," Mama whispered back.

"I know what you are," I said. I could no longer hold back my words. "You're not my mama. You're a thing from Outside. You're going to kill the village and blame it on her. My real mama is strong and brave and beautiful. My real mama would care if something was following her that could kill us all. She would do something about it."

Mama didn't scream. She didn't turn over the table again. She put down her food very deliberately.

"I am your mama," she said. "Please believe me. I have always been your mama. I married your Daddy at midsummer and we built this house, and it only had two rooms the first time we built it, because we had hardly any treasure then. I gave birth to you in a mountain pass, with Auntie Kingba and Uncle Paca holding my hand, because we had been trapped there months longer than anyone planned, and I hadn't realized you were in my belly when we set out. You were reaching for the hilt of my sword, from the sling at my shoulder, by the time I found my way home. Your Daddy fainted when he saw you. Your first word was 'cow'. You said it all stretched out, trying to match the sounds they made."

She went on and on. In a low monotone, she told me every story she used to tell the aunties and uncles about me, and a few we had kept between us, like the first time I got moonsick over a boy. By the end of it, tears were running down her cheeks.

I sat transfixed. I did not understand how this could be. No wizard or demon could know everything my mama knew. But Mama would never tell the stories this way, not even while she was keeping her voice down to avoid disturbing Daddy and the elder. Mama had always laughed and preened, keeping her sword close by.

I glanced at her sword while she talked. It was lying in the corner, leaning carelessly, just where she'd left it three days ago, before she screamed at me.

I had not noticed before. But she had not picked it up in all that time. Her sword was how she did battle, and she had never even clasped the hilt to raise it against us, not even in her worst panic. She was not here to hurt us. She had screamed and screamed, and overturned tables, but she had never gone for her sword.

"I am your mama," she said at the end, as though it was an incantation. "But you. You are not my Kejiu. My Kejiu is brave and clever and loyal. My Kejiu loves me. If I fell terribly ill, my Kejiu would care for me. Not run from me. Not hurt me. Not blame me for things I didn't do."

I started to cry, too. I couldn't lie to myself anymore. This was Mama, my real mama. Mama wasn't waiting for me out there in the adventurous world, ready to destroy the evil and set things right again. This was the only Mama I had. I had been so cruel to her because I couldn't believe it. And, kind or cruel, I didn't know how to stop what was happening.

"I'm sorry," I whispered. "I'm sorry."

Daddy closed the door. The elder had gone away.

"He says the creatures..."

"Followed me. Yes." Mama raised her face to him, the tears stilling on her cheeks. Resigned.

Daddy shook his head.

"They came to the west side of the village. Both of them. Pajo's house is just at the west edge, and so is Aba's. They came from the west. Don't you remember, dear? When you walked here, you came from the east."

Mama's face contorted and she looked back down.

"I could have said so to him myself," she said, her voice wavering in a very un-Mama-like way. "But who would have believed me?"

Daddy knelt and took Mama's hands. "He says Outside is perverse, and something may have been waiting for this time. Not following you, but waiting for you to arrive, so that you would be a scapegoat. You would distract us from what was really coming."

"What will we do?" said Mama. Her arms shook like leaves, even with Daddy holding on to them.

"He is pulling a group together. One from every household, for now. More if we can spare them. And in the meantime, sending runners to other villages. To other lands. Because, if the creatures keep coming, we will need all the help anybody can give."

One from every household.

I suddenly realized that, if creatures came, Mama could not fight them. Not anymore. Her mind was broken, like Teacher Sounin had warned me, and if they came, she would only scream and scream. But the creatures had to be fought. Someone had to. Someone who knew their way around a fight.

I couldn't believe I was doing it. But I stood, when Daddy said that. I crossed the room and picked up Mama's sword, the metal she'd told me never to touch, cold and powerful in my hand.

"Then I'll go," I said, and my voice sounded like a stranger's.

"This will be hard," said Elder Degu, through the dark smoke of his fireplace, while all of us knelt with our swords. Me, boys and girls my age, fathers, mothers, grandmothers. Some only with wooden swords, or with sharpened plowshares.

I wondered how many of us, by next midsummer, would have tentacles for legs, like in Auntie Houngba's stories. How many of us would be screaming like Mama.

How many of us would live that long at all.

"This will be the hardest thing you have ever done."

Some of the boys' eyes glinted with excitement. They were stupid. This would not be an adventure like the ones Mama came home from happy, full of treasure, surrounded by hale and healthy aunties. This would be an adventure like Mama's last.

None of us was safe. Me, I could beat any boy in a fight and most of the people Mama's age, too. But that did not make me safe. It meant I would be chosen for the most dangerous things of all.

It meant I would go the way Mama went.

I felt sick.

"The first thing we must do is follow them back to the west. To figure out where they are coming from. There will be a breach somewhere; a natural one, or one that someone has put there deliberately. We must close it. And we must deal however we can with what has already come through. The lives of the whole village, the children and the ill and all future generations, depend on this."

Mama had wept when I picked up her sword. She had sobbed so loudly that I worried she would start screaming again. Knowing, I guess, why I had to, and that she could no longer fight for herself. Knowing better than anyone what might happen to me.

At last she had crushed me in a hug and said through her tears, "Kejiu. Kejiu, my only daughter. You are braver than anyone."

Kejiu, my only daughter.

Forgiving me.

Elder Degu made us kneel before we left his house. Made us pray for deliverance. But deliverance would come at a cost, even if it came. Nothing could be the same as before.

I touched the hilt of Mama's sword, cold and strangely heavy at my hip, and I knelt.

Hippocamp

Flea-bitten ox, knees splashing,
tired of tugging a skeletal cart
into the rising sea

Moon Laws, Dream Laws

I was in temple, mixing libations for the Lady of Blood and Stone, the night the moon did not rise.

Even here, where we worship the moon, it took too long to work out what happened. We are too used to the Un-God, his demand for knowledge and order instead of worship. We talk to each other on phones with his bright little screens. We forget that all the gods but him are still wild as beasts.

It was an overcast night. We chanted the Moon's Awakening unknowing, with nothing but a blur of cloud on the projection screen at the temple's apse. The ceremony was long over when Friana, the Acolyte of the Telescopes, ran in.

Friana is always running, tripping over the hem of her blood-red robe, her hair in disarray. It's usually nothing. But she ran past the sub-altar where I was measuring wine and oil, and her panic cut through me. Sharper than Friana's usual panic.

She ran all the way to the High Priestess. I put down my sacrificial dishes to watch. She spoke breathlessly, and I couldn't make out the words.

The High Priestess's voice was clear: "You what?"

And then, "You checked every instrument? The radio telescopes? The laser optics?"

Friana bowed her head, mumbled.

Then, "That's impossible. You've mixed up the coordinates again."

"No." This time Friana was loud, shrill. "I double-checked that! The moon didn't rise. It *disappeared.*"

Everyone looked up at that. The High Priestess glared around, then picked up her robes and swept off with Friana. "Back to work. We'll sort this out."

Terrified chatter burst out in all directions.

The Lady of Blood and Stone *is* the moon — in a way. She is also a stern maiden, and also... Well, with gods, you could never finish counting the things that they are. But the moon is what we weave in our tapestries, praise in our poetry. The moon is our livelihood.

That is why the others were worried. It is not why I suddenly had trouble breathing. The world blurred, and the libations ceased to matter. All I could think was a name.

Trulia.

I remember saying goodbye to Trulia. I clutched her in my arms and kissed her, on the launch pad, breathing her sharp scent while her separation anxiety tangled painfully with mine.

"It's only a year," she protested. "Then I'll be back." But no one had tried to live on the moon before. Anything could happen.

"Call me whenever you can. And dream of me."

"Yeah."

She didn't mean it. Even waking up next to me, arguing over breakfast about what we remembered, she had trouble believing in dreams. I had tried to teach her to travel that world, but there hadn't been time. At least we had phones.

I let her go. The Un-God's rocket flared to life, and she flew away.

I called Trulia over and over again. All I got were error messages. A few priestesses gave me sour looks, which I felt more than saw — I ought to have been readying the wine and oil for the next ceremony. I didn't care.

When the High Priestess strode back into the sanctuary, she had changed clothes. The silver-and-white diadem of the Highest Days crowned her head. Blood-red ribbons draped her limbs, and new crimson lines — real cuts — stood out on her face. Her fear was even worse than Friana's. It startled me, feeling that sting from someone so outwardly serene.

Her amplified voice echoed in every niche. "There is no reason to panic. Remain calm."

There was no calm. Hysterical murmurs rose at the corners of the room.

"I have gone into trance and spoken to our Lady." The High Priestess's voice was crystalline, betraying no trace of the fear underneath. But that is how we choose High Priestesses: they must be cold as space, celibate, queenly and unshakeable. "She is hidden for a time. She is angry, but not at us. We will continue our duties. That is all we need know."

That is all?

She knew about Trulia. She did not meet my eyes.

Voices rose in chaos as she swept out. But only I was reckless enough to follow.

Trulia didn't mean to go to the moon. She disliked my Lady, even though I could see a resemblance, a moonlike hardness in Trulia's eyes at times. Her supervisor guilted her into adding her name to the recruitment list, promised she'd be a fifth-string backup at best, just some quick training and a prestige point for the university. We didn't think anything would come of it.

Then exotic-materials engineers started bowing out — family concerns, sudden illness — until Trulia was the only good candidate left.

"I can't go," she blurted when the colony's recruiters came knocking. "We're having a baby."

"You're what?"

We weren't really. We'd talked about it, decided we wanted it, even though Trulia would be barred from my Lady's temple for nine months. We'd drawn blood for the Changing God's rites — turning my woman's cells into something that could burrow into Trulia's womb and make life. But those rites, like anything of the Changing God's, are experiments. It takes months before the cells get it right, and we'd only just started.

We stopped the rites. We stopped making love. The recruiters tested Trulia's urine. They waited a month, and she bled like any woman. Trulia never understood how barrenness could be beautiful and holy. But she knew that it was important, that strict rules had been laid down before my Lady would allow humans on her surface at all.

"The colony needs you," the recruiters said. "It's only a year."

I bit my tongue till it ached. I wanted her here, having our baby. But Trulia believed in rockets the way I believed in blood and solitude.

"They need me," she said. And I let her go.

I couldn't disturb the High Priestess in her Highest Days regalia. She must be utterly untouched in that diadem: even a tap on the shoulder could bring down my Lady's curse. I waited by the vestry until she had disrobed to a white linen shift.

"Trulia," I blurted, once it was safe to speak.

The High Priestess turned to me with tired eyes. "I don't know, Viola. The Lady of Blood and Stone didn't say."

"You didn't ask."

She snatched up the red silk cap she wears for everyday duties. "There were fifty thousand souls up there. Do you think I am one of the Un-God's sociopaths? Do you think I didn't ask?"

I took a deep breath in and hissed it out until I trusted myself to speak.

"I'm sorry," I said. "But you know what she is to me. Give me the afternoon off. I have money saved. I'll ask the Herdsman of the Dead–"

"No."

The answer was so sharp that it froze me.

"Our Lady has forbidden us to know. Whatever she is doing isn't finished. And if you pry, she'll curse you. You know our Lady needs privacy."

There were no tears. I was genuinely surprised when my voice cracked. "Then give me the afternoon off to grieve."

Her pity was a pool now, cold and dark. She had seen more bereavement than any of us. She knew its shape.

"Take it if you like," she said. "But I think it won't matter."

Trulia was a woman of numbers and careful measurement. She had the usual range of feelings — love, fear, rage, joy — but without numbers, she could not understand them.

"Look at that man," I said once, pointing to an image on our home video-screen. I was trying to teach her. "How is he feeling?"

Trulia squinted at the screen. "He looks tired."

It was a public health announcement, the Lady of Mercy and Discipline's propaganda. He was an actor playing a drug addict, wracked with regret and despair.

"Look at the quirk of his mouth. The way the corners turn down."

"What about them?"

"It means he's very sad, Trulia."

She sighed in disgust. "I don't even know how *I'm* feeling."

She never understood dreams, but she dreamed as everyone does. I built a tower of numbers in the dream world, every floor built from the angles of a single digit. More often than not, when we slept side by side, she found it. "Did you build this for me?" she said, and the familiar phrase shocked me lucid.

Sometimes she refused to believe she was dreaming. Sometimes all she wanted to do in a dream was make love, which is like making love in real life, only sometimes the bed turns into a giant piano when you aren't looking.

Other nights, a light went on in her head. "Let's go flying. I've always wanted to fly." Those were the good nights — hand in hand, soaring into the clouds.

Every morning, I asked what she had dreamed. She said, "I don't remember." Or sometimes, "I remember a cloud."

"We flew, Trulia. You met me in a tower of numbers. We flew over a city and into a cloud."

"That's what *you* dreamed. I just remember a cloud."

I tried to explain. "That must be it," she would say, humoring me. "That must be what we did." But she never really believed.

She promised to dream of me, but I knew it was hopeless. The tower of numbers stood empty.

Day turned to night, night to day, and the moon did not appear. My hands shook. I spilled wine and oil and had to start over. I bumped into walls and scarcely noticed. All I could think of was Trulia. Any second now, Friana might come running back in with news.

I knew my Lady would curse me for looking. I didn't care. I pulled books brazenly from the temple library, downloaded the colony's plans and schedules, searched for news with my phone. No one stopped me. I did my duties one-eyed, hunting vainly for clues.

Everyone had noticed the moon's absence by now. There were headlines, frantic arguments, tearful interviews with others who knew someone up there. Self-proclaimed scholars declared that this was nothing: it would blow over like all my Lady's moods, though perhaps not with all the human lives intact. I found nothing useful in the news, and turned to the oldest stories.

There were no stories of the moon disappearing, but there were some of the sun. The Lord of Fire and Sky, my Lady's father, sometimes tried to marry her to a god or a mortal hero. Enraged, she pushed him out of the sky.

The Un-God told us, later, that this was a lie, and that the sun's disappearance was astronomy and optics. But a story can be true and not true, just as my Lady is the moon and not the moon.

I thought about that, singing the Moon's Awakening over a moonless horizon. My Lady was the moon and not the moon. Could Trulia be alive and not alive?

One suitor, the Lord of Green and Crawling Things, was unusually persistent. He chased my Lady and sang songs of beautiful, many-limbed children. She cast him into darkness so complete that the other gods could not find him, but within the week, there he was, cavorting under a mossy rock.

"I plucked a leaf from my hair," he said, "and it found the ground. Leaves know how to fall." But he never chased my Lady again.

I could hardly even read. I would get through a page, or half a page, and Trulia's name would abduct me. Was she alive?

Once the Herdsman of the Dead sent a bleating messenger to ask my Lady a question. It found her asleep amid her stones, unclothed, with trickles of blood running down her divine limbs. It did not want to wake her. Bleating, trusting, too stupid to know better, it curled up against her thighs and joined her in sleep.

When my Lady woke up, panicked by the unfamiliar presence, she picked up the messenger and threw it off the moon, into a comet so cold that it broke and burned. Its bleats became screams, and it never stopped screaming.

I meditated every evening, willing myself to find Trulia somewhere in the twisted dream-world. It didn't seem to be working. Tonight I dreamed of a wailing darkness.

Cold, inexorable currents tugged at me. The gods can't enter dreams, but other dreamers can, and sometimes stranger beings. The current could have been theirs — or a part of my mind I didn't want to deal with. I thought of forcing myself awake. But what would I have then? An empty room and a head full of fear. So I let myself drift.

I washed ashore in a tower of numbers.

It was not quite like my tower. Mine was made of black numbers on a blue and salmon seashore, reaching the clouds. These were white numbers floating in the dark. Through their curving forms I could see stars.

I scrambled to my feet.

"Trulia!" The darkness swallowed my voice. I knew, deep in my gut, that she had made this place for me. "Trulia!"

No one and nothing answered me. I gathered my breath for a scream. "Trulia!"

"I'm here."

She was suddenly behind me, buzzing softly with concern — and relief. I turned and crushed her in my arms. "You're alive."

"I missed you," she said. Her hair twirled around her face, longer than I remembered. Her belly was distended in a familiar way; we had often dreamed she was pregnant. Dreams can be like that: wish for something and it's so. She nuzzled me, warm and solid. I could smell her shampoo, feel her affection all around me. "It was a whole year."

"No it wasn't. Love, you're dreaming."

"I'm what?"

This is how it always went. She scowled at the dream-world as though it had lied to her.

"See? The tower of numbers. You're dreaming."

She took a deep breath, and her eyes grew a glint of mischief. She lunged and kissed me, covering me in the taste of her — the warm blush of desire inside her. "Well, if this is a dream, let's..."

Everything in me snapped to attention. I missed her so badly it hurt. But I couldn't. "Wait. I need to ask–"

She only kissed me more firmly. "Ssh. It's been a horrible month. Just let me touch you–"

"Trulia." I pulled away, held her at arm's length. "One of us might wake up. I need to know quickly. Where are you? What happened to the moon?"

"They're going to kill me. That's what happened." Her desire was ebbing into frustration, uncomfortable against my hands. "Why can't I touch you?"

I fought to keep my voice calm. "Who's going to kill you? Why?"

"I don't want to talk about it."

"I know about the moon. I can help you."

"No, you can't. You're just a dream. I'll forget you in the morning."

"*I* won't forget. Please just tell me–"

But then her phone's cheery ringtone blasted the air. A wake-up call. She startled, and in an instant, she was gone.

As the days crawled by I decided my Lady wasn't going to curse me. If she cared, she would have done it already. Her curses are swift and unsubtle. Even when there isn't screaming and sky-falling, there is always blood.

Once, on a slow afternoon, the High Priestess knelt beside me.

"What are you looking for?" she asked. "Even if you work out what happened, what makes you think you can do anything?"

I choked down a retort.

I really didn't know. I wasn't even sure, deep down, that the Trulia in my dream was Trulia. I had often woken up with memories she didn't recognize. Just because we *could* meet didn't mean we *had* met, and with me wanting her so badly, fearing for her so badly...

I had touched her, smelled her. But I was frightened enough to doubt my senses.

"I have to know," I said. "Even if that's all I can do."

That night I found the tower of numbers again, and Trulia was crying.

If she was Trulia. If she was real.

I put out my arms and embraced her. She buried her face in the crook of my neck. Her grief and fear felt real. Her body was as soft as ever, though her belly was too big, and her smell...

"Tell me what's wrong. Who's going to kill you?"

She sniffed. "All of them. It's the only way to bring the earth and the stars back. They didn't want to, but your Lady said they'd die if they didn't. So they're going to launch me in a ship and let me suffocate in the blackness."

Her fear cut worse than Friana's or the High Priestess's, worse than any fear I'd felt before. Maybe she was only dreaming that she'd die. But that would mean she'd dreamt it last time, too. More likely, this was real, or at least a reflection of something real.

"A human sacrifice." We hadn't done that for centuries, not since the Lady of Mercy and Discipline threatened to stop healing the other gods' followers over it. Could they have regressed so far, so quickly? "What for? And why you?"

"Because it's my fault. I hurt her."

She clutched her belly, and I suddenly understood.

It was impossible, but there was a terrible warmth mixed with the fear.

Mother love. Stronger than I'd ever felt it from her before. She wasn't dreaming of being pregnant. She was really...

Of course the Lady of Blood and Stone was having a fit. She was a goddess of chastity and solitude. Pregnant women weren't allowed in her temple. To let one walk on her very body — well, that was why they'd done the tests.

I opened my mouth to protest. It couldn't have happened. She would have to have slept with a man as soon as she left, and Trulia didn't even *like* men.

Unless...

"It can't be mine. They did the tests when we stopped trying. You weren't pregnant."

"Not then." She gave me a wobbly smile. "But it's the Changing God, and it always takes him months to work it out. Maybe he was working it out *inside* me. Maybe your cells were there all along, changing, and..."

She really believed that. I still half-thought this was my own mind, dreaming things up. But it was the truth to her. There hadn't been anyone else.

That only made everything hurt worse. If she'd stood her ground and said *no* to the recruiters, we'd be together now, having a baby, and we'd be so happy. Now they were both going to die.

"There has to be something we can do."

Trulia teared up again. Her despair was painful, and I had to concentrate to hear her words. "This is what she always does. You of all people should know. They won't see the earth again unless they put me on a ship and send me *nowhere*. Like the sheep in that story. Like the Lord of Green and Crawling Things."

I stared at her.

"The Lord of Green and Crawling Things survived. He had a leaf."

"He what?"

"He had a leaf. Leaves know how to fall."

"How the hell does that help me?"

I was babbling. I had no idea if this even worked for mortals, but it was the only thing I had. "Listen, Trulia. This is the most important thing I'll ever tell you. You're going to wake up, and you have to remember. Find leaves."

"What are you talking about?"

I squeezed her hands so hard that she winced. "As many leaves as you can. From the hydroponic gardens or wherever you can find them. Don't let anyone take them away. Hide them under your clothes if you have to. Then pray to the

Lord of Green and Crawling Things."

She squirmed. "I hate bugs."

"It doesn't matter. Pray to him. I don't know that he can see you now, but the leaves will find him, sooner or later, on their way to the ground. Leaves and prayers, Trulia. Remember that. Leaves know how to fall. They'll guide you home."

She shook her head. "I won't remember. I never remember my dreams."

"You remember little things. Clouds. Do you remember dreaming of clouds?"

"Yes, but—"

"Then you can remember this. Find leaves. Leaves know how to fall. Remember."

Tears leaked from her eyes, but she nodded. "Find leaves. I can remember. Find leaves."

I held her as close as I could. We repeated it to each other, over and over, until the tower's every wall became a green, growing branch.

That day I walked around in a blur, not knowing if the dream had been real, if my words had saved her. The next night, I didn't dream, but I woke up aching. I rubbed my eyes, and my hand came back dripping red.

Blood. Pain. My Lady's curse.

But why curse me now? Why, when I'd been defying her for days?

I stumbled to the bathroom, peered blurrily into the mirror. My skin was a clotted mess. I showered and scrubbed myself spotless, but within the hour, the blood was oozing its way back.

I met the Acolytes of the Curse, outside my Lady's temple, with lowered eyes. They shook their heads. Everyone had seen this coming.

"You have to wear bandages," said the junior acolyte, as if I didn't know. "And never go in the temple of any god. You will be alone." She looked at me full of pity. She was even younger than Friana, and freckles dotted her nose. Her voice shrank to a whisper. "Was it worth it?"

By my Lady's rules, I couldn't answer. I wiped my bloody hands and shuffled away.

Here is the thing.

Some gods work slow. The Herdsman of the Dead's plans last lifetimes. The Changing God tries at random, for months, until he gets it right. But the Lady of Blood and Stone sees with terrible clarity. She acts in a moment.

Yet she didn't curse me when I looked in the books against her orders, when I sought Trulia in dreams, when I told her about the leaves. She didn't seem to care that I defied her. We both knew it was useless.

And this morning she cursed me anyway.

Something must have changed.

She wanted to punish Trulia. I think I must have stopped her. The moon hasn't risen yet; the sky is still black. But I won't doubt anymore. Why would she curse me now, unless Trulia found the leaves and slipped out of her grasp?

I don't know if the blood will drive her away, when she sees me again. It surprises me how little I care. It's enough to know that she's alive, that our baby is alive.

So I pace our apartment, washing as often as I can, scattering green leaves over the floor, so she'll fall here, and not some other place. I pray to the Lord of Green and Crawling Things, though I'm not used to his liturgy, and even when the pain is at its worst, I am happy.

Trulia is alive, and she's coming home.

Memo From Neverland

Lost boys take finding; take watching;
take hauling their weight from the snickering surf
when the pixie dust runs out too soon.
I built this place one tree-house plank at a time.
The vines you bat aside, the sword-storm of pirates
and flight through stars: that's all by design,
love. That's the cleverness of me.

I fell out of my crib with nothing.
Now the mermaids and tigers are mine—

And you say I never grew up?

Goblin Love Song

Sink your claws in deep, though skin resists,
and lay me down on spine-contorting stones.
Shrug away these rags and bare your wrists:
I want to suck the marrow from your bones.

Busied with the cleaner world above,
my greeds and yours have been too long apart.
Crush me under fangs and tongue, my love:
I want to gnaw the innards of your heart.

Atavist

When she pecks at the ground she dreams of teeth.
When she scratches the dirt she dreams of claws:
sleek feathered bodies with meat-hooks for toes,
running in packs
before time gave them wings.

Lady Blue and the Lampreys

Lady Blue likes everything just so. Second table from the far window at Old Benny's Pub, the dark wood shining clean and the drapes half down, an Electric Lemonade in a frosted highball glass just off-centre. No menu, no salt shaker. This is Lady Blue's spot, and Benny saves it for her every Wednesday, Thursday, and Saturday night, with a second chair pulled out discreetly for Lady Blue's dearest husband, whether or not he arrives.

He is here tonight, of course. The latest model is a Jason, young and clean-cut, with gym-rat muscles and a mischievous little beard. His eyes are hazel. The girls at the bar can tell he's Lady Blue's property from the way he hangs on her gestures. That, and the bright silver key on a bright silver chain round his neck. Lady Blue's husbands get keys, not rings.

That's the tableau. Lady Blue impeccably neat, in a sky-blue evening gown, with her hair up to bare a slender neck. Jason, in the half-light, leaning in to her whispers. Men in old brown coats around them, drinking and drinking, and girls in a little less than that. Everyone's huddled together, night like tonight. Benny says there's a sea-storm coming.

"Hah," says a girl all in red: the hair, the lips, the dress, the heels. She's playing cribbage with the boys, two tables down from Lady Blue, and she's just won two nob points for dealing a Jack. "Clear sky, not a drop. Anyway we're tens of miles inland."

"Doesn't matter," says gap-toothed Shaun, who's been at Old Benny's Pub longer than a girl like Red can remember. "Benny's never wrong."

"Nobody's never wrong," says Red. She snaps down a card. "Five."

Then it comes.

It's a wind that whips through Benny's half-open windows. A visible wind, a dirty brownish-blue, smelling of brine. It leaves a scuff on Jason's glass, like someone's rotten-tooth breath.

"What'd I tell you?" Shaun hollers. He points to the frigid swirl at the centre of the room, which grows more visible by the second, thickening into something like limbs. Shaun loves it when Benny's right. Benny just shakes his head, keeps washing the bar.

The wind thickens and thickens, and then the howl isn't wind through branches but an unearthly trill in the throats of what's standing there.

They're men from the solar plexus down. Above that, something slimy and finned twists up and up to a blind head. Each one gapes with three black lamprey mouths.

Lightning flashes, flickering off of their thousands of teeth.

Everybody's looking now, even Jason. Bloody Tom Jackson with the long sideburns, fingering the switchblade in his back pocket, is the first to rise.

"This ain't your town," he says. "Get going, you."

Bloody Tom stares down the lampreys. The lampreys, eyeless, gape back at him.

Jason edges a little closer to Lady Blue.

Then there's a lunge. Nobody's sure if it's Bloody Tom who strikes first, or the lampreys. There's just a whirling howl, a wet smacking noise, then Bloody Tom lies limp in a lamprey's grip, his knife knocked out of his hand. The creature dips its mouthy end as if about to kiss him. One sucking mouth latches on to the hollow of Bloody Tom's cheekbone. One at the base of his jaw. And the third, the largest one, at the base of his throat, between the collarbones.

There is a sound like a child sucking a milkshake through a straw. Bloody Tom's body shrivels.

Jason clutches at Lady Blue's hand. He's shaking, poor thing. Lady Blue trails a fingertip along his knuckles. She is not fool enough to interfere, but she rather wants to stay and watch. Lady Blue is not afraid of anything.

The lamprey drops Bloody Tom's body to the floor. Its mouthy end looks different now, rounder, with something rough at the edges like a parody of sideburns.

"My name is Bloody Tom," it says, all three mouths speaking in unison. "Everyone knows I beat my wife. Nobody knows I beat my children. I want them to be tough enough to get *out* of here, see? But they fuck up and I lose control. Then I beat myself. I think I never really had control, not in my whole life."

The other men, poised at first to defend Bloody Tom, back away.

"My name is Bloody Tom," says the lamprey again. "Does anyone else have a problem with me?"

And no one's dumb enough to say they do. The lamprey stomps to the bar and orders a Jim Beam, Bloody Tom's favorite. Benny's the kind of bartender who doesn't say anything. Just slides the glass across and takes his money.

The other men make excuses and leave: some with terror in their eyes, some saving up murder for later. Lady Blue would like to watch the lampreys a little longer. The one taking Bloody Tom's name looks like his head is imperceptibly unrounding, gradually losing Tom's features. She'd like to see how that works, what it means. But Jason is practically in her lap now, clinging to her, though he's man enough to pretend that's not what he's doing.

"I got to get you home, honey," he says. "I don't think it's safe for you here."

Lady Blue's house is the biggest in town. There are rooms for breakfast, rooms for lunch, pantries and dining rooms, bathrooms, shower rooms, hot-tub rooms, guest rooms, storage rooms, linen closets, wardrobes, rooms full of appliances, rooms for television and board games and stacks on stacks of books. There is the one little room where Jason must never go, and there is the big bedroom, the mountainous canopy bed where he waits every night, naked but for the key round his neck, the way Lady Blue likes. If he were a dog, he'd be wagging his tail.

Tonight when he gathers her up in his arms, his forearms quiver. "What *was* that tonight,

honey? Where do things like that come from? Do you know?"

"Not a thing," says Lady Blue, which is the truth. "Smart men learn not to look too hard for answers."

Jason has an adorable way of multitasking when he's drunk. He tugs at the buttons of Lady Blue's dress while he talks. "God, when I think of anything happening to you—when I think of you in the same room with those things, I just get..." He reaches the last button. The thick blue silk falls away, and he falters midsentence. Falls to her creamy skin instead of talking, kisses and bites the curve of her breast. "God. Oh."

Lady Blue smiles indulgently, weaves her fingers through his short hair. "You get frisky, honey?"

"No! No, that's not it, I just get–" Whatever he gets is lost in another set of incoherent noises. He clutches her waist, pulls her closer and kisses his way up to her mouth. She leans in over him, hands at his shoulder blades, makes him lean back. "I want to keep you in here," he says in snatches, when there's room for his lips and tongue to make anything but kisses. "Safe here. Forever. All mine."

Lady Blue doesn't talk back because there's no need. Jason knows just how to please her. She tells him sometimes, when they're done and lying puddled together, what a good boy he is. How he makes her shine from the inside out. But she will never admit the other thing she feels. The way she looks down at him sometimes and dares to believe that he's perfect. After all these years and all these husbands, this one will stay good to her. This is the one she can keep.

If anything ever scared Lady Blue, it would be the way she gets that feeling every time, even knowing better.

The lampreys don't go away. They skulk on street corners gaping at passerby. Working mothers pull their children close to cross on the other side of the street. Men — specially no-good men like Shaun — glare at the lampreys and growl.

On Sunday, three of Bloody Tom's friends jump on a lamprey, figuring three men with blades drawn are a fair match for three mouths. The lamprey doesn't think so. There's a whirling of wind. Now it's three men and seven lampreys. No one sees those men again, but everyone hears their voices in snatches of three-part harmony.

"My name is Lou, and I'm so lonely I sleep with my arms wrapped around the radio."

"My name is Cal, and when my sister died, I knew who'd taken her. I never told. I was a kid. I thought he'd come for me next if I said anything."

"My name is Mack, and I was lying when I said I wanted to stab that lamprey. I was drunk, I just wanted to sound tough, and I didn't think — Please. I don't give a shit about Tom. If I hadn't lost that factory job, you think I'd be here? You think I'd care about you lowlifes? I hate you all. Please. God. Please, let me go."

Some folks look at the lampreys with pity when they say those things — though the pity is not for the lampreys. Most folks, even the ones who thought they loved Cal and Mack, draw away. Most don't want to know the things at the bottom of a dead man's heart.

On Monday there's another fight, and no one in town agrees what side started it. On Tuesday, the lampreys take the local seamstress and her baby son. When a lamprey crosses town declaring that its name is Ollie and it misses its mama, the game changes. Conquest now, not vengeance. Families hide in their cellars. Leave the window open a crack, or a knot-hole unguarded in the wall, and there's a chance they'll come shrieking in on the wind.

On Wednesday night, Lady Blue slinks into Old Benny's Pub and takes her usual seat. The pub has been unofficially divided, with lampreys to one side. A few of the shabbiest regulars, still alive, huddle at the other and nurse their cheap liquor.

Benny raises an eyebrow as Lady Blue enters. "Where's the husband?"

"Safe," says Lady Blue. Benny puts down the usual Electric Lemonade, and she raises it to her lips. "Doors weatherstripped, windows shut, snug as a pin. I mean to keep this one a good while yet." And she means it. Poor thing — when she suggested going out, he said yes, but he shook like a trapped rabbit. It's a good enough reason for missing their date night, she thinks. This once. As long as he's waiting for her when she returns.

"Yet you're out here."

Lady Blue takes another sip. "I want to understand what's happening. A lady doesn't do that by hiding at home."

"So what's your grand plan?"

"Observe."

Lady Blue looks away from Benny. The man's seen a lot, and there's a wariness in his voice when he talks to her. He avoids looking straight at her, even while he's setting out the highball just the way she likes. Lady Blue finds this tiresome.

The bar's quiet, but for lampreys murmuring in their wind-whisper way and human drunks muttering in despair.

Lady Blue strains to hear if there are any human words in what the lampreys say. Lady Blue does not believe in God, but it strikes her that the lampreys are like little gods, judging every soul that goes in. Or pretending to. She wonders if the human words in those mouths are even true. She wonders which is worse, calumny or exposure.

While she is thinking, a new man walks in.

You can tell he's from out of town by the uniform, the crisp-cut walk. No one walks so clean and straight in this town. Even spotless Lady Blue tends to slink or to glide, not to march like a fool soldier. The man's clean-shaven, with hair so short it must be military, and a wooden cross round his neck. His eyes are bright green.

"Evenin', sir," he says, nodding to Benny and Lady Blue. "Ma'am."

"Evening," says Lady Blue, nodding back.

"What'll you have?" says Benny.

"Nothing, sir. My name's Abner. I'm from the Department of Emergencies. There's been reports of some disturbance here, sir, so I was sent..."

He trails off, his Adam's apple rising. "Reports of some disturbance" hardly covers it.

"You think you can do anything?" says Lady Blue.

"Ma'am," says Abner, "with the good Lord on our side, the Department of Emergencies can always do something. Can't say I've seen a case quite like this, but there's always hope."

Lady Blue takes a sip of her Electric Lemonade. "What if the good Lord is on the lampreys' side?"

Abner laughs. "Wash out your mouth, ma'am."

"And spoil the taste of a good highball?"

"Fair point." He smiles. More intrigued than offended. "Night like tonight, though, shouldn't a dame like you be home, where it's safe?"

"I can take care of myself, thank you."

One of the drunks in the corner grins up at them. "Toughest dame in town, that one. Richest, too."

This seems to perk Abner's interest. Or his worry. "You're not from that big house up on the hill, ma'am?"

"I would be, yes."

His brow furrows. "You... You don't have a spouse or dependents in that house, do you, ma'am?"

Lady Blue looks at him levelly. "What's it to you?"

"Ma'am, I went by that house and there was a front window wide open. You better get back there, round up your people, if they're still there. Beggin' your pardon, of course."

Lady Blue's gaze becomes a stare.

She is sure that she closed every window, sealed every door. Lady Blue pays attention to the details.

"I can walk you there, ma'am," says Abner. He's subtler about it than most, but his eyes have been on her since he came in, more than on the lampreys. Men see Lady Blue and they want to stay with her, protect her. "Not sure what I can do beyond that, but if you need a pair of hands—"

"No," says Lady Blue.

She puts down her Electric Lemonade unfinished and pays, leaving Benny his usual tip. Then she slips out of Old Benny's Pub and runs up the street, in her long blue dress and high heels, as fast as she's ever run to anything.

Jason is silly, not stupid. He knows what will happen if he opens a window. He cannot have done it carelessly, and Lady Blue knows she did not do it herself. He can only have done it on purpose. To hurt her. To hurt himself. In some mood so shattered that he no longer cares for his soul.

There is only one thing that makes Lady Blue's husbands betray her.

She hopes she is wrong. Jason is so new. He hasn't started with a single one of the warning signs. He has never toyed idly with the key in her presence; never cast long, brooding looks at it; never asked the wrong questions. Lady Blue will never admit it, but there are tears in her eyes. She does not want the lampreys to have this man. If she is wrong about what he has done tonight, she will protect him with everything she has. She hopes she is wrong.

She knows she is right.

She reaches the house on the hill. The front window is wide open. She unlocks the door, lets herself in, closes it behind her, and shuts and locks the window.

The anteroom is silent and dark. Lady Blue flicks on the lights. She does not see any lampreys, so far.

She walks head held high, no sound but the click of her heels, through the five halls and the countless rooms. She thinks she hears something wailing faintly, now and again, but she is not certain. She does not see lampreys. She does not see Jason. She pauses by the door to the one little room where he can never go. It is shut and locked, but that is no proof of anything.

She checks the closets, even the cupboards. She pauses in the kitchen and draws her best carving knife from its drawer. She saves the master bedroom for last.

On the great canopy bed, Jason is waiting for her, naked, just the way she likes. But he is weeping. His eyes are puffy and red, and the key round his neck drips, fouling the sheets with blood that is not yet his.

Lady Blue goes very still.

"Jason," she says.

He starts towards her, then cringes away.

"Explain this to me, Jason," says Lady Blue without a hint of emotion.

He struggles to speak through his tears. "What did you do to them?"

"To whom, Jason?"

"Your other husbands." The words wrench their way out of him, halfway between a sob and a shout of rage. "All of your other husbands! All h-hanging there, dead, dripping. How could you do it, honey? How?"

"Why did you go in that room, Jason?"

"You were so c-casual. All the time. With the lampreys. And I thought — I thought you must *know* something. I know I promised you I wouldn't look, but the whole town is dying. If I saved the whole town, you'd forgive me, wouldn't you? God would forgive me. Maybe things wouldn't be like they were, but— He hiccups, chokes briefly on his tears. "But there was nothing about lampreys. There was just them."

"And the window, Jason?"

"I was so scared. And angry. I could hear them wailing outside. I thought, if they want to kill us both, why not? Why should I want to live?" He sniffs loudly. "But they didn't come. And you're going to kill me now, too, aren't you?"

Lady Blue makes no effort to hide the carving knife. Neither does she do anything with it yet. She sits on the edge of the bed next to him. He shies away, but she catches him under the chin with one finger, makes him look in her eyes. "If I didn't kill you now, honey, what would you do? If I held you gently and explained in small words how it started, said I was sorry for scaring you like this, promised not to hurt you so long as you kept my secret? Could you live with me? Could you still be my dearest husband and make me shine from the inside out?"

Jason pulls away, and that's when she knows for sure. He can't meet her eyes, but he sniffs and mumbles, "Yes. Yes, I'd still love you. Please. It could be like before."

"You'd listen to everything I told you? You'd keep it all a secret for me?"

"Please..."

Lady Blue strokes back along his cheek. Tangles her left hand lazily in his hair, like she does every night, when he wants to put his mouth on her. "Then kiss me, honey."

She doesn't draw him closer. She waits for him to move, and he does— away from her, bucking against her grip. They all struggle like this, in the end.

"What did you do to them?" he demands again, his voice rising to a shriek.

"This," says Lady Blue. She cuts his throat, spilling his blood over the bedspread.

Then she puts on a little light music.

Lady Blue is a creature who mourns. Just not the same way as most women. Most of her rage and grief at losing Jason is in the carving knife, the one swift cut that brings closure. The rest must be dealt with in other ways. The essential thing is to keep herself moving and orderly. There are rituals: care of the body, washing of hands and sheets, cleaning of knife, lighting of candles. And there is music. Lady Blue's only real friend at these times is her old vinyl record of Verdi's Requiem. Verdi understands about punishment, about actions having consequences, even if Lady Blue's husbands never do in the end. She has everything timed, so that when the last strains of the *Libera me* fade, her house is spotless. Except for that one little room.

She washes her hands as the choir softly murmurs, and then she gets to work. She fetches a coat hanger from that one little room and hangs Jason on it like a suit jacket. The hardest part is carrying the body down the hall and not leaving a trail of blood. She always fails at this, a little, and has to use steel wool and polish to get it off the hardwood, which is factored into the schedule.

Three feet from the door to that one little room, she hears a wailing like wind.

She pauses. Jason's body lolls in her arms.

"I have no quarrel with you," she says to the walls. "Leave me alone."

The wailing fades, or seems to. It's hard to tell under the music. Lady Blue stands in place and breathes for a moment, considering. She could turn off the record, but that would mess up the ritual. Anyway the *Kyrie* is winding down, with longer and slower pauses between each phrase, and maybe if she waits a moment—

Yes. There is silence. She cannot hear either music or lampreys.

Then the record gets to the good part. She does hear wailing now: the choir wailing in the hands of an angry God, the strings wailing in answer. The wind wails, too. A lamprey materializes in front of her, flexing its mouths with greed.

"I am not one of the men who attacked you," Lady Blue says through her teeth. "I am not your enemy." But she readies her carving knife all the same. She knows that speech is useless, and that it will lunge at her.

Instead, it lunges at Jason.

She is not ready for that. She swipes with the knife and misses. Jason is borne out of her arms, kissed by those hungry toothy mouths. She stands frozen. His body withers before her eyes. The lamprey lets go, dropping him to the floor. There is a bit of a shape to it now, a bit of Jason's cheekbones and his mischievous little beard.

"My name is Jason," says the lamprey, its three mouths shouting to be heard over the despair of the choir. "And I loved you, you bitch. You were my whole life. I'll never forgive you. I'd kill you back if I could. I loved you. I hate you."

Lady Blue grabs it and cuts all three of its throats. Its blood is not red but black and sluggish, like the silt at the bottom of a river. She slices four, five times to make sure, until its mouthy end hangs off the rest of it by a tiny sliver of skin.

She feels confused. This is not how the ritual ought to go. She did not make time for cleaning up two bodies, and she'll never get that black blood out of the hardwood floor.

She tucks what is left of Jason carefully into that one little room, on its hangar with the others, even shriveled and small. She closes and locks the door, then cleans the key. She decides she will clean up after Jason completely before dealing with the lamprey. He deserves that much.

There is wailing outside the house now, very loud. At some moments it drowns out the Requiem. It shakes the windows, batters the eaves. She's killed one of their own, and the lampreys are angry.

She ignores them. She has sealed up the house. There is nothing else she can do.

The best way to get blood out of bedsheets is quickly, with ice water and salt paste, before the stains have time to set. Lady Blue works diligently until her hands change color with cold. When she has exhausted the first bucket of ice water and is heading to the kitchen for more, she passes the lamprey's body again.

In its pool of sludge-blood, it's twitching. Its throat re-forms, and its mouths strain to form words again. "My name is Jason. My name is Jason, my name is Jason, and I loved you..."

This time Lady Blue cuts off its mouthy end completely. Then, to be safe, she cuts the rest of it into pieces and seals each one in a separate Tupperware container from the kitchen. Her carving knife wasn't designed to slice through bone, but it is the best she has. It is long, ugly work. By the end of it, Lady Blue is filthy and twitching herself. The sea-wind has only grown stronger.

She is all the way to the *Sanctus*. She should be most of the way through the cleaning now, not making more of a mess. The choir taunts her, singing in mock-joyful chords drowned out by diabolical, chromatic strings. Whatever they are praying to, it is not the nice tame God that the man from the Department of Emergencies wears round his neck.

The lampreys will kill her eventually, Lady Blue knows. As soon as she ventures out of her sealed-up house. Jason and his open window will get to kill her back, after all. Very well. She will face them like a lady. Perhaps she will take a few with her.

Lady Blue stacks the Tupperware containers and puts them in the room with her husbands' bodies. Jason's soul is in there somewhere, after all. Then she trudges back to the anteroom, carving knife in hand, leaving a trail of black blood which someone else will have to clean.

Lady Blue flings open her front door.

The lampreys fly in. Dozens of them surround her. Lady Blue moves without much thought. She stabs with her carving knife, dodging their drooling mouths, and they fall and fall around her. She does not have time to really kill them. Only to keep hurting each one until it can't move closer.

She has no sense of time passing apart from the music — fickle music, pleading and raging by turns. She is surprised to last even a minute or two, but the music goes on and on, and there she is, fighting. Bloody Tom's friends couldn't have lasted this long, and they had three times as many knives.

Lady Blue is not like the others. Doesn't she know it.

It's still a matter of time. For each one that drops, two more sail in on the wind. Finally she doesn't spin fast enough and they blindside her. Six lamprey necks wind around the hand with the knife. Eight more at the other arm — she is suddenly immobilized. She can see nothing but mouths.

The music builds to its final, tragic chorus.

These things are pitiless just like Lady Blue. Like looking in a hideous mirror. Lady Blue has only ever done what she had to, but the lampreys will not see it that way. They will eat the excuses and drink the darkness underneath, the thing even Lady Blue cannot name. Then they will pour it out on the town like it's all she ever was. Maybe it is. For the first time in her life, Lady Blue is terrified.

Mouths latch on to her filthy skin everywhere, not just three but a mass of them. She kicks wildly and accomplishes nothing.

Then there is a scream.

First one lamprey turns back into wind, then another and another, until the horde around her is nothing but a screaming flight, fleeing into the night sky and gone. Lady Blue falls to the floor in a puddle of black sludge.

She puts a hand to her neck, stunned. She is not withered. She does not even feel much pain. She does not seem to be injured apart from one small, round laceration, the kind that only needs a drug-store bandage.

She does not feel triumphant, like a thing that scares gods. She feels hideous and tired.

The music is more or less over. "*Libera me, Domine, de morte aeterna, in die illa tremenda,*" the alto spits in a bitter monotone, as if she already knows there is no redemption. There are a few, soft chords, and the recording ends.

Well. The floor is absolutely unsalvageable. She'll have to buy an industrial-grade steam cleaner and refinish the hardwood. Tomorrow.

She washes the carving knife in dismal silence. Then she throws her bloodsoaked dress in the kitchen garbage and takes a scalding shower, scrubbing for what feels like hours until she no longer feels lamprey sludge in her pores.

She emerges into the wide, tiled bathroom, haggard but dripping clean. She wipes the fog off the mirror, leans against the sink, and looks sideways at herself. She feels very old, but she is still perfectly smooth, perfectly curved.

She meets her own eyes.

"My name is Lady Blue," she says to the mirror, unsure if it's even true. "I do not know what else I am. And I wish that someone — just one person, just once — could look at my soul and not flee."

On Thursday night, Lady Blue does not appear at Old Benny's Pub. But on Saturday night, there she is, splendid in something new and midnight blue. She does not feel much like speaking to men, or speaking to anything. But one must keep up appearances.

No one has seen any lampreys since Wednesday night. Red and the other girls say that the monsters must have seen the cross round Abner's neck and fled.

He's still here. The admiring girls seem to make him nervous. Sweat drips down his from his buzz-cut temples. He makes an excuse and disentangles himself from the girls, walking to stare out the window at the night street.

He must know that the girls are mistaken. Lady Blue wonders what else he knows. What else he's hiding.

He isn't a poorly built man. Strong, not with gym-rat muscles like Jason's, but in an understated way that suggests long treks through the woods. Clean, apart from the sweat. White nails. Not even a hint of stubble. Still, Lady Blue is not in the mood to admire men for long. She takes care not to come too close.

"You," she murmurs.

He looks up, startled. "Oh, I recognize you. I hope everything was all right the other night, with the... the window, and all."

Lady Blue takes a sip of Electric Lemonade, cool as you please.

"You don't really know what happened, do you?" she says, low enough so the other girls won't hear.

Abner sighs. "No, ma'am. I'd appreciate if you didn't spread the word around, but I don't. That's why I'm still here. I can't give the Department of Emergencies the all clear when I don't know why those things are gone, or whether they want to come back."

"Wise choice. But your secret's safe with me."

Abner takes a sip of his rum and Coke, looking back out the window. "I can't say for sure without proof. But I like to think the good Lord did come through. The cross is just a symbol when you get down to it, and those things ain't vampires anyway. But we prayed, we hoped, we stepped in to try to help, and He sent *something* to pull us through. That's how He works, isn't it? Probably sent help in the last place anyone'd think to look. I reckon I can find it."

Lady Blue can't help but smile. It's so cute when they have hope. It ought to be sad, but it draws her in every time, like a moth to a candle. Even — or especially — in the midst of her grief.

Abner looks at her, perplexed. Unconsciously, he fingers his cross. "There's something different about you," he says. "Beggin' your pardon, ma'am. But there's a type of young woman who comes to this sort of place alone, and you're not that type. No, forgive me, ma'am, that's an inexcusable way to say it. Just that it's been two drinks, and I'm trying to figure out why you're here at all."

"I'd like to know that myself," says Lady Blue.

He looks at her ringless hands. "You married, ma'am? Gettin' away from the husband?"

"Widowed," she says, quite calmly.

He blushes. "Oh. Oh, I'm sorry, ma'am, I shouldn't have — I'm sorry."

Lady Blue smiles again. "As penance, why don't you buy me a drink?"

And he does. They're all the same. She sits in her spot, second from the far window with the drapes half down, and Abner brings her a second Electric Lemonade in a frosted highball glass, just the way she likes.

A Certain Kind of Spider

The male of the species swings as he walks.
He puffs his eight-armed leather jacket
(unknowingly inside out).
The male of the species knows we want him.

He calls me, signing with eight virgin hands.
I love a strong woman. A warrior.
Come here, you Amazon, come to me
and I'll savage you like a man should.
He beckons. He flexes his chitin.

Of course I come to him, jaws open,
just as he asks—

and two minutes later it's *Oh God, my head,*
my head, you ATE it — you crazy cannibal bitch,
what's wrong with you, what did you do to my head?
Your head? Oh, my darling—
as if you'd ever used it before!

The Siren of Mayberry Crescent

1

She's not much to look at.
Pinch-faced, tight-haired,
buried in a muffler
she storms past polished lawns
same as anyone.

Only when it's bursting, panicking,
pounding on the inside of her mouth
does the smallest note slip past
through her lowered lips
and into — not the air!—
but the neighbor's hedge.

She looks back.
Not at a straight green line
but a wave, root-trapped,
straining to follow her.

She snaps her jaws together.
Silence is golden.

2

In dreams she strides a rocky shore,
years ago, laughing aloud,
singing to dash fluttering fish on the stones
for easy supper.

Ships' bones for shelter.
Sailors for pleasure.
Duets, trios in the wreckage,
earsplitting and heavenly.

In dreams she plants herself treelike
in among the cliffs, draws breath forever,
and screams.

3

Why did she leave that rocky shore?
Why does a girl leave anything?

He scaled those rocks with his ears stuffed.
Laughing, brave and long-limbed,
no trance-led obedient beast
but a leaping dancer, like her sisters,
and he tilted the world in his wake.

He picked up his oars still smelling of her,
and she climbed in, unseen,
to see this other world
where men had minds.
Past the horizon he turned, startled.
Like she was a ghost.

I hope you know what you've done,
he said — his first words. *I hope you know,*
where I'm from, you can't sing.

Ask any sea-witch:
your voice is a pittance.

4

He was good: bought her a ring,
a house, a white leg-tangling gown.
A food processor with maelstrom blades.
The neighbors peeked in,
scowled, shook their fingers.
She was good: kept her mouth shut.
A whole year until the words clawed her head,
and she shrank her breath to the smallest sound,
alone in the dark with him.
I don't want this anym—
He turned away and the words died.
He'd kept his ears stuffed all along.
Later she tore atlases, unlettered,
for a rocky shore like hers,
breaking her eyes on the lines
until the bookseller shut them.
Your husband don't sail anymore,
lady, you can't go back.

5

He goes to work. Reads the news.
Doesn't even laugh now, deflated
by her wordless stare.
She wears no bruises, no broken bones,
just silence and silence and silence—
until, in a week like any other,
she takes a left, stops the sedan,
climbs atop its roof like an animal,
heedless of human stares—
and sings car-crashes, splintering glass,

bloody handprints on crushed metal,
telephone poles crashing down.
Widening crowds claw over car-knives,
trample each other to reach her, to reach her,
until someone has the presence of mind
to call the police in their checkerboard cars,
which smash, the first few times,
blaring lights music-drowned.
The third time, they plug their ears with wax,
but by then the whole block is gone
and she refuses to raise her hands.
This far in, there's no compromise,
only silence and song,
and she sings.

Evianna Talirr Builds a Portal on Commission

Here's the thing. Atoms lie.
This ring of golden gears I've built,
spread like a pool before your feet,
the interlocking click of parts too small to see
and the roaring night inside — this is the twin
of the tunnel of light seen by dying men,
the rush of air when certain beings disappear,
or a simple wooden door.
Only atoms stroke your ears
and whisper that one place is not like another.

(Feel that?
The wind on a knife edge,
the howl of hungry air from the floor.
It's a long way down.)

Common portal-operators, idiots,
slaves to geometry — they can't do what I do.
They push pins into star-maps,
pull wires taut between, and lucky you
if you can work out a zigzag heading
from you to your goal.
I am more direct. Hence a hundred fools before you:
Evianna, take me to a forest
that the gods have never seen. Evianna,
find me the largest corundum vein
in the galaxy. Evianna,
take me somewhere they can't find me.
They pay, at least.
(As you did — *Evianna,*

take me to my vanished lover.)

Where is she? Wrong question.
Where will you go? Remember,
atoms lie. Circuits and prayers
are not so different, all places are one
and you and whoever she is:
likewise. What's love but a kind of seeing,
piercing past the lies of your bodies
and knowing nothing really separates you?
There — the smile. You've seen her that way.
Now think, if you could strip away the lies
and leave your core, not the body,
but the part that always knew these things — Yes.
You understand, though your hands shake.

(There *is* another way. It involves a contract
for your soul. Interested? No? Good.)

Brush the burnished threshold with your toes.
Let the wind tear your hair. You won't die.
The fall will flay you. I can't help that.
But I've found a world where atoms tell a different lie.
Have a look around you
once your bones have worn to sand,
and I promise you,
she'll be there.
Now.
Jump.

The Mother of All Squid Builds a Library

For Bogi Takács

1

In the Fourth Year of the Hydra, the Mother of All Squid built a library.

This, according to the whales, was foolishness. The Mother of All Squid sent fifteen of her bodies to the whales, asking them for stories from their journeys, or perhaps a bit of ambergris or a songbook.

"Foolishness," said the whales. "Libraries are things of the upper worlds. Their books are made from weeds which would wither in the deep. And they must be read in the blinding light of the sun."

"Do you think," said the Mother of All Squid, "that I cannot build a thing in my own way?"

She had heard the whales speak about libraries before, after all, and she saw no reason a creature of her stature should not have such a beautiful thing.

"Foolishness," said the whales again, and they swam back to the upper worlds, eating two of her bodies on the way without even saying thank you.

2

The Mother of All Squid built her library out of crushed clamshells and stone from the deepest vents. She allocated six thousand bodies to the task, three thousand picking up seamlessly when the other three thousand needed rest.

There was no rest for her mind. While she assembled the walls, she took one hundred more bodies as emissaries to the flame-eels, who had only one body apiece and who were covered in ever-shifting lights. Of the species who spoke with light, flame-eels were the brightest and most beautiful — at least everyone thought so apart from the whales, who said the best lights belonged to the upper worlds.

The Mother of All Squid requested a tribute. Because she was beneficent, and because she had shared her wisdom with the eels and made treaties to keep the whales away, several eels volunteered, all young and at their brightest.

The flame-eels staged a festival to mark the occasion. The volunteers paraded through a canyon, decked in trains of bone and sand. The rest of the flame-eels sang songs of praise. All their lights flickered in unison, wishing the volunteers all the dragonfish they could swallow in the afterworld.

Then the Mother of All Squid took them, hooked the barbs of her tentacles under their skin, and flayed them.

Each volunteer took pains to say something important as they died. One told half the tale of an ancient war, while another sang a lullaby, and a third shone with the passion of courtship. The Mother of All Squid was precise, and took care to keep them alive until the last of the skin was removed. The resulting skins were beautiful and clear, each message perfectly preserved.

Finally the Mother of All Squid stretched the skins against the library's smooth stone, holding them in place with discarded barbs. Flame-eels came for miles to see it. They wept with delight, rainbows shivering from their teeth to the tips of their tails. And the Mother of All Squid — who, admittedly, had a bit of a vain streak — was pleased.

3

"Foolishness," said the whales. "This is not a library."

The Mother of All Squid pointed out that she now had twenty eelskins, containing everything from family sagas to treatises on cell biology. In the Mother of all Squid's opinion she was doing very well.

In the whales' opinion, the Mother of All Squid was only useful as a snack.

She endured their hunger and then, with a remaining body, called to them from a safe distance. "Well, do *you* have any libraries?"

"We need none," said the whales, "for we have the finest songs in the ocean, instead."

"Goodness," said the Mother of All Squid. "That does sound very nice."

"It is far better than eel-lights."

"It sounds extremely nice," said the Mother of All Squid. "If only my library had a song like that! That would be real knowledge, the likes of which I have not seen, since I am so small and live so far down in the dark."

The Mother of All Squid had been around a long time, after all, and she knew the pride of whales. She spoke winningly to them until one small whale said,

"Perhaps I can stay here and help. I have lived my time and fathered sufficient children. I am known for my songs, and content to be remembered through them."

The other whales protested, but he had made up his mind, and one by one they swam away.

"Sing to me," the Mother of All Squid urged. So the whale sang until she memorized every note.

"Thank you," she said. "That was so beautiful. It is just what I need." Then she hooked her barbs into the skin behind his unresisting nose.

"This," she said kindly, "might hurt a little."

4

The Mother of All Squid spent a long time arranging corals beneath the whale's skin, allowing water to whistle through them. For months she tuned every note, deepened the timbre, and amplified the highest peals.

"This will be foolishness," said the whales when they returned. "It will be nothing." But the Mother of All Squid lifted a curtain, and a mournful, beautiful song poured out. The flame-eels cavorted, but the whales were silent a long time.

"That is him," they said at last. "You have made him immortal."

And they swam away.

5

If you ask the whales now, they will say this:

Yes, the Mother of All Squid has a library. The lights of a thousand flame-eels dance on the walls. She did well.

They do not mention music. But every few years, a whale swims down to that place and does not return, and his song is heard across the sea forever.

Turning to Stone

I'm slowing down, or else the city's
speeding up around me. Paint-bright people
whirl along the many-cornered streets.
Your walk, my friends, becomes a fire-dance.
You point, you lean to whisper with each other.
Neon lamps play tango with your eyes. I struggle
forward. Once or twice you break your stride
to question me.

        (Stone woman!)

How do I like these violet candies in
the storefront? Or these cartoon-colored speed-line
cars, too far outside my skin to dream
about? You want to watch my belly hatch
the words. I try. I draw a breath. Time flees,
and when the sound begins, you've run too far
ahead to hear.

        (Madwoman!
        What shall we give you?)

I cannot walk. I'm looking at my leaning
hand against the red brick shop-side wall.
The knuckles stiffen. Nails grow thick as marble.
Something gray and cold spreads underneath
the skin in place of blood. My eyes crust over.
Mind and body slow and stop together,
and the world is only motion. Maybe
you've returned by now. I wonder if

I hear you shouting:

> (Show yourself! Speak to us!
> Can't our hands soothe you?)

I think the sounds will drown me. Something hardens
in my lungs. I have to stand as still
as possible

> (Have you found wisdom
> in unending silence?)

and fling my mind behind me
to remember

> (Stone woman! Snake-caught,
> what punishing god
> have we mocked
> to deserve you?)

how
to
breathe

Crocodile Tears

They slide from my lashes to my cupped hands.
I ball them like salty snow, aim just right
and pitch them into your pitiless eyes.

The Self-Rescuing Princess

You drew the chalk lines, lit the candles,
asked for me. Are you surprised?
Did you expect this: matted hair,
dress in the unsexy kind of tatters,
holes at the elbows and filth in the seams,
fingernails black, face scarred?

I've broken my own hands to slip
a sacrifice's shackles. Torn the eyes
from the dragon's sockets.
Stabbed a wicked prince's throat,
wrenched myself off the railroad tracks—
and where were you?

Writing in your book about
how women are strong now.

But with these bloody, callused hands,
I still can't strangle shame.
You think I'll pose for that camera?
Think I'll paint my face and smile
in Wonder Woman's chains?
Try making a world
where princesses don't need rescuing.

Watch me walk out of your chalk circle.
I'm on a quest you know nothing about.
I'll learn to love myself,
rule myself, guard myself,
but I will never speak the lines

you feed me. I am not
your heroine. I am
a goddamned
survivor.

The Dragon-Ship

My lover gave back the ring and I ran to the docking bay: watched the great ships writhe against the night. We had so often stood here with his palm brushing mine. A dragon-ship glinted in the solar wind, spine spiraling, scales glittering turquoise and gold in the station floodlights. Half-alive, prow cruelly pointed, undulant through the slow current of spacetime: these were the ships that slipped like sea-snakes into galaxies no chemical thruster could reach. These had minds, hearts, cold-cortex dreams untranslatable to mortals. This one turned. For an instant, its diamond eye reflected into mine. A choice quick and final as a laser pulse. I would go. What reason did I have, now, to stay? I ran through cold steel to the ticket-office, counted the little salvage I had ever saved, offered it up. The dragon-ship rolled over in the darkness. The teller shook her head. I turned back and pressed my palm to the frozen porthole as the ship slipped prettily out of the world. Leaving me a too-slow fool full of coins, watching a fading yellow smoke-ring and the stars.

The Screech Owl Also Shall Rest There

By Ada Hoffmann and Jacqueline Flay

"Close your eyes. Sing."

Tiqu, the new boy, does as he's told, standing tense in the temple's centre with Ishka poised in front of him like a lover. He opens his lips on a wordless melody. It doesn't matter what the song is, only that it distracts him. The comb will hurt worse if he's thinking about it too hard.

The temple is a monumental thing, carved full of lion-gods, eagle-gods, even beetle-gods. Ishka usually does this under the trees or the stars, wherever her pack happens to be. But the temple was close this time, and she could not resist it. She is old enough to remember when this was pure blasphemy. Imagine gods that stay in one place, not roaming freely like every other creature! There were wars over this temple once. Ishka still smells blasphemy when she visits, and she likes that, even if the humans no longer remember why.

Tiqu's brow furrows. He repeats his melody, a chant to match the carvings.

Ishka dips her sharpened obsidian comb into the bowl of ash in front of her and looks Tiqu's nude body up and down.

Then she drives the comb into the flesh of his thigh.

Tiqu flinches. The melody catches in his throat, but he doesn't cry out. Good. He's a man, though a young one. He'll learn to crave this soon enough.

"One," she says.

Blood oozes out around the comb, which Ishka pulls out, making him flinch again. She leans in and kisses the blood away with the delicacy of a lover, which she will be, before the night is up. It's rich, healthy, free-flowing like most young blood. She swallows and lets go, leaving a small raw line of marks with something black at its core.

"You belong to me," says Ishka. This is the real ritual, the one for her, not for these silly rocks that are supposed to be gods.

Tiqu squares his shoulders. "I belong to you."

There is a murmur of agreement from the sides of the temple, where the rest of Ishka's pack watch. Okbu, the man who brought Tiqu here; greying Elgeia, her daughter, and her three younger sisters; Alqet, next-youngest to Tiqu, whose eyes blaze with recognition, seeing this ritual from the sidelines for the first time. Others, too, holding torches. All human, apart from Ishka. All sworn to her. When Tiqu's initiation is finished there will be thirteen, counting Ishka. Enough that she can sustain herself on sips of their blood without harming them. Not enough to make it difficult to feed them in return.

Ishka watches Okbu out of the corner of her eye. He is older even than Elgeia, and has been here the longest. His shoulders are still broad and his muscles taut, despite his age. Okbu and Tiqu are lovers, and Ishka knows it is Okbu, not her, who convinced Tiqu to run away with this pack. That is acceptable for now. He will learn.

She drives in the comb again. "Two."

Tiqu gasps, but does not open his eyes.

"You are my sustenance," says Ishka, when she has tongued the blood away. "I am your sustenance."

"Three." This time he whimpers shortly, a tiny sound he tries to cover up with another song. His breath is coming faster now. "I am the one who provides for you."

"You are the—"

He cuts himself off with a grunt of shock. This time she hasn't bothered to wait.

Ishka grins, her white fangs glinting in the torchlight. "Four."

Ishka's tattoos are patterns of dots and lines, not drawings in the usual sense. The patterns mean things only Ishka can translate. Generations ago, they were simple tally marks, reminding Ishka how many humans she'd taken (and, on a bad day, which was which). But tallying for hundreds of years is boring. She has learned to add flourishes and inconsistencies, which serve as mnemonics. A particular line does not stand for a concept, or even a sound — nothing that sophisticated. But something of Ishka stays in the patterns. Years later she can look at a tattoo and remember just what she was thinking when she made it.

Tiqu's upper left thigh says:

You are mine. Your hunger is mine. From now on I'll feast secondhand on whatever you steal. Your love is mine, even if you don't know it yet. Your life is mine. And, darling, new darling, I take what is mine.

Thirty incisions. That's as much as most can take their first time. They learn stamina later. Okbu has a pattern across his chest and shoulders which runs into the thousands. Ishka has seen Tiqu run his hands over it when he stands with Okbu, and she likes that. The way he gets scared and intrigued, like he's wondering if he'll ever be so brave.

At the last of his first thirty Tiqu shivers and scrunches his eyes. Ishka doesn't tell him out loud that it's over. She kisses her way up to his mouth, his blood still hot on her tongue.

Tiqu stumbles. Ishka catches him before he tips over. She pushes him up against a pillar carved with sharp-beaked birds, and she kisses him again. This time he's aware enough of what's happening to kiss back. A long groan escapes him, not entirely one of pain.

Only then does Ishka whisper: "It's over now, love. The pain, at least, is over."

Of course, she doesn't let the others watch after this. She drags him to a secluded corner for the last of the ritual. But no one is confused about what will happen. Everyone in the pack, male and female, has been through it themselves: the wild, half-panicked pleasure of Ishka's love, with their body still barely scabbed over.

Tiqu doesn't last terribly long, but he runs his hand along her jaw, afterwards, speechless, like he really has seen a god. She smiles thinly and leaves him. She can feel the sun coming up outside, and the exhaustion of day coming over her. In the daytime, Ishka sleeps like the dead in the deepest crevice she can find, and only Okbu ever follows.

Okbu was once young like Tiqu, of course. His oldest tattoo, the one at his upper left thigh, says:

You, boy, barely a man. Do you know the world is changing? A human can live his whole life and not get from one end of the change to the other.

You are strong for a human, good-looking, and able to kill. But there are strong young men like you in every band. Do you know why I chose *you*? Because the band that birthed you is old still. You do not have a staying season. You do not even weave nets, bless your hearts. The day is coming when no one will live this way. I will miss it. So let me keep you on my tongue, new boy, for as long as you last.

Ishka stretches awake at sundown. She rolls over, but Okbu isn't at her back. Probably gone to comfort Tiqu. Okbu's allegiance is to Ishka, but Tiqu may be lonely or frightened, and Ishka doesn't mind if Okbu loves him a little on the side.

Ishka's pack has a routine. Travel and hunt at night; rest in the daytime, though most humans don't need as much sleep as Ishka, so if they wake early and begin something useful, that's just as well. It's staying season, when most humans huddle in temporary houses, trusting the plants around them to provide until the summer drought makes them move on. In staying season, only packs like Ishka's move from place to place, creeping into human fields and taking what they can. Ishka's humans eat the fruit and roast the livestock, and Ishka drinks the surplus from their blood.

Ishka remembers when there was no staying season. She preferred things that way. It is ludicrous for a human to keep a patch of ground the way one keeps a garment or a lover. Humans did not make the ground, nor does the ground know loyalty. A little banditry now and then will perhaps remind them of this.

She rises and walks through a maze of passages into the temple's main chamber, ringed by lions and beetles. Her feet make no sound on the cool stone, but her voice does: a barely-formed tune, echoing Tiqu's voice the night before. A casual summons.

No one answers.

The temple is empty. The pack is gone: all twelve of the humans, even Okbu. An intriguing surprise. She is alone...

She sniffs the air. No, there are humans around. A pair at the outskirts of the temple. But not any humans she knows.

Ishka creeps to the edge and listens.

They're quiet. Not worshippers; not lovers on a tryst; not a pair out to walk and talk companionably. They're standing still, like they don't want to be heard. Like hunters.

Hunters of humans? Has someone learned to do this without Ishka's help? Hunters of animals, though few venture so close to the temple? A raiding party in some feud between bands? Followers of that frightening rarity, another vampire?

Or is this a coincidence?

Ishka creeps around behind them.

A man and a woman, both dressed like hunters. A spear at each side and a knife at each belt. Amusing that they think one knife each can protect them.

A deer stirs somewhere, and the woman looks towards it for a moment. In that time, Ishka leaps, grabs the man, and wrenches him back towards the temple. He barely has time to struggle. She twists his head and arms backwards painfully until he can't move.

The man cries out. The woman looks at him and shrieks. She pulls back her spear, ready to throw it, but Ishka cranks the man's neck back another notch, and he screams. "Don't, Ethibi! Don't."

The woman—Ethibi—lowers her spear. She suddenly stinks of terror. "Who are you? What are you trying to do with the temple?"

"I'll ask questions, not you." Ishka tilts her head. "Answer quickly and I'll let him go. If I still wish to, by then."

The man groans.

Ethibi bares her teeth. "What do you want to know?"

"At sunrise yesterday twelve humans were with me. They would not have all left me unbidden. Where did they go?"

"Today is a forbidden day. Did you not know?"

Another tug. Another scream. "Answer my question."

"No one must enter the temple on days when the moon is half-grown, for the moon-goddess and the lion-god do battle on this day. Anyone in the temple may be harmed. The day-guards came to enforce this rule and found a band of twelve. They took them back to Eddik. We... We didn't mean to hurt them, it was just forbidden for them to be there, so..."

Eddik. The settlement closest to the temple. Ishka's pack would have raided it today. Eddik is on very fruitful land: often it doesn't dry out even in the leaving season. The last few times Ishka visited, Eddik had no leaving season at all. The humans lay in place year-round, growing small and indolent.

"Forbidden?" says Ishka. "How can it be forbidden for humans to go where they like? No one was using the temple when we arrived, so we did not even inconvenience you."

Ethibi mumbles something.

Ishka thinks she understands. For generations, Eddik has grown greedier and greedier. In their long staying season, they have tried to tame the land like a dog. To make it better than it was. The more the land is tamed, the more possessive the humans are: *We made these olives grow, not you. We kept these flocks, not you. You cannot have them. You cannot enter this land.* Not that any human can stop Ishka.

Somehow, someone in Eddik must have decided that the temple is theirs. Even though the temple is generations older than Eddik, built hundreds of years ago. No one now living in Eddik built so much as a basin in its halls. It was meant — by those who didn't call it blasphemy — as a holy space for traveling bands to pass through for the night, every so often, to see and touch the gods' likenesses and make offerings if they wished. Yet now even the gods are human property.

It is so blasphemous that it takes Ishka's breath away.

"You mean to say the temple is yours," she says, to confirm.

"Not mine," says Ethibi. "It belongs to the gods. But the High Priest knows what goes on with gods, and the High Priest says that on days when the moon is half-grown..."

It is just a roundabout way of saying that a human made rules about when other humans could and couldn't be here.

"What if I say that I am a High Priest," says Ishka. "What if I say the temple is mine now?" She yanks the man sideways, making him stumble a few steps, to illustrate her point. "Who could stand against me? Would that make me the High Priest?"

"A blood-drinking abomination could never be High Priest," says Ethibi, who seems to be regaining her courage. "You are not fit to set foot in our glorious city."

"And who would stand against me if I did?"

Ethibi falters, but the man in Ishka's arms, his face contorted with pain, grunts out an answer.

"Armies," he said. "Our armies would stand against you."

Ishka, in surprise, lets the man go. He stumbles to Ethibi and turns back towards Ishka, gaping. Neither of them attack her. They have worked out what she is. They know it would not go well for them.

"What is an army?" says Ishka, perplexed. "Are you an army?"

The man shakes his head. "We are temple guards. The people in an army are warriors, not guards, but it is a great deal like being a guard, and there are many more than two of them."

"What is a guard?"

She recognizes the root of the word: there are *guardians* who keep wolves and lions away from the sheep, *guardians* who shoo wild herbivores away from Eddik's crops. *Guardians* who are the first to retaliate when an enemy band steals a woman or harms a child. But for a temple, the word does not make sense. There is nothing to guard. It is not as though Ishka plans to make off with the pillars and carvings.

Ethibi explains what a guard is.

"I don't think I like guards," says Ishka.

Then she stabs them both to death, drinks as much of their blood as her belly will hold, and leaves the half-drained bodies in the brush.

The top of Okbu's right shoulder says:

I am writing on you now because I am angry and you are frightened. There were wolves chasing us for our kill today. Not the kind that hangs around human garbage heaps, but real wolves, hungry. They cannot yet tell the difference between a human scent and mine. Poor wolves. But they did plenty of damage to Elgeia, and more than enough to Kesdi, before I could finish them off.

Wolf blood does nothing for me. It is like stale water. All I really had today was the bright blood running from Kesdi's arm. He kissed me, trying to draw it back into his body through his mouth. I was careful, and took nothing that would not have come out of him without me. Still, he may not survive.

I do not like it when humans mourn. You are temporary; it is your nature. What are we but wolves among wolves, roaming the land, taking what is ours? I have chosen you for this. You are fortunate. Do not whine to me because your fortunate lives are shorter than mine. If you must cry, then cry blood for me, Okbu. Cry me something I can understand.

Okbu expects to be killed in Eddik. He does not let the guards drag him there without a fight. Some of the younger ones do — Tiqu, heartbreakingly, does — but Okbu throws punches until they have immobilized him in a hunting net.

So. They will kill him. That's what Ishka would do to a human who tried to hurt someone in her pack. And Okbu has broken a rule of that size. He has taken something that is theirs, the way Ishka's pack is hers — though he does not understand how, merely by sleeping in an empty temple, he can have done this.

He is not the only one who fights. Young Alqet throws herself at the guards. She is restrained only after knifing two and being stabbed deep in the upper arm. There is blood everywhere. Blood like Kesdi's. Then the guards take her away, out of sight.

(Okbu has seen many deaths. Lovers, enemies, friends, friends' children. Kesdi was not a lover, but he was a confidante when Okbu was young. The only one Okbu dared trust with his doubts. Then, scarcely two months after his initiation, there were the wolves. His arm. Blood everywhere. The wound refused to heal. It brought a fever in its wake, and Kesdi died raving. Ishka had no patience for Okbu's grief. She left Kesdi's body for the real wolves to eat.)

Ishka's pack are wolves among wolves. They should not fear death. Ishka reminds him of this constantly, teasing him with his old man's griefs. Kesdi's death is not the bloodiest Okbu has seen, nor the youngest, but it is the one that plays behind his eyes when he thinks of death. And now, with fierce young Alqet, it is happening all over again.

Okbu wants to strike down the people of Eddik, break their skulls, feed them to Ishka. He wants Ishka to pierce his skin, swallow his tears, ride him to exhaustion and remind him in that mocking voice how little he knows about time. But Ishka cannot come until sundown.

Without her, he is the oldest. He is responsible for the others. The guards push them into a house made of tree-trunks and clay, covered over the top, with a hearth in the middle. Those who have gone along without fighting slump in the corners. Tiqu rises after a while and untangles Okbu from the hunting net. It is slow work, and his hands shake.

"This is not defeat," Okbu says.

"It looks a lot like defeat," says Tiqu.

"They have taken us here to kill us," says Okbu, "but they are fools. They should have done it quickly. Instead they have given us time to prepare. We can make this space into a death-trap. We can kill them, or frighten them into letting us go; and if we can do neither of those, we need only hold them off until tonight. Then Ishka will come and wreak exquisite revenge."

This only makes Tiqu shake harder.

"We are wolves among wolves," Okbu says. "Remember? Look at them, these small, inbred people who stay in one place. They do not deserve our submission."

"I'm not a wolf," Tiqu says miserably. "Not really. I only had my first marking yesterday."

"Then you are the best kind of wolf," says Elgeia's youngest sister, who has been leering at Tiqu from the sidelines since she first saw him, though Tiqu— as far as Okbu can tell—has no interest. "The kind who still has to be taught wolf things."

Before long Okbu has coaxed them into work. He is impressed by the hunting net. He wants to drape it over the door and catch anyone coming in, but there is no sensible way to keep it stuck there. It's hard to keep the pack organized without Ishka. Everyone is still arguing about the net when the guards return. An old man of Eddik, even older than Okbu, walks between them.

These people really are small, shorter than all but the smallest of Ishka's pack. They move differently. Even with the warriors, there is no prowling, no guardedness. The city people are more like deer. Okbu would use the word *gentle*, but he knows better. They have murdered Alqet, haven't they?

They have knives, but it scarcely matters. Okbu roars and charges towards them, fists raised.

"Stop," says the old man.

It is the tone, more than the command itself, that brings Okbu up short. There is no fear, no anger, not even the contempt that creeps into Ishka's voice when humans challenge her. The warriors have not yet drawn their knives. The old man speaks to Okbu the way he would speak to a beloved but errant friend.

Okbu stops.

"I am sorry," says the old man, "for the haste in bringing you here. I understand that you do not know why we took you prisoner. That you do not even understand what trespassing is."

"What have you done with Alqet?" Okbu demands.

The old man nods. "A fair question. Again, I apologize for the haste. We had to treat and bind her wounds quickly. I will show you."

Another group of warriors guide her in: Alqet, alive and walking, even smiling, though it is a bewildered smile. Her wounded arm has been bound with clean, white cloth, much tidier than anything a pack on the move could provide. There is a red stain in the cloth, but it is no longer growing.

After the wolves bit Kesdi, he never looked this healthy. Not even in the brief reprieve before the fever. He never even walked unsupported again.

"Hello," says Alqet, relieved but uncertain.

Tiqu and the other young ones rush to her. They put their hands on her, as if she might be a ghost. Kaben, the next-youngest man after Tiqu, even touches the bloodstained cloth, though Alqet flinches away from that.

"It's a trick," Okbu barks. "They've forced her to pretend to be healed."

But he is not sure he believes that. Kesdi could not have moved like this, with force or without. All Okbu knows is the city people did this to gain some advantage, and he has no advantages to spare.

"I'm all right," says Alqet. "I'm... confused, but they haven't harmed me. They've been very respectful. They said they'd let us go back to Ishka once we listened to them."

"It's a trick," Okbu says.

But no one moves to attack the city people again.

"I understand this must be difficult," says the old man. "You are bandits — so Alqet tells me. You are here to steal the food that keeps us alive. But I have known bandits before. Bandits steal because they do not understand what stealing is. Is that not so?"

"We take what is ours," says Elgeia, who hasn't moved a step past Okbu.

"And that is where we disagree," the old man continues. "It is not yours. But it *could* be. You do not understand the glory of staying in one place. Owning a thing you can pass down to your family. Building things that bring joy and comfort to others, not merely grabbing what will keep you alive. So I have a proposition. Walk with us today. We will not harm you. We will show you what it is to live in Eddik. At the day's end, you may choose if you would like to stay. We will not punish your trespassing, nor your violence — though, if you leave, we will not let you steal from us again."

The younger ones look to each other, confused.

"Those are pretty words," says Okbu. "I do not trust them. What would you be saying if Alqet had died?"

The old man spreads his hands. "We would express our sorrow and offer her a place in one of Eddik's graves, should the rest of you stay."

There is silence.

"What is a grave?" says Tiqu.

The old man explains. When the young ones object, he explains all over again. Okbu is silent. He thinks of Kesdi, and how they left his body behind. Young Okbu asked Ishka how he would be remembered, when all his friends and lovers but Ishka were gone, and Ishka scoffed.

The sun creeps quietly over the sky.

The curve of Kesdi's left shoulder blade, before the wolves ate it, said:

Sometimes I think even I do not understand time. I am as prone to boredom as anyone. Yet life consists of things that happen over and over again — sunsets, fights, meals, markings like these, and love. I have never grown bored with these. Only avoidable things bore me: Long conversations. Etiquette. Certain humans. Not you, of course. I wonder if humans would grow bored if they lived this long.

You bite me bluntly, sometimes, during love. You say you wish you could live forever. You do not really know what you're asking. You are beautiful, and your blood tastes sharp like your temper. But you would not take to my kind of life, and even if you did, who is to say I would not grow bored with you? I think you will be beautiful when you are old. There is an extra beauty in finiteness. Trust me, and be content with that.

The tip of Alqet's chin says:

I love that you are fierce, that you growl and snap at your prey. I love that you sometimes taste your enemies' blood, though you cannot live on it as I can. It reminds me of something — I cannot think what. Some scrap of old writing that I must have left behind.

Ishka is so angry she thinks her fingernails will catch fire. She loves this feeling. She has forgotten what it is to swallow down so much human life that it stuffs her. Little sips from Okbu and the others keep her alive. But this? This is more than living. For a moment after draining the guards, she cannot believe she chose to be different from other vampires, to cultivate humans who love her instead of stealing, raping and eating them whole.

But then, there is a reason other vampires are rare. They cannot work together as humans and wolves do. Even to Ishka, other vampires are only competition, and to most vampires, humans are only prey. But a once-human part of them grows lonely for something prey can't provide. Vampires die of loneliness: after centuries on their own they go mad, lie down in the sun, and burn to ash. Being full like this, flaming with blood-strength, is not worth risking that death.

Okbu and the others are what stave off Ishka's loneliness. She needs them. Especially Okbu. She will fight to take them back. And she will love every blood-spattered second of the fighting.

Eddik is bigger than last time. More crops. More *kinds* of crops. Ishka gleefully tramples the plants as she goes. Just outside the buildings huge fields of hulled wheat lie over the land. At the edge of one field stands a guard. Ishka grabs hold of him as easily as plucking one of the plants.

The guard screams until she slaps him quiet. He takes a stunned breath, and she digs her nails in below his collarbone. He's already dropped his spear.

"Abomination," he whispers.

Ishka rakes the skin with her nails until blood comes and he screams again. "You hid twelve prisoners somewhere in this city. Tell me where."

"Abomination," he says again. He spits at her.

Ishka finds this amusing. She tries a few of her other tricks. Hitting him in the testicles repeatedly doesn't break him. Snapping two of his fingers does.

"Stop," the guard whimpers. "Stop. They're in the House of the Snake."

Ishka tugs a third finger nearly into snapping position, but not quite. "You may have noticed I'm not from here. Say it in a way I'll understand."

"T-third house in the innermost circle, counting east to west from the big fig tree."

"That's better." She tilts her head. "Now call me an abomination again, will you?"

He blinks, his eyes fluttering in terror. "A...bomination?"

"Good." There is a snap from his third finger, then a crunch from the whole hand. By the time he stops screaming, she has vanished.

In central Eddik, there is no space between the huts. To get anywhere, the city people must climb a ladder and walk across the logs of the roofs. Ishka vaults up in one easy movement. These people are too easy: they scream when she hasn't even done anything. Old men cower. Mothers pull their children into the corners of their huts.

And a group of warriors converges. Five — no, ten more — twenty. The biggest group Ishka has ever seen outside of all-out war. An army. These are the only ones not screaming, the ones with knives, spears, and bolases. Two have crude bows and arrows.

If someone shot one of those arrows at Ishka, she might get hurt. That idea excites her. She is in no serious danger — she doubts either of the bowmen could hit her heart before she took them down — but she might get cut and bruised. One or two of her opponents might even get away. It's been a long time since she faced odds like that. She is in the mood to face them again. The bowmen notch their arrows. She leaps...

"Stop," says someone.

The familiar voice jolts her out of battle-rage. It's Okbu, standing atop the third hut from the fig tree. Beseeching her with his eyes.

Ishka pauses. Why is he not a captive?

"Don't shoot her," says Okbu.

"Spoil my fun," says Ishka. She knows what a sight she must be to her pack, eyes glowing, blood from the temple guards drying at her chest and sides. Okbu knows her well enough not to cringe. The others... Well, she is saving them. They will be grateful as soon as they work that out.

"Please," says Okbu. "I beg you. If we have found any favor with you at all, don't shoot her."

Ishka looks quickly between Okbu and the warriors.

"Really," she says, "I don't mind killing them. It isn't exactly a hardship."

"We were never meant for this place," says Okbu. "Don't you see? You have shown us wonders. But we belong with her. We made that choice long ago. Please do not bring punishment on yourselves. Please."

There are hurried discussions. Ishka suddenly has the feeling that she does not understand what is happening here.

"You really wish to live with that abomination," says one of the oldest among the warriors.

"We have already chosen her," says Okbu.

And the townsfolk let them leave peacefully, shuffling out across the roofs and climbing down into the fields. Ishka doesn't like that. Where can she vent her rage now? She thinks of lashing out at the crowd that parts to let them pass, hurting a couple just for fun. Then she thinks of what Tiqu would say, and the other young ones, and she holds back.

The small of Okbu's back says:

How long have you lived with me, darling? I forgot to count years until tonight when I looked at your hair. We had raided half the sheep from a shepherd boy, who tried to drive us off by throwing stones. I let him live. He was so young and weak, he did not deserve to be acknowledged as an enemy. I think he will survive with the sheep we left him, but I do not truly care.

Tonight I watched you butcher the biggest sheep. (The rest, we will drive before us until we have need of more meat. They will last a few weeks.) Blood got into your hair, and I realized that, when cleaned, your hair is fully silver now. I wonder how much longer you will last.

It would be shameful to say this to your face. We have argued so often about death. If I grieved for every lover who left me, I would go mad. But you are so strong. You have run beside me in my battle rages. You have held enemies down while I carved obedience into their skin. You have seen the parts of me that terrify most humans, even the rest of my pack. Yet you still reach out for my love. You still groan in pleasure when I mark you, and curl your belly against my back when we sleep. You know I do not share sleep lightly.

I think, Okbu, darling, that when you die I may miss you a little. I may be out of sorts for a week or two. It has happened before, rarely, and how the pack mocked me when it did! But if I have an occasional human feeling, that is not surprising, is it? Hundreds or thousands of years ago, I was one of you.

Nobody thanks Ishka for saving them from the stupid, sickly, decadent little city.

She's led them to a hilly meadow with some cavelets where she can rest. Now they all twelve mope around the fire. They haven't had time to hunt, but there is a decent crop of wild mushrooms in the meadow. They appear to have been fed in Eddik also. Yet no one smiles.

"It can't have been that bad," says Ishka, who by this time has cleaned the blood from her skin. There is still a fire inside her, but the sun will come up soon, and her eyelids are heavy. "I don't see any broken bones. What did they do to you, exactly?"

"Nothing," says Okbu. His face wrinkles up, more haunted by this than any atrocity. As if it never occurred to him that a band could take captives and not hurt them.

"Do you wish they had done something?"

Okbu shakes his head.

"We need to talk," he says. "I mean the others in the pack and me. And you."

"We're talking now," says Ishka.

"I mean there are decisions to make."

"For you, maybe. *I'm* going to sleep. When I wake up, I expect to see you this time. I've worked up a lot of frustration, darling, and we've had a very eventful night. I'm going to draw something new in your skin. Then I'm going to bite you, scratch you, and fuck you until you can't move. Maybe a couple of the others, too. Maybe Tiqu. Then we move on."

Normally Okbu loves it when she talks like that. But he's staring into the distance.

"Have you ever heard," Okbu says, "of a grave?"

"No." And now is not the time to get sidetracked learning new words. She's tired.

"In Eddik they put the dead underground, away from the sun, instead of leaving them to be eaten. It's... I can't explain."

Ishka shrugs. "Good for them." She doesn't understand why the details of corpse disposal would bother Okbu like this. He must be tired, like her.

"Have you ever heard of an army?"

"Recently, yes. I almost went up against one tonight. It was hardly a threat."

"No, it wasn't a threat today. I think there won't be an army that can hurt you in my lifetime. But think of the long view. Isn't that what you do? Eddik will grow. One day, if it's big enough, won't it have an army big enough to hurt you?"

"Never."

"Are you sure?"

"Never ever. Not in as many generations as there are blades of grass in this meadow."

On the inside, she's not sure. Maybe it could happen. A bigger army in and of itself wouldn't do it: only so many people can get close enough to knife her at once. Only so many can aim spears without getting in each other's way. But someday, there may be new weapons. New ways of fighting.

The city must really have done something. Otherwise Okbu wouldn't be imagining this: a repulsive little world in which stupid, weak humans band together to drive Ishka out. Something has happened to this man. When the sun goes down, she'll pummel him until he tells her what it was.

"But, you see," he says, "Eddik may still be there after that many years. After everyone who lives there now is forgotten."

"So?"

Okbu sighs. "I think... I think some of the younger ones like that idea. Some of them are tired of being doomed to vanish while you live forever. Maybe... even if they still have to die in their bodies, some of them want to be part of something that stays."

Really? Could they actually want to go *back* to the city? It's preposterous. She has been good to them. All the love, all the blood, all the spoils of weaker and stupider bands: she has held back nothing. They are ungrateful. She has spoiled them. Maybe she needs to teach them gratitude with a fist and a sharp stick.

No, she is worrying over shadows now. They won't leave. Maybe a few of them. Maybe stupid little Tiqu. But not Okbu. He has Ishka's ink all over him. He has been hers ever since he was a man at all.

So all she gives him is a contemptuous stare. Then she slinks into the cavelet to rest.

Okbu cannot read the lines on his body. But he knows there is meaning there that only Ishka can see. Sometimes when she looks at him, she isn't feasting her eyes on his body: she is looking at those marks, remembering what she was thinking when she made them.

The noonday sun beats down on the pack as they finish their preparations and leave. Okbu is last. Tiqu is hurrying him to go on, but Okbu pauses by the dead ashes of the campfire. He picks up a stick, hardly knowing what he is doing.

Okbu thinks that, if he ever sees this place again, he would like to remember it.

He writes, in the deadened hearth:

I'm sorry.

He tries to think of more words. He wants to explain how this is inevitable. The world has changed. He has ignored it a long time. All his life. But the new ways are better than the old. They answer a question he has never quite been able to ask. In Eddik, the longest-lived do not always win. There are other ways to be remembered: other things besides the living that can last.

Ishka must have known it would happen someday. It isn't fair to her, but it *must* happen: the world must change, or it is hardly alive. He can see in Ishka's eyes, sometimes, that she has gone too long without having to change.

He knows what he is to Ishka. He might have stayed, for her sake, and accepted a death without remembrance, the way he always planned. But the rest of the pack is unanimous, and he is the oldest. They need him. Tiqu, in particular, needs him.

He is inexperienced. He doesn't know how to say these things out loud, much less write them. So he writes:

I'm sorry.

And that is all.

It's very quiet when Ishka wakes.

Okbu, again, is missing. She half-expected that. No doubt the twelve idiots have been up all day, talking about what happened to them in the city.

She crawls out of the cavelet.

The meadow is empty. There are no humans anywhere. The campfire has died down to ash, and the breeze moans.

She sniffs the air.

It's true. No one is here — not since hours ago.

Not even Okbu.

Deer in the distance, wolves, rabbits in rabbit holes. But no Okbu. No humans at all.

In the ashes of the fire, someone has drawn a pattern of dots and lines. A parting speech which Ishka cannot read.

She turns on her heel and runs for Eddik.

Can she wrest the whole pack from the city and bring them back by force? She wants to. But what good will it do? This is not another kidnapping. They have gone back by choice. If she takes them again, they will escape again. If she binds them to her to stop their escape, it will be a resentful binding. Her pack will not be her partners, the wolves who run at her sides. They will be slaves. They will fear her and hate her. It makes no difference what Ishka does: these people will not love her again.

This must have been growing in Okbu all along, and she never saw. Maybe he never saw it either, until the city found it and took him.

She hates him. She hates them all. She wants to stab them all and bloat herself with their blood.

She runs so fast the tops of the grasses scratch her calves.

They are children. The future opens its arms to them like the babies they are, full of promises that they need not hurt or be hurt. Yet no one ever stopped to ask what place Ishka has in that future. Not even Okbu.

The people of Eddik would not welcome her, even if she wanted that. Abomination, indeed.

All animals kill or are killed. Usually both. It is the essential hubris of humans to think they can get away with doing neither.

Towards the city, Ishka slows. She could slaughter everyone inside and bathe those wooden walls in blood. It would be easy. But she will not.

She could collect dry grasses, set them out in a wide circle around the city, rub two sticks together and burn the whole thing to the ground. Pick off the fleeing survivors. She will not.

She makes her way with a lightness of foot only vampires and cats know. She slips past the guards, who do not so much as turn their heads. Shrouded in her hair, she is a black figure in the moonless black night. She creeps along the roofs of the houses and gazes down inside.

It is not long before she sees Elgeia and her sisters, asleep by a hearth, as though they've already forgotten her.

She could slip into their beds and kill them. Oh, yes. She could find Okbu and make even him, with his stamina, die screaming. Begging for mercy. She very much wants to.

But she will not.

She could take revenge in all sorts of ways on these little humans. Or she could take the long view. Of the people who have ever mattered to her, she alone will live as long as Eddik.

It is Eddik that deserves her revenge. If she kills Okbu for hurting her, he will be forgotten long before she stops hurting. And it is not really Okbu who has taken her pack from her. It is Eddik. Eddik lures humans in and leaves Ishka outside. Eddik plans to bloat itself as the generations pass, growing wide like a fat old tree. Squeezing out the places where someone like Ishka can live.

She does not look for Okbu.

Instead she creeps along until she finds a hut full of children. Three young women — one pregnant — two men, and six little puppy-humans, far younger than the youths Ishka normally takes, tangled around the hearth with their thumbs in their mouths.

Ishka creeps down the ladder into *that* house.

The youngest human here is a baby, which has rolled out of its mother's grip to dream on its stomach. Ever so quietly, Ishka lifts it to her. She will not hurt this one, much as she dreams of hurting everyone. This one will live a long, full life. But not in Eddik. It will live with her, the start of a newer, crueller pack. Or as a foundling in some other city, if she tires of it.

The baby does not wake.

It is not the last baby she will take from Eddik. Let Okbu explain why the city is cursed. Let him explain why children vanish in the night, why grown men turn up naked with their throats torn out. If humans will no longer love Ishka, let them fear her. Let them tell stories about her to their children. Let them make her into one of the beasts in the temple. She will be part of the soul of this city, whether the city likes it or not. She does not plan to let the city like it.

In the hut with the six children, Ishka bites her fingertip and smears blood in lines and dots against the side of the ladder.

The blood says:

You have chosen your fate. You have fenced yourselves in, thinking, this is the good place: if we stay in this place, we are safe. You have created an inside — and an outside.

You used to understand darkness and wildness. Now they are things you shut out.

I chose to be kind to humans: I took them with me, shared what was important to me, and kept them alive. But for you this is not good enough. You would rather have night creatures at our most dangerous, lonely and starving for blood, so long as we are outside. So long as you do not have to think about us.

Understand, then, what you have done. You have invented an outside and bequeathed it to me. And, darling city, I take what is mine.

Ishka examines her handiwork. The baby's mother stirs in her sleep, draws her arms closer to her belly, as if still holding what has been taken from her.

Ishka tiptoes up the ladder, child in one hand, and is gone.

Taylan

Taylan was everything I wanted him to be. Never a hair out of place. Never a dull-edged quip or a dim smile.

Eda was everything I loved, once. Knees stained green from chasing fairies through the playground's long grass. Fingertips purple from expressionist marker monsters. I had hooked my pinky in hers, one sunlit afternoon, and sworn to be best friends forever.

But that was years ago, and glamorous adulthood beckoned. Colleges cast their greedy eyes on our young flesh. Taylan changed for them. I changed. But Eda still ran through the fields as though nothing had happened. She came to prom like that, not in a proper dress but in something like a fairy's mantle of leaves, green and rough-edged, her feet bare.

She expected me to dance with her. Innocently, like we had when we were two little girls in the fourth grade. Like Taylan, prince among boys, was not on my arm.

I glanced up at Taylan when she asked. He said nothing, but his nose wrinkled.

"Sorry," I said as I steered us away, but I wasn't sorry. Not really. I had chosen Taylan over Eda, elegance over imagination, long ago.

Lament for a Faithless Prince

See, I have made you a hall of ruby,
the length of it bright as blood, cold as stars,
and a white bear's skin for you to lie on.
I would sing to you there as I once did.
The wardrobe stands in your bare, dim hall
where it always stood, and I am sure my highest peals
still reach your world — *Come to me!*
But you will not come, you will not.

I am full of palaces and fragrant glades—
fear-frosted nights, too, for I know
your inner dark, and you know mine.
You have ridden, hounds baying, through these lands.
Silver-eyed nymphs have kissed your lips,
abased to your will, and there is more—
my love, you have not seen half of me.
But you will not return, you will not.

I have seen you call me Never Never Land
with a left-handed smile, as if to say:
There could never be a hall made of ruby.
Your lips appease the bearded scholars,
the rationalists who own you now,
but the lie goes deeper: you kissed me,
not the nymphs but the very stones,
the night you barred and locked the wardrobe.
And you will not return, you will not.

See, every door to me is a gnashing mouth.
If I could, I would gulp you down whole

and chain you with gold in my belly.
I've dreamed a thousand of you, pale ghosts,
held them in my glittering depths.
But every one has faded to glass, to smoke,
until I cannot feel them, and must call:
Come to me, love. I have made you these things.
But you will not come, you will not.

Ekpyrotic Theory

I must not mourn these torn-through stars.
I need only wait through a bottomless hour
for your membrane to shift
once more against mine

and make light, campfires,
Australia, Saturn, the Prose Edda,
broccoli, albatrosses, icebergs,
you and me.

Feasting Alone

Martin uploaded his soul to the servers late. "A month," he'd said at the outset. "Just a month so I can set my affairs in order." But with our minds newly augmented and running on exaflops, a month may as well have been a lifetime. Whole movements had risen and fallen in six-dimensional art by the time his ID pinged at the arrival depot. Ponderous volumes of time-poetry had been written, revised, debated in the common halls and spawned rivals. We'd long ago abandoned the silly conceit of human avatars. Most of us were not wholly embodied at all: we were intricate fractal shapes on gossamer wings, or shadows that glistened with subtle colour.

Martin was hideous. Martin was one of those shambling masses of flesh that we'd left behind. And he quailed when he saw us.

"Demons," he said.

Well, we sorted that out, but not a soul on our server had the patience to teach him more. He couldn't understand time-poetry, let alone see in more than three dimensions. We tossed manuals his way, but he ignored them. He sat in a corner, holding his virtual head — as if anyone still suffered *pain* in here.

When we had left him alone for long enough, something rose from his virtual body that we thought we had forgotten.

Oh, God. The chewing, smacking sounds. The smell. Someone had taken pity on the man and given him a program to call up the virtual ghost of food. He squatted on the floor, guzzling obscenities: salt pork, chocolate cake, rigatoni, grapes. He gaped, all tonsils and teeth.

Then, as we gathered to stare at him, he burped.

We flew away into the aether. "Freak," we said. "Pig." To wallow in sensory indulgence and ignore the beauty at his feet! We drew caricatures of him in lines of pure light and hid them in the dimensions he couldn't see yet, tossing them to each other and giggling.

But when the others tired of that game, I turned back.

Why was I drawn to him? What was it that I wanted to understand? It was so hard to remember the old, bad world.

Martin swallowed his tiramisu and stared at me.

His voice was dull, thick and organic, though if he'd read the manuals he could have given it the sinuous emotion of a violin. "Are you here to laugh at me again?"

"I don't know."

Why was he so familiar? Why, through my disgust, did I feel sorry for him?

"I thought I was ready," he said. "I thought reading about it before the upload was enough. But I don't understand anything here. Least of all you. At least the food's programmed to taste like..."

Home, he didn't say.

He looked at me like I was warm bread. Like he needed me.

"Would you like..." I shook my head. What could a man like Martin want? "Help looking at the manuals?"

"I can't yet. I look at them and I want to vomit. You're all so far ahead of me that I'll never catch up."

I flitted backwards in case he did vomit. I didn't know if he had a program to let him do it, but I didn't want to find out.

"Can't you just sit with me?" said Martin. Pleading now. "Just for a minute. Just eat with me. Like we used to."

Like we used to.

Why couldn't I remember? And why did I want to? How could anything in the dull, physical past be relevant to me?

But that look in his eyes. He knew me. We must have been friends. We might have been...

Lovers.

Oh, God. Yes. I dimly remembered. We had been lovers. We had wanted to be in this world together. I could hardly fathom it now, but somehow despite all the sweat and slime of the act he had been important to me.

Had anyone in this swarm of enlightened souls been important to me? The art had been important to me. The time-poetry. The sheer joy of living unfettered by physical limits. What were other people in comparison to that? None of us were anything to each other apart from what we made.

And suddenly I was mildly uneasy about that. Enough to take a risk, though a small one, in trying to understand.

I racked my memory for a body with biological processes. To eat virtual food I needed a virtual mouth, teeth, a tongue, an esophagus and stomach... The change came over me with a shiver, as easy as any other, though it felt strange and unwieldy having insides again.

I knelt beside Martin. Picked up a grape. Bit back my disgust, flicked it onto my tongue, and chewed.

The taste was... physical. It was a mild pleasure, but one I had grown unused to, and I frowned as I swallowed.

I still didn't understand, but his food no longer disgusted me.

"We need to teach you," I said. "Slowly, and in a way you can understand. It will take a long time. But maybe you need to remind us of something in return."

I hesitated, and then swallowed my pride. "Could you pass the chocolate?"

He met my eyes, bewildered, grateful. And we ate.

Synchronicity

So many times I sketched an outstretched hand,
like glass, twisting the light
of street-lamps through its palm,

then shook my head
and buried the page with old magazines.

Later, unknowing,
you crept in anyway. You said,
"I dreamed of a woman made of glass, like this,"
laid out a page in your own hand,
and met my eyes.

How My Best Friend Rania Crashed a Party and Saved the World

Rania Mehanna was my best friend, so when I bumped into her crying in the stairwell at lunch hour, I was stupid enough to rush right to her. She freaked out and shook her head, trying to brush her eyes off all clumsy. Rania didn't cry much, and she didn't have the hang of it.

She hadn't picked the spot at random, of course. She'd crumpled up in one of the blind spots where the school security cameras don't quite see. She didn't want the world to *know* she was crying. World Savers don't cry alone in corners. I had to be careful not to blow her cover.

Everyone knows this stuff. But when your best friend is hunched over sobbing, basic stuff slips your mind.

I stopped, then grinned and hopped over the rest of the way, like I was just happy to see her. Rania glared at me, but she stopped trying to jam her fists into her eyes.

"Hey," I said.

"Hey, Emma."

"You want to be alone?"

She hesitated. "No."

I slid down beside her. "What's up?"

"Nothing." She shook her head.

"'Kay, then. I got us movie tickets. Two seats. Rania Mehanna and Emma Cruz for *Catgirls vs. Pterodactyls*. Opening night. I mean, if you still want to go."

She sighed. "Yeah, I guess."

"With Suman Bachchan as the pterodactyl trainer."

"Yeah whatever."

It wasn't like Rania not to squeal over Suman Bachchan. She scowled even deeper when I said his name. Boy trouble, then. I lowered my voice. "It's Jacob, isn't it?"

Rania buried her face in her hands. "He stood me up again. That's all. I should be used to it by now."

"Bastard," I said.

"Like you'd know."

I hated when she needled me about that. I never got into the "guys" thing. Or the "girls" thing. Dating wasn't my scene. But I knew what it meant to care about people. I had friends I'd take a bullet for — Rania first. Even when she was giving me the death glare from Mars.

"Hey," I said, "if you promised me *Catgirls vs. Pterodactyls* tickets and stood me up, I'd be pissed too. I get it."

Rania snorted and shoved me. "That's not a date with me. That's a date with Suman Bachchan's cheekbones."

I shoved back. "Then *Stephen Hawking: Space Pirate.* Same analogy."

"Dude. I'm allowed to stand you up if the movie sucks."

"Filmgate gave it 8 out of 10."

"Filmgate is full of Numbers Fiends. They'll give 8 out of 10 to any pile of crap with a space pirate."

"So who says it sucks?"

"Moviedock." Which was as full of World Savers as Filmgate was full of Numbers Fiends. "No female characters in the whole movie. Not even a waitress or something. Just a bunch of white dudes with speech synthesizers blowing things up."

"But you don't have a problem with all the bikinis in *Catgirls?*"

"Yeah, well." She waved me off. "Suman Bachchan. Shut up." Now she was smiling, at least. "Did you hear the Infallible Cloud changed his label? He's not a full World Saver anymore, just a World Saver slash Pleasure Seeker. Can you believe it?"

I shrugged. "I don't know the guy, except for his cheekbones."

"Yeah. Stupid raters." She pulled her knees up to her chest. "Stupid *everyone.*"

"Rania," I said, "how long has it been since you and Jacob talked?"

Rania plopped her head down in her hands. "A month now. I mean, I text him. I post on his wall. Nothing stalkery. But he's all 'Oh hey, I'm out someplace, talk to you later.' I ask him to come and see me, but he ignores it."

"So go see him anyway. He's got GPS, doesn't he?"

"You *know* why I can't go see him."

I did. Jacob was a Pleasure Seeker, all jokes and persuasion with nothing on the inside. Which was fine, as long as he and Rania were happy. But his dad had a new job and the family had moved to Brightside: one of those prissy gated communities in the suburbs, full of Upward Movers and Monocle Men. World Savers did *not* go to parties in Brightside. Rania couldn't go to him without losing some serious personality points. And Jacob wouldn't go to her.

"So don't go see him. Set your AllBook status to Single. It's not like he deserves any better."

She snapped back up straight. "World Savers do *not* break up online. That's a sign of poor empathy and lack of respect for your partner, and if you don't even respect the person you're dating, how can you—"

I raised a hand. "Stop. Respect goes both ways, remember? Right now you don't owe him any. Besides, everybody's got little marks on their record. Even the Pope."

"Easy for you to say. You're a Relator. You can make friends in any cesspool of privilege you like."

"Sorry," I said. "It sucks. You're right."

She closed her eyes and breathed in and out.

"I wish I was a hacker," she said. "I wish I could just go see him, cuss him out, break things off, and then erase it all from the system and still be a World Saver and get into pre-med at Harvard. I'd do that."

I wanted to tell Rania that even the rudest breakup in the world wouldn't stop her from being a World Saver. She was the real thing: single-handedly raising thousands of dollars for World Hacks one month, volunteering around the world in another, and keeping her grades up high the whole time. She didn't quit: her only problem was that she couldn't set out to fix her personal life with the same zeal as fixing everything else.

But Rania had her eye on some picky colleges. The kids who got in had records spotless like you wouldn't believe. These were kids who never went through a Delinquent or Self Destructor phase, not even something semi-respectable like Beta Girl. They'd been World Savers since they were two years old and their parents posted about how fast they'd learned the alphabet. I had a theory those kids weren't the actual best World Savers, but they looked great on paper. By those standards, one mark on Rania's record was a pretty big deal.

I knew those problems went way deeper than what I could deal with. I knew I should sit tight, let Rania cry on my shoulder, validate her feelings. But all of a sudden I had a bright idea.

"Do you want it that bad, Rania? 'Cause I've got a lot of Numbers Fiends on my friends list."

She shoved me again. "You've got a lot of *everybody* on your friends list."

"Yeah, and I bet someone in there knows how to sneak into Brightside without the Infallible Cloud knowing. I bet we could do this, Rania. If you wanted it enough."

She looked at me sidelong. "We?"

"Of course."

It was like a Suman Bachchan movie. Me and Rania on a heist, beating the computers at their own game. I had a lot of smart people to draw on. We could do it.

She thought about it. Then she hugged me ridiculous tight. "Let's."

Jacob Harrington [Pleasure Seeker] wrote
Can't WAIT 4 Julia's party. Gonna be awesome, robot camels and 360 degree TV. For real, her house has everything. <3 Brightside!!
Yesterday at 2:38 pm | Comment | Like

Emmett Lancaster [Upward Mover] wrote
U gonna bring Rania? Dying to meet her. Looks great in ur pix.
Yesterday at 3:16 pm

Jacob Harrington [Pleasure Seeker] wrote
she's busy
Yesterday at 3:54 pm

Parker Austin [Upward Mover] wrote
Not according to her profile. Dude, you haven't met her at all this month. Love you to prove me wrong, but twenty bucks says you're keeping her around for the personality points.
Yesterday at 4:25 pm

Caroline Ward [Monocle Man / Numbers Fiend] wrote
Bad strategy if so. Strong relationship good sign if desired
transition to Upward Mover but in yr case many more
pressing issues judging from profile, e.g. grades?
Extracurriculars? Dating life minor in comparison esp. at
our age, & for actual strong relationship, rl interactions with
gf are expected.
Yesterday at 5:07 pm

Parker Austin [Upward Mover] wrote
Dude, Caroline. Nobody asked you.
Yesterday at 5:38 pm

I didn't know a thing about sneaking past the Infallible Cloud. But I had
two thousand people on my friends list, give or take. Maybe forty of them were
Numbers Fiends, and twenty of those were local. AllBook would log anything
we said online, so I had some face-to-face schmoozing to do.

I had plans that evening already, of course. Bowling night with my friends
at yearbook committee. So I typed out a bunch of heartfelt apologies and
cancelled those. Then I got to trolling for Numbers Fiends. Gita Jha, my
favourite, was out of town, and the next two had their schedules bricked right
up, but I got a hit with number four: Deborah Hendrix, a frizzy-haired girl I
played video games with every couple of months. Numbers Fiends aren't picky:
a quick query if she wanted to hang out tonight, and I had her.

Deborah had the kind of house that smelled like old pizza boxes and chips,
with her parents holed up in home offices all night, but she led me all perky
through the mess to the den. In here, there was enough clear floor to move
around. Three of the walls were plastered with wide-format screens, and a
patched-up maroon sofa leaned against the fourth. Deborah took out an old-
fashioned handheld remote.

"The arm controls are broken," she apologized, pointing at the sofa's
raggedy arm. "You know how it is. I got a new platformer, though. With alien
battles! You still like those?"

"Sure."

We clicked our way through the login and into the new game. Pictures popped up on the walls: a maze of golden walkways, gears, and ramps over a steaming green sea. We ran in place, and our avatars on the big central screen ran through the maze — or the maze moved around them. We jumped from one walkway to another, grabbed power-ups, sometimes pushed each other into the water to see what would happen. (Answer: You die.) We dodged the flocks of flying 8 balls. On the first big stairway, with a mean-looking alien at the top, I moved one of my arms wrong and the stairs folded up into a slide. My avatar fell all the way down and landed in a green bubble-blowing machine, which swelled me up and popped me into nonexistence.

Deborah giggled. "Oh, man! I missed that — I never died that way. Try it again."

I held my arms out straight and tried to do the biggest steps I could up the staircase, but I couldn't get it right. By the fourth bubble-popping death we were both hunched over laughing on the floor.

"You suck at this," said Deborah.

"I'll try again when the room stops spinning." The alien on the wall fidgeted, and a *return to last save point?* window popped up, but I ignored them. "Hey, while I was here, I wanted to ask your help with something."

"Yeah, sure." Deborah waved me aside, still giggling. "You've got to get to the top of the stairs, though. The alien battles are awesome. They've got all these tentacles and you have to — Wait, what do you need help with?" She scowled. "I am *so* tired of people using me as a math tutor. I like you because you spend time with *me*, not my textbooks. If this visit is about math, I swear—"

"No, no. Not math. Do you know Rania Mehanna?"

"Sorta."

"She and I want to crash a party."

I already knew it had to be a party. Showing up at his house would be creepy, and his parents would see us.

Deborah raised a bushy eyebrow. "A party? And you asked *me?*"

"It's not just any party. It's in Brightside. If the Infallible Cloud gets word Rania went to a party in Brightside, it'll lower her World Saver rating. She's extra worried about her rating. Wants to get into Harvard, you know. But her boyfriend's in Brightside and she needs to talk to him. So we need to get to the party, do what needs doing, and get out again, without anyone knowing. And for that, we need expert help. You in?"

Deborah scowled. She didn't have the best dating life either. Mostly she'd gone for the boys — and a few girls — who asked for her help with their math homework, despite the way she complained about them, and they tended to dump her in the spring when math class ended. "Why's Rania dating someone in Brightside?"

"I don't know. Animal magnetism. Four months ago they did Model UN and she babbled nonstop about the way he swaggered around pretending to be the Russian Federation. Then all of a sudden they were dating. He didn't used to be in Brightside, you see."

"Oh."

"But now he's standing her up all the time and he won't change his status back to Single."

"Oh, and she can't change it herself without a face-to-face meeting. I've heard of that." Deborah tugged on her hair, thinking it over. "Yeah, I guess it's worse than not dating. You sure you have to go into Brightside to find him? He never goes out to the movies or something?"

"Yeah, he goes to the movies. At the Brightside Cinema. They've got everything in there, trust me. Logic says he'll run off on vacation at some point, but that could be months, and even then he might not go anywhere Rania can reach him. He might head straight to the airport and jet off to Tuvalu. So to get to him, we've got to go in."

Deborah thought it over.

"Okay," she said at last. "I'm in. On one condition."

"Yeah?"

She grinned and sat up straight, which swung her avatar's head right into an oncoming 8 ball. "I want to go to the party."

Celebrity Sues Over "Fraudulent" Personality Rating

The Infallible Cloud is not so infallible according to Sadie Clare Wolfe, star of *Electric Mermaid* and *Babes of the Apocalypse*. When her personality rating changed from Upward Mover to Beta Girl, Wolfe sued the six major rating consortiums, calling the decision "fraudulent" and claiming that the change would cost her hundreds of thousands of dollars in lost fan revenue.

The rating consortiums stand firmly behind their product, saying the change to Beta Girl was simply an honest algorithmic assessment of her behaviour. But Wolfe and her legal counsel claim the models behind personality ratings are subtly flawed. Two other B-list celebrities, Sophie Xu and Dimitra Panagiotopoulos, have filed suit on similar grounds.

The furore has led some to speculate that Suman Bachchan, the heartthrob star of *Catgirls vs. Pterodactyls*, may also speak up. Bachchan, noted for his philanthropy and charity advocacy but also a regular at Hollywood parties, was recently reclassified as a World Saver / Pleasure Seeker, rather than simply a World Saver.

At press time, Bachchan's agent had not responded to inquiries.

Rania's house was the opposite of Deborah's: it looked like something out of a furniture ad. Cozy, mind you, with cushions and blankets over the armchairs, and it smelled like cinnamon and honey from the kitchen. But Rania's mom had a fit if anyone so much as got crumbs on the floor.

Deborah was already sprawled out on the carpet by the time I got there. Rania was perched on the edge of the couch. She looked worried that I hadn't found someone better. I had to introduce them and convince Deborah to sit on a chair like a normal person. Then we got down to business.

"First thing you do," said Deborah, "is leave your cell phone at home."

Rania flinched. "But what if I need to call—"

"No. Trust me, it does GPS even if you turn it off. Leave it here. Same with whatever else you've got. Tablets, book reader, music, even your ID. And no ultra-good clothes. Secondhand is best. Nothing with an RFID."

Rania nodded slow.

"That'll stop the Infallible Cloud from tracking you. Next thing we have to do is block face recognition."

I raised an eyebrow. "They've got face recognition at the door?"

Deborah sighed like she was talking to idiots. "People are taking pictures at this party, right? And posting them? It's not a Luddite party? Even if you stay out of trouble, you're going to be in the background of someone's photo. Soon as they post it, AllBook runs face recognition, auto-tags you, and links to your account. In case someone goes 'Who was that girl?' and wants to friend you. So we need to give you a face AllBook can't identify. Got any interesting makeup?"

Rania made a face. "Can't I just wear big sunglasses, or..."

"Obvious disguise attempt is obvious. No. You want something that screws up the algorithms, but doesn't *look* like you're trying to screw the algorithms. Best thing is dressing you up like a World Hating Poet. They're all drawing spiderwebs under their eyes, right?"

"Yeah."

"So you wear your darkest, laciest clothes. I've got a lace trim hat you can borrow. And Emma paints you with the biggest, most asymmetrical spiderweb ever. Darken the cheekbones and nose, brighten it up above the eyes, and with any luck AllBook gets so confused it can't tag you."

"But I'm not a World Hating Poet," said Rania. "I can't have that on my record."

"Which is why," said Deborah, talking slow. "We're getting. The computer. Not. To tag you. Got it?"

Rania sighed and nodded. "I've got an eyebrow pencil in my bag."

I leaned back. The couch was solid: didn't even creak. "This is all great for the computers, but people are gonna manual tag her."

Deborah shrugged. "I got nothing. You're the social-skills girl. Just try not to get in a photograph."

"Oh, sure," said Rania. "How do I do that?"

"Luck," I said. "And stay away from dancing, big groups, cool balconies, anything photo-oppy. Keep your body language closed-in and boring in case someone's taking candids."

Rania sighed. "Yep. World Hating Poet. And we're going in your car, Debs?"

"*My* parents' car." My mom was a doctor; we weren't Upward Movers, but we had enough money to park in their street, and taking the bus was too risky. "I drive. We go in, find Jacob, Rania takes him aside, I stand lookout, and you enjoy the party. Everyone's happy, right?"

"Right," Deborah said fast, and Rania nodded, but that worry in her eyes was getting worse.

I chewed my lip. "You want moral support?"

"And a witness. So he can't blow it off."

"Okay. Deborah, would *you* stand lookout?"

She sat up straight. "I wanted to see the party."

"You can still see it. We'll even wait around in the car when we're done if you want extra time. You just need to stick with us for a little while and let us know about anything suspicious."

"How would I know?"

"People pointing. People gravitating towards you. People saying 'hey, where's Jacob, I think he's in there.' The usual, obvious stuff."

Deborah raised her chin. "Sure. I'll do the social-skills stuff. See if I can't."

Suman Bachchan [World Saver / Pleasure Seeker] wrote
Wore an old suit for *Catgirls vs. Pterodactyls* opening night instead of buying new. Donated the difference. Still look GREAT! Dunno why everyone's still talking about the Pleasure Seeker label. Just a label, guys.
Yesterday at 12:31 pm | Comment | Like
1542 people like this

The party was ridiculous fancy. Deborah's gaming system was space-cool by my standards, but this was from another planet. Not just screens on the walls, but 3D projections outward and inward all over, making the whole place an ultra-real projected desert full of postcard dunes. The resolution was so good you could see through the walls, into the distance, where the dunes went on forever and ever. We would have all bumped into the walls if someone hadn't projected pictures of railings on them.

Lots of the guests were wearing imitation desert clothes to match. Girls with Jell-O shots tripped past us in headscarves and belly-dancer pants, and pale blond Monocle Men fiddled with their keffiyehs.

Rania wrinkled her nose. *Orientalism,* she mouthed when I caught her eye, and I nodded. *Ew.* Rania's mom wore a headscarf for real, and most of these people in fake hijab would've whispered and called her a terrorist outside this party. Too bad it would have wrecked our disguise if she said anything. I guess this was why World Savers didn't go to these parties.

Deborah stared around at everything making fish faces.

"Ohmygod," she whispered. "Look, look, this is top-of-the-line early adopter stuff. Musta cost more than my parents' car. And what's th—"

A robot camel the size of a Golden Retriever slammed into her. I winced. How much money did you have to waste to get custom robots just for one party? But Deborah made a wibbly face, like it was a kitten, and threw her arms around it. "Ohmygod, Emma, *look!* It's so realistic. Look how they did the joints, you can hardly tell it's motors under there and not muscles. The fur, even. You're not looking."

"Real camels aren't two feet high at the shoulders," Rania muttered. "And real houses don't have camels *indoors.* God."

I got the sense Deborah had never been to any parties at all.

I nudged her. "Yeah, it's good craftsmanship. I like the nose." Rania glared. "But remember we're trying not to draw attention."

Deborah blushed. "Oh. Yeah, okay." She straightened and tried to look cool and bored.

"In to find Jacob, in to talk to Jacob, then out," I said.

"Yeah," said Deborah, tossing her frizzy hair. "Whatever."

I stifled a laugh.

"Recognize anyone?" I whispered to Rania.

"A little. Seen a few of them in Jacob's AllBook photos. Never in person."

We sauntered around, avoiding the photo-ops, and Rania found a redheaded boy browsing the retro-cool paper bookshelf.

"Hey," she said. "You seen Jacob?"

"Yeah." He pointed. "Kitchen."

In the kitchen Deborah started bug-eyed grinning again. The place was like a posh cooking show, all sterile metallic lines and big spaces. A hot desert sun beat down above the oven, and a cool oasis powered the sink. A steel screen door led out to the back porch. Jacob and like twenty other people stood around talking beside it.

Jacob had the most ridiculous outfit in the whole party. Not just a keffiyeh, but a whole costume from that godawful remake of *The Sheik*. Trying too hard. That would get him Beta Girl if he kept at it, but not Upward Mover.

Rania started at him, then paused. "If I go get him, people will realize it's me. Is that going to be...?"

"Yeah, I'll do it. You two wait outside."

I sauntered in and spent a couple minutes joining the crowd, laughing at the jokes, pointing out movie references. Easy peasy. Jacob noticed me and frowned, but it looked like he didn't want to make a scene, either.

"Hey, Jacob?" I asked after we'd exchanged a few not-so-*bon mots.*

"Yeah?"

I did a flirty head tilt. "Wanted to talk to you outside for a bit. You mind?"

I never flirt. Jacob knew me well enough to know. But Jacob never *didn't* flirt, and the others in the crowd grinned, poking him to follow me.

He sighed. "'Kay, sure, whatever. 'Scuse me, guys."

I led him out the screen door. There was a bigass back yard, the kind with a pool and a porch *and* a big dog-walking lawn full of cute stands of trees. He got pale when he saw Rania and Deborah. "What is this, some kind of girl-mob?"

"Those trees." I pointed. "Over there."

"You're ganging up on me?"

"*I'm* ganging up on you," Rania said. "Emma is here as a witness. And Deborah... is here."

"Standing lookout," said Deborah.

"Why are you dressed like that?" said Jacob.

"Long story," I said. "Let's just get to the trees."

He gave me a nervous look, but he let Rania and me frog-march him into the trees, away from the splashing, chlorine-smelling pool crowd.

"First thing," said Rania once we were out of sight. "I'm not going to be seen talking to you in that."

Jacob couldn't have taken off the whole costume without stripping, but he took off the headdress, at least. "Nag, nag, nag. This is why I don't call you more often. You're so busy being a World Saver you can't have fun."

"So you're tired of me?" said Rania, folding her arms. "You don't want to see me anymore?"

Jacob blinked.

"Um," he said. "I mean, it's not that simple. I was going to call you, it's just that things keep coming up."

"Then you *do* want to see me?"

"Um," said Jacob.

"You see, the last six times you said you wanted to see me, we set a date and you never showed up. It kind of gives the impression you don't. Isn't that right, Emma?"

I shrugged. I knew a script when I heard one. "Sounds right to me."

Jacob scowled. "Okay, maybe I don't."

"Then we're breaking up?" said Rania.

Jacob paused.

"Look, you don't know how it is for me. Everyone here's been an Upward Mover for years. I've got to work quadruple to fit in. At least if I've got a girlfriend, that gives me something to talk about."

I raised my eyebrows. "You talk to them about Rania? There's nothing to talk about, at the rate you two have been going out. Unless you're making things up."

I wondered if he *was* making things up. It was the sort of thing he'd do, and it might cost Rania more personality points than she thought. Boys like Jacob made up weird sex stories, or even crime stories, to get attention. That kind of gossip might change her label for real.

"Please," said Jacob, ignoring me. "If you find someone else, then sure, that's cool, but why not keep our status at 'Dating' till then? For show? It would help my personality rating. And I know how you feel about *your* personality rating. I know you understand. I need this." He reached out and rested a hand on her shoulder. "Save the world for me a little, Rania, sweetie. Just for a while."

Rania wavered. She bit her lip.

I looked around quick, trying to squint through the tree needles and assess the danger. Clumps of people all over the backyard, and a big splash-war in the pool, but nobody dangerous close. Not even Deborah.

She'd wandered off. I thought I saw her frizzy head in the distance, talking to someone. Flirting, to judge from the body language.

Duh. I should have seen it coming. Deborah might not go to another high school party ever. How could I expect her to stay in the trees, missing it all?

"I don't know," Rania said. "Maybe..."

I wanted to run and drag Deborah back, but Rania needed me here more. Her weak spot was weaker than I thought.

"You think it's saving the world," I said, "helping you swan around in those clothes? You think the world will improve one bit because you, Jacob Harrington, were an Upward Mover?"

"Well, sure," said Jacob.

Rania rallied. She raised her head a bit higher. "And you think I owe that to you? You want me to give up my personality rating, my chances at a good college and a World Saver job, and most of my chances at finding someone *better* than you — all so, what, you can impress people at racist parties?"

Jacob raised his voice. "You think you can call me racist?"

"I think I can tell you," Rania said, raising hers to match, "that World Saving has as much to do with this as pigs do with the International Linear Collider. And that you are no longer my boyfriend, as of now. You can put that on AllBook!"

"Because why?" He was shouting now. "Because you're on your high horse about the clothes at this party? Who even invited you? I didn't!"

"I don't have to explain anything to you!"

"Guys." I was starting to freak out. Yelling like this was a good way to get noticed fast. "Guys, can we quiet—"

Jacob shouted past me. "It's *my* love life, and you owe me an explanation! This is the worst thing about World Savers. You prance around deciding who's worthy of help and who's not, and you think you're so *good.* But when an ordinary guy needs a little bit of slack—"

Rania wasn't looking at me either. "Don't you tell me what World Savers are like. You've never been a quarter of the way to World Saver in your life!"

"And damned glad that I—"

There was a quick rustle in the branches, then a click and a flash.

I turned. A whole gaggle of Upward Movers in imitation hijab stood there giggling, snapping pictures with their phones.

Rania turned the color of feta cheese.

"I'm going home," she said in a strangled voice, and she rushed out of the trees.

Ethan Waller [Upward Mover / Beta Girl] wrote
LOL guys, drama going on at Julia's party! UR MISSIN IT
Today at 10:24 pm | Comment | Like
3 people like this

I didn't chase Rania down right away. She didn't like to talk when she was that upset, and she wasn't going to get far without a wallet or bus pass. Instead I pushed past the Upward Movers and ran to Deborah.

She was flirting, all right. At least the trollop who'd distracted her was well-dressed. No costume, just a smart vest, boots, and slacks, with boyish bowl hair.

"Deborah," I said through my teeth.

She startled. "Oh, hi, Emma. This is Caroline. We were just — I mean, is everything all—"

"A horde of Upward Movers walked in on Rania and Jacob and me while you were gone. So no, everything is not all right. Thanks for asking."

Deborah flushed bright. She knew what she'd done.

"Walked in?" said Caroline. "What were they doing in there?"

"Breaking up," Deborah moaned, burying her face in her hands.

"Why on earth would you need to break up with nobody watching? For that matter, if you needed to break up with nobody watching, why on earth would you try to do it at a party?"

"Long story. C'mon, Deborah." I tugged Deborah's wrist. "We've got to take her home. You can look Caroline up on AllBook later."

"But—"

Caroline waved a vague hand. "It's all right. I'll probably look you up before you even get home. Have fun."

"Bye!" Deborah called as we hurried away.

We found Rania pacing the sidewalk. It was a well-lit street, no traffic, but it looked like she'd remembered she didn't have a bus pass or taxi money, and it hadn't improved her mood.

"I'm sorry," Deborah said. "I'm really sorry!"

"Don't talk to me," Rania snapped. She had this apocalyptic redness under her eyes.

"I'll drive you home now," I said. "I've got the keys. It's going to be okay."

"Don't. Talk. To. Me."

But she got in the car.

The ride was hot and silent until we dropped off Deborah. After that, Rania started throwing words like bricks.

"My life," she said, "is ruined."

"Maybe not." I'd been trying to figure out what to say ever since starting the engine. "Maybe you lost a couple of points. Maybe not going would have been worse, in the long run. Maybe his points would have rubbed off on yours."

"I should have just changed my status to Single. I shouldn't have let you talk me into this."

"You did a good thing, Rania. You confronted someone who'd been hurting you. It would have worked if not for Deborah and the shouting. You were brave."

"Fuck brave." Her knuckles paled around the arm rest. "You ruined my life."

"Rania—"

"You ruined my life, Emma." We stopped, and she unbuckled. "I'm *unfriending* you."

I stared at her. She was my best friend. She had the biggest, most tempestuous heart. But she was no World Hating Poet. She didn't do the "leaving forever!" thing lightly.

She slammed the car door and stalked off.

Deborah Hendrix [Numbers Fiend] wrote
ARGH. No wonder I never get invited to parties, I screw
EVERYTHING up.
Yesterday at 11:01 pm | Comment | Like

Caroline Ward [Monocle Man / Numbers Fiend] wrote
Nonsense. 138 people tonight by last count, incl. crashers.
Each on average participates in dozens of activities. Hardly
any of these screwed up, most not by you. Also enjoyed yr
company. Thinking of mtg again at more intellectual venue.
Shame about angry friends though. What happened there?
Yesterday at 11:15 pm

Deborah Hendrix [Numbers Fiend] wrote
It's private. Emailing you...
Yesterday at 11:23 pm

Mario Cantu [Numbers Fiend] wrote
u went 2 a party???????
<u>Yesterday at 11:55 pm</u>

Mario Cantu [Numbers Fiend] wrote
nvm, found pix
<u>Today at 12:00 am</u>

Caroline Ward [Monocle Man / Numbers Fiend] wrote
Ah. Received email. Thinking over reply. Possible I can find
a way to help...
<u>Today at 12:02 am</u>

School sucked. I mean, I had plenty to do: I passed notes in science class, giggled with the Beta Girls by my locker, organized up a storm with yearbook committee (with constant apologies for missing bowling night), and kicked butt at volleyball practice. But I kept seeing Rania out of the corner of my eye, slumped over her desk, puffy-eyed. Glaring when she caught my eye.

It wasn't all my fault, but she was hurting, and it had been my idea. I had to make it up to her. And groveling empty-handed wasn't going to work. World Savers are about results.

I knew I had twenty-four hours: the Infallible Cloud's average latency. The pictures of Rania at the party — yelling, red-faced, with a World Hating Poet spiderweb on her face — had gone up last night. The makeup must have worked, because AllBook didn't automatic tag her. But Jacob sure as hell knew who she was, and *he'd* tagged the picture in the wee hours of the morning.

"What's on your mind?" said my friend Isabella while we toweled off after volleyball. "You've been out of it."

"I hurt Rania," I said, rummaging through my clothes. "Didn't mean to, but I overreached and screwed things up."

Isabella wrinkled her nose. "So it's, what, one of those World Saver spats? She yelling at you?"

"No, she *unfriended* me."

"Yikes."

What could I do? I wasn't Deborah, and even Deborah couldn't hack a system like AllBook. I was a Relator. I just talked to people.

So.

I was a Relator. I had two thousand AllBook friends. How many of them could I talk to in an evening?

Emma Cruz [Relator] wrote

My friend Rania Mehanna is a World Saver. Top of every social science class. You should hear her talk about her fundraising for World Hacks or the volunteer trip she took to India. She's ambitious. Wants to change things.

We need World Savers because things need changing. Always will. We build the best systems we can, but one way or another we'll always need better.

Rania's ex-boyfriend, Jacob, used the system against her. He wanted all the social points of a girlfriend and none of the responsibility. So when he moved to Brightside, an Upward Mover community, he stayed there. Rania couldn't visit him without risking her World Saver points, and he refused to visit her. If she dumped him online, that would have risked her points too: let's face it, breaking up via text is still a dick move.

So with a couple of friends, Rania snuck into Brightside and stood up to him. She had Numbers Fiend advice for the sneaking. Turned out that wasn't enough. Now Rania's despondent because the pictures are up online and her World Saver label's in danger.

But World Saving shouldn't just mean doing the right volunteer work and having the right opinions. World Saving is risky. Rania Mehanna had to choose between fixing her personal life and saving her reputation. That choice is *itself* unjust. But when it was reputation or justice, Rania picked justice.

This is the principle World Saving works on, big or small. It's not Big Oil or the rainforest, but this is what it looks like.

Rania thinks the Infallible Cloud doesn't agree. But the Infallible Cloud's *supposed* to reflect what people think. Which is why I need you all to click "Like", and repeat this yourself:

Rania Mehanna is a World Saver.

Spread the word.

<u>Today at 4:36 pm | Comment | Like</u>

<u>1663 people like this</u>

The next day I couldn't even get to my locker past the crowd of people saying:

"Oh, wow, your post!"

"I wish I had the balls to post something like that."

"Go Rania!"

Just like in the comments. So far, so good. But Rania pushed past them all and howled, *"Emmmaaaa!"*

She hugged me and everyone crowded in.

"It was the least I could do."

"No, no. Emma. When was the last time you looked at your AllBook feed?"

I started paranoid-imagining everything. Trolls. Death threats. AllBook shutting the page down. "This morning before breakfast. So, like, seven maybe. Why?"

She took a minute to get the words out, and by then other people chimed in.

"Oh. I think I saw this too."

"Saw what?"

"Let her tell it, dude."

Rania took a huge breath and shrieked, *"Suman Bachchan!"*

At which point everybody started cheering and talking so fast that it took like ten minutes to get out my phone and check AllBook. I thought I was going to lose Rania in all the high-fiving. But there it was:

> **Suman Bachchan** [World Saver / Pleasure Seeker] wrote
> Everyone keeps asking why I'm not up in arms about the
> label change. Maybe I've got other things to worry about?
> Just maybe?
>
> On that note, a friend linked me to **this.**
>
> Go read it, guys. She says it better than I could.
>
> Rania Mehanna is a World Saver.
>
> <u>Today at 8:19 am</u> | <u>Comment</u> | <u>Like</u>
> <u>4324 people like this</u>

I stared at my phone. I like to think I'm a supportive friend. But the first
thing I thought was, "Oh, God. I'm going to be *swamped.*"
Then I started laughing.
"How the heck? How did that happen?"
Rania made her way back to me. "That stupid Monocle-Man-slash-
Numbers-Fiend who was talking to Deborah. Her uncle knows Suman
Bachchan's dad. Can you believe it?"
I hugged her again.
"So we're still friends?"
"Total friends. And we're still on for *Catgirls vs. Pterodactyls.*"
"Awesome."
She hooked her arm in mine, and we marched to science class. Rania was
what Rania was, and there was a lot of world left to save.

The Parable of the Supervillain

Don't think I didn't watch the news, sister of mine,
in those days. Don't think I didn't see you
in that mountaintop palace strewn with blood-red bones,
the mosasaur moat, the horned, hooved footmen.
At four in the morning with the baby biting me,
I watched you call the President of Australia
from his velvet bed
and feed him to the army ants.
You were never satisfied. Money, sex, guns, velociraptors:
Mother only wanted your voice on the phone.
You wanted the world.

Evil, they said. Pray for her soul, they said,
for her to step down meekly right this instant
and join some convent, or die. But I clung to the television
not knowing what I felt, at first,
pretending to change diapers and scrub sheets,
not knowing half of it was envy.

They broadcast that final battle of yours—
you remember, I'm sure — and I scratched tic-tac-toe
in my arms to wake myself.
I often dreamed they'd murdered you because I'd put a foot
        wrong:
I'd made the wrong face
or whispered your name to my son.
Those grim, strapping, blue-pyjamas men:
I watched them fly. They shattered stones with their hands
and cracked wise like you were nobody's sister.
That last explosion, like a nursery-school

spilled can of paint, Golden Yellow and Clementine
licked with Sea Green.

Of course they never found your body.
Finding people is a black art, sister—
ask me about the time I lost my husband.
One morning, the squeeze of his sweaty arms:
the next, nothing. Bedclothes in disarray.
It took a month to find him:
lazing in the U.S. Virgin Islands
with a younger me whose voice didn't choke
when they broadcast endless sparkling parades
for your defeat.
I get it, sister.
I know the rage that fills a woman,
swelling you up cumulonimbusly
until not even the President of Australia
could be enough.

So don't grovel like that on the doorstep.
I can't offer much:
I don't keep army ants
or a bathtub big enough for your mosasaur.
But the guest room's clean.
Don't beg for forgiveness like I'm one of them, sister,
like I'll put on blue pajamas and blow you to smithereens
if you cry the wrong number of tears.
You don't know what you did for me
in your old defiance. Please, come in.
There's tea in the kettle, soup on the stove,
and a six-year-old, chocolate-smudged nephew I'd like you to
      meet.
We can talk until sunup and past,
if you like. Don't sorry me. We're sisters.
You're home.

The Company of Heaven

Blinding light bathed the remains of the Worcester State Hospital's old Kirkbride building, the one Cassie passed every day on the way to her psychiatric clerkship. The angels who had gathered there cast black spots on the eyes: so tall, so bright, as if anything that touched them would burn. And they were singing.

Cassie shielded her eyes as she passed, crossing to the other side of the street. Angels gave her the creeps.

"*Sing praise to the Lord,*" Their voices were strange, like crashing bells in the tallest steeples, but the hymn was familiar. "*Thanksgiving and song to him be outpoured all ages along!*" They danced, if you could call it dancing, gliding in eye-searing circles.

"Cassie," one of them said, in that same struck-iron voice. "Come sing with us."

Cassie hunched her shoulders and hurried on her way. "I'm already late."

She had two more texts from Sheridan by the time she checked in. Bastard. She deleted them unread, then turned off her phone. She needed to review her patients' charts and make four sets of assessments before noon.

Cassie loved the hospital: the bright lights, the bustling halls, even the chemical smells in the air. So much to do. So many surprises.

Mr. Ježek was hallucinating again today. He was a weatherbeaten old man with a craggy, gray face and scarred knuckles.

"It's the Nazis," he explained. "I saw them in the hall again. They're coming to get me."

"I know, Mr. Ježek," said Cassie, checking his write-up. His dosage had been stable for a while. It might be time for an increase. She would mention it to her supervisor. "It's all right. You're safe now."

"I saw angels, too. Angels on the lawn in front of the Kirkbride. Singing. Nurse Verena couldn't see them, so I must be crazy, eh?"

Cassie swallowed. She looked down at the write-up.

"I couldn't say, Mr. Ježek. I'm not your diagnostician."

She did not want to talk about what she had seen. Especially not if the nurses couldn't see it. She had seen other pedestrians stroll past the angels like nothing was there. And at this stage in her clerkship, she could *not* afford to be called crazy.

Mr. Ježek gave a good patient's trusting smile. "Well, if the angels were real, I'd tell them to do something about the Nazis. You do that for me if you see them, will you?"

"Of course." She turned on the television for him as she left. Mr. Ježek liked television.

The angels were still singing after five, as she rushed to get to painting class. Twilight only made things worse. They seemed bigger than before, sky-filling shapes of light, chasing the evening's deep blue to a faraway corner.

"Cassie. Come sing with us."

"Not on your life."

Cassie stuffed her hands into her jacket pockets to disguise the shaking. Her right hand slipped into a fist around her phone. She couldn't say why the angels frightened her. They swelled with too much light, but so did the sun, and she didn't cower away from that. Maybe it was the way they said her name. Like another thing that knew her. Another that wouldn't leave her alone.

"Heaven is here, and the angels of Heaven."

She raised her chin. "Is that so? Are you angels of Heaven?"

"Yes. Come sing with us."

"Then why aren't you doing anything about—" She paused. Nazis seemed a bit far-fetched. "Curing schizophrenia. Or wars."

"The world holds more than one kind of work, and more than one kind of angel. As for us, we are made to sing."

The words rang out in those bell-like tones, and Cassie shivered. She refused to believe it. They could not possibly be as perfect as the light made them look.

Maybe she shouldn't be talking to them at all. Maybe someone would see and decide she was crazy. Hell, maybe she *was* crazy.

"You're not even singing proper angel songs. You're borrowing ours."

"Is that a problem?"

Cassie's phone buzzed in her hand. Another text message. Flipping the phone open and deleting it, she looked back at the angels. "Tell the other kinds of angels they're doing a terrible job."

She made it to painting class on time. Students lounged in front of their easels, fussing with brushes or mixing colors. She paused to delete the three other messages from Sheridan that had shown up on the trip over, then got to work.

Luisa dropped into the chair next to Cassie, her dark brown hair up in a ponytail. "Hi." She looked perfect as always — not a hair escaped. Cassie had an irrational urge to muss her up, to run her fingers over Luisa's well-behaved scalp, kiss her forehead, smell her shampoo. But she couldn't, of course. She and Luisa hadn't said much, other than classroom small-talk, since that evening two weeks ago at the Viva Bene.

"Hello."

Luisa began to paint from a photo: a lion curled and sunning on a rock, his mane tumbling around him in unkempt waves. Cassie was still on her preliminary sketches.

"Did you hear Ginns identified a gene associated with canine compulsive disorder?"

Cassie's hands roved across her sketchpad, trying to figure out what was missing. The assignment was to paint a real person or animal. She had tried for a standing human, but something about it wasn't quite right, and anyway it was hard to concentrate when talking to Luisa. Her pencil traveled in aimless arcs. "I knew he was working on it."

"They finished the study and approved it for publication. There'll be a piece in the news tomorrow talking about it."

"Well, congratulations to them."

Luisa leaned over to peek at Cassie's sketch. The sudden proximity made Cassie's skin tingle. "So what are you working on so intently — Oh."

The aimless arcs behind the standing human had coalesced, while Cassie wasn't looking, into wings, and a wide nimbus like the light of the angels.

Cassie pulled the easel away. "It's nothing."

Luisa stood motionless. Paint dripped unheeded from her paintbrush onto the floor. Her eyes were accusing.

"It's not like that," Cassie said. "It's not... I'm not..."

Crazy, said one part of her mind. But she wasn't sure that was really what she meant.

Luisa sucked in a breath.

"That's it, isn't it? That's why you wouldn't talk to me after that evening. You think this is a sin. You think I'm going to hell."

"No, it's not."

"The assignment was to paint someone real, Cassie. Are you going to tell me you believe in those things?"

"No, I just — No. It's not like that. It's not anything like that. I don't even *like* them. It's... That's not why." She bit her lip, tongue-tied. "I like you. I don't think you're evil. It's... It's nothing."

Luisa looked down. Relaxed a little, but her voice was gloomy.

"Can't you see that it hurts me? That you won't even talk about whatever it is?"

Cassie flinched, thinking of text messages. "Yes. But I can't."

It was the closest they'd come to talking about what happened at the Viva Bene. Maybe it was a step up from silence. Luisa didn't keep pressing the way a boy would. She just nodded, sighed, and went back to her painting, and the room kept on with its busy silence.

They'd been giddy, that evening at the Viva Bene, laughing at each other's jokes, stealing bits of each other's entrées, talking about medical school minutiae, art, music, sports, other people and each other. There was something electric in the air, in the way Luisa's hands found Cassie's, the way their feet came together and their eyes met. They weren't just friends who were girls, out for dinner. This was something new.

"We should do this again," Luisa said, late in the evening. Their table was clear and their glasses drained, but neither one wanted to stop talking. "Soon."

"We should. Soon."

"When are you free?"

"Oh, hardly at all." Cassie pulled her day planner out of her purse. "I can do next Saturday evening. Or Thursday after next. Wait, no. That's Access to Essential Medicine group." She giggled a little. It wasn't like her to giggle. "I can skip Access to Essential Medicine group. It's not for credit. This once, I can."

Luisa, digging in her own purse — sleeker and trendier than Cassie's — made a face. "Oh, I forgot my day planner. That's not like me."

Cassie just smiled. "You'll see me at painting class tomorrow. We'll figure something out then."

They talked for another half an hour, while Cassie took the cheque and walked Luisa home. Luisa squeezed her hand, told her what a wonderful time she had, and kissed her on the cheek. Cassie stood speechless, suddenly flushed and very aware of her own skin. Luisa said goodbye and ducked inside, leaving Cassie with the road back to her own apartment.

It was only a couple of well-lit blocks. It should have been fine. But in her giddy daze, she took out her phone and turned it back on, out of habit. Five more messages from Sheridan stared her in the face.

He'd said *I'm sorry* in the first few messages. She'd never believed it. Sorry people didn't harass you with texts every minute of the day. They didn't call you *bitch*, in the same texts, a few days later when you still hadn't replied.

She made a list when she got home, to stop everything from whirling around in her mind. Wrote it all down. *I really liked last night. I like you. I like everything but it's happening too fast. I just got over a bad breakup and I didn't think I wanted something new this soon and I didn't even think I wanted to do this with girls until last night and my mother would NEVER approve and it's not bad, just confusing, but I need to think...*

But when she saw Luisa again, when she tried to recite everything on the list, it wouldn't come out.

"Hey, you," Luisa said. "I'm free Saturday evening."

"I'm busy," Cassie blurted. "Busy then. I'm too busy."

Because it wasn't just the things on the list. There was another thing she hadn't dared to write down: the idea that, a month or a year or five years down the line, Luisa would be clogging up her phone with messages, too.

Her marks were falling in painting class. It was so hard to concentrate with Luisa on one side and all this emotional baggage on the other. It was no wonder she'd strayed off the assignment and started drawing angels.

"What about the bad breakup?" Luisa prompted after a minute.

"Still bad. That's all."

"Is there anything I can — I mean, do you need a new place or the police or—"

"No," she said quickly, and then wondered why she'd said it so fast. The police had never even occurred to her. Sheridan, uninterested in her school career even when they were dating, hadn't bothered to track her down in person. He'd never actually uttered a threat — at least not in the messages she'd read. Maybe he crossed the harassment line despite that. Maybe the police had actual jurisdiction. But what would they say if she went to them? She had no evidence. She'd been deleting it all.

"It's not *that* bad," she added, after a moment. "But thank you."

Luisa started filling in the tawny colour on her lion's mane with broad, luxurious strokes. "What's he doing?"

"He just won't go away."

By the time she passed the Kirkbride again the next morning, she was starting to wish she hadn't deleted those messages. If she'd kept them, she could have shown them to someone. She could have gone, "See, here are five hundred and seventy messages from the past four weeks. All the same guy. He is seriously interfering with my quality of life." Then they could have done something. Cassie itched to make an evaluation, fill a prescription, stitch up her entire personal life and fix it. She had to do something. She just didn't know what.

"When peace, like a river, attendeth my way. When sorrows like sea billows roll; Whatever my lot, Thou has taught me to say, It is well, it is well, with my soul."

"You don't even have souls," said Cassie. "Do you? How does that work?"

"Come sing with us."

"Stop it." Cassie made a fist. "Stop telling me to do a thing I can't do. You think I can make those bell sounds and shine like a light? You think I can have anything to do with you?"

"We think you can sing."

"What if I did sing?" She couldn't stop her voice from rising. "Who would that help? You know what would happen if put on some choir robe and tried to sing with you. I'd waste an afternoon singing and it wouldn't make any difference. You'd still drag me off at the end, because I'm *wrong*. I can't love the people I'm supposed to love. You know what I mean, if you're really angels!"

"My sin, oh, the bliss of this glorious thought..."

"You *know*!" Cassie shouted.

But they only kept on singing. Cassie stared at them, then turned on her heel and kept walking. The hospital was only a short distance away.

Everything apart from the angels was disgustingly normal. The trees were green, the hospital was white, the sun was shining, and Cassie's phone was ringing. A real call this time. Not a text message.

She looked fearfully at the caller ID, but it wasn't Sheridan. With a sigh, she flipped open the phone. "Hi, Mom."

"Cassie. How wonderful to catch hold of you! I've been feeling so out of the loop."

"Sorry. How are things?"

She had a few minutes, so she sat down on a bench and listened while her mother went over the details of church meetings, PTA, town hall and tiny details of social slights done to others. She got out her notes for the day and went over them while she listened.

"And one other thing," said Cassie's mother. "I got the saddest phone call from Sheridan the other day. Cassie, I couldn't believe it! You never told me the two of you broke up."

Cassie swallowed hard and put a hand on the side of her notes, careful to keep them from dropping. "We broke up."

"Oh, I know, dear. He told me all about it. He's really the sweetest boy. I know he can get a little angry sometimes, but really, Cassie, not even returning any of his calls? I've always said, all he needs is a nice girl like you to teach him—"

Cassie clicked the phone off and sat staring at it in rage for a moment. She took a few deep breaths. Then she returned the notes to their rightful place, stood up, took a few steps towards the nearest trash can, and threw the phone in.

The force of the throw and the strength of the clanging sound surprised her. But she was fed up. It felt, at that moment, like everything wrong with the world came at her through the phone. So the phone had to go.

She took two more deep breaths. She could still hear angels in the distance. They were from heaven. They would never understand.

She stared at the trash can, and something small and rebellious bubbled up inside her. She had told the angels they would drag her off at the end. Was she sure? Her phone was lying there in the trash can with dirty napkins and cigarette butts and no one could tell her how to feel anymore. She would feel what she liked. Was she sure of that?

"All creatures of our god and king. Lift up your voice and with us sing."

Maybe she could. Maybe, even in front of these terrifying creatures, she could.

She took a breath and joined in, tunelessly, like anyone would mumble in the pews on a Sunday. Hoping they wouldn't hear, because she really wasn't sure of this at all. "Alleluia. Allelu—"

And the world did a flip underneath her. The sky was full of music. Music swelled in her ears, suffusing her blood. The road underneath her, the hospital building up ahead, the stupid ornamental trees by the sidewalk, even the trash can was music. The squabbles, the fear and the heartbreak, they were a faint jumble of little discordant notes. When they finished, they vanished. The music went on.

And Cassie was part of it. Even frightened, even doubting, with her tuneless imperfect voice. She had been welcome to it all along. With every flawed tremble of her vocal chords, she was more and more part of it.

This was what they had been trying to show her.

Alleluia! Allelu—

The next moment, everything was back to normal.

Cassie stared at the angels. They sang on as though nothing had happened. She stared at the street around her. People still walked and drove. The ornamental trees, the asphalt, the bricks and the ruin of the Kirkbride were all just the same as before.

Nothing had changed. Nothing was fixed.

So why did she feel like everything was fixed?

Cassie stayed a minute or two extra with Mr. Ježek that day. She had time. "No trouble with Nazis last night, Mr. Ježek?"

"No." Mr. Ježek gave her a jowly little smile. "But I'm still seeing angels. Nurse Verena says it's the craziest thing she's heard from me yet."

Cassie paused. Technically, she was not supposed to do this. But she *didn't* feel so concerned, right now, about what she was supposed to do. She went to the window and opened it halfway. "I see them too. Right down there. By the Kirkbride. Are these the ones you see?"

"You're making fun of me," said Mr. Ježek affably, as though this made Cassie an adorable scamp. And he craned his neck to see. "Yes, that's where they are. And..."

Cassie gave him a moment to think. She slipped a hand into her pocket and touched the empty space where her phone had been. She would get a new one and Sheridan would never know the number.

But Luisa would know. At painting class tomorrow night, she would explain it all — not just her phone, but the angels. *Everything.* If Luisa didn't shout or call her crazy, well, then, they would see what happened from there.

And if Sheridan tracked her down again, she would keep the messages this time. She would talk to someone. No more of this bustling around pretending it hadn't happened.

Mr. Ježek was smiling more broadly than she'd ever seen before. An old half-strangled melody escaped his throat.

"Amazing Grace. How sweet the sound..."

It only lasted a moment, and then he looked back at Cassie, eyes wide.

"I knew they were singing. I could see it from how they moved. But no one believed me."

"I do," said Cassie. "I believe."

Abominable Snowman

Stomped brown, watery-sick,
bites the heels of furcoat girls
who never look down

Nightmare I

a grayscale giant
glimpsed through glass

(do not look,
do not see him)

the night becomes a game of not looking

when i see him he will rush to me buffeting
and never let go

(here he is,
here he comes—)

my eyes refuse to close
my hands can't find the curtains

i have seen
this grayscale face
before

i know him
i know
there is nothing i can do
but scream

Ribbons

When they put Marnie in solitary she started to pick at her
fingertips. Nervous habit, congenital, nothing to be ashamed of;
besides, better to think of the skin on her fingers than the silence and
the fear.

When the blood started to well, it hurt, but not as much as she'd
expected. She wondered how long it had been. Ten minutes? An hour?
How many long minutes of silence and fear if she stopped?

She did not stop.

When they opened the door to collect her, they found ribbons
of skin, rivulets of blood. But Marnie was nowhere at all.

Blue Fever

Athba had a death to sing.

She stood straight and tall at the front of Lord Keloth's small, nervous group of court musicians. The smell of jasmine, orange flower, and oakmoss rose from dim braziers at the corners of the banquet hall, mingling with the scents of roast meat, delicate sauces, and sweets. Courtiers whispered and jibed, no doubt forming and breaking alliances even as the banquet's courses were changed. A clockwork servitor's gears clicked incessantly as it rolled with an insectlike gait from table to table. It paused and pointedly brushed a crumb off Athba's skirt before rolling away again.

She breathed deeply, willing herself not to tug at her thick black hair or to fuss with the robes hiding her voluminous figure. Style was everything with Lord Keloth, and though he had not disliked a song of hers yet, she could guess at the penalty for failure. He perched heronlike on his throne, draped in scarlet silk, his eyes fixed on hers.

"Athba," he said, "do you have something to sing me?"

It was a silly question. Of course she did. Her deathsongs were the sole reason she enjoyed Lord Keloth's patronage. She nodded, and he gestured to the group. As the lead violinist drew her bow, Athba drew breath.

The song began with a wordless, plaintive tune on Nanu's violin. Athba sang her first verses soft and menacing, in a tone that hinted something else lurked underneath.

"Sunlight glinting red
Off of ruby-tinted scale:
Teeth, claws and wings
Worked in intricate detail..."

Slowly, she sang the story of a gift: a life-sized dragon worked from rosy glass. This was not an ordinary royal gift, but something deposited mysteriously during the night, with nothing but an enigmatic note. In reality, Keloth's guards would never have allowed such a thing; in the song, it could be explained away as magic.

Lord Keloth, in the song, found it on his morning walk to the throne room. (The tempo increased slightly; Nanu took up tense repeated notes, hypnotic and nearly dancelike.) Anyone bestowing such a gift would know he had reason to fear glass sculptures; but Keloth was no coward, nor a poor sport. He had it installed in his courtyard.

The tempo continued to increase. The other violinists took on the repeated notes, while Nanu played an urgent modulating bridge, swooping high and back down again.

The sculpture came to life. It crept up the stairs, in the dead of night, and into Keloth's bedchamber.

The accompaniment was frenzied now, and Athba no longer held back. She put her voice's full power into the sharp-edged melody as she sang Keloth's battle with the beast. It growled threats; he made dry little jokes. He cracked its limbs; it bit his throat. He shattered its head with a heavy book from his bedside table, and at last it died. Shards of glass clattered across the chamber like cobblestones.

(A sudden slowing. The wordless, plaintive tune recurred, and Athba drew herself back, returning to the menacing voice she had at the first. There was a new tone in it, too, a bittersweet acceptance.)

Keloth had won, but the bleeding was too heavy, and from too many wounds. Knowing nothing could save him, he refused the attentions of healers. Instead he sat down by the remains of the glass dragon and murmured to it.

He died smiling, without regrets.

Athba held her pose for a moment as the strings died away. Then Keloth applauded, and the rest of the room followed suit.

She curtsied, breathing a sigh of relief. She always worried that one day she would have nothing new to say about the single word, *glass*, no remaining way to satisfy the court's morbid tastes. But that day had not yet come.

A whirring servitor rolled over to Keloth, clearing his plate and depositing a plate of lime ice. Keloth picked at it, but his eyes rested on the musicians. "Athba, will you do something for me?"

Another silly question. "I am at your service, my lord."

"A week from today, Lady Irathi arrives to discuss an alliance against Lord

Ulan. Compose and perform one of your songs for her."

"My lord?"

"A deathsong. That is what you do best. The words on which to expand are *blue fever.*' That is all."

Athba's rather hefty stomach turned to ice. Morbid lords like Keloth could commission their own deathsongs as much as they liked. But to commission them for someone else? This was never done. Lords of the same standing never mentioned each other's deaths. It would be taken as a threat: *I know how you will die. I can make it happen quickly if you like.*

But one did not say no to Lord Keloth — particularly not when one had gone to the clacking clockwork machine in the highest tower and spilled one's own blood. Keloth had seen the parchment predicting Athba's death before permitting even Athba to read. He rarely passed up an opportunity to remind her, or any of his other servitors, that he knew what would kill them.

"I will do as my lord commands," said Athba, and she wondered if this next deathsong would be her last.

"Can you believe it?" Athba said later in the practice room. She paced through mountains of unattended sheet music, scattering paper through the velvet chamber. Nanu could not even control her frizzy red hair, let alone the volumes of paper she needed, but she was a good confidante for all that. "Because I can't."

Nanu shrugged her scrawny shoulders. "I heard that Lady Irathi never commissions deathsongs at all. But I'm sure Keloth has something planned. He wouldn't throw away an alliance just to amuse himself."

Maybe not, Athba thought, but he would certainly throw away a courtier who displeased him. The deathsinger before Athba had once sang a deathsong in which Keloth was dragged across shards of glass while comically tangled in his horse's reins. He was forgiven, or so people whispered, for the grisly description, but not for making Keloth look foolish. In any case, no one ever heard from him again.

If Irathi was displeased, Athba would go the same way.

"I heard she kept her death secret so no one could use it against her. I'm surprised he even managed to find it. Why's he blurting it out in front of the whole court?"

Nanu chuckled. "Who knows? Maybe she's changed her mind. You remember how you got when you first had your death read. It takes some getting used to, you know? It is morbid."

"These are morbid times."

Athba's death, predicted by the clockwork machine, was *grapes*. She had avoided fruit with amused horror for several weeks, but she couldn't keep it up. Keloth made a point of serving Athba his best wines. Not as a punishment, he said. Merely to keep her on her toes.

Nanu did not know her own death, or claimed not to, though Keloth assuredly knew it. She had closed her eyes while the machine spun its clacking gears, telling the lord she preferred uncertainty. He had humored her by making *everything* uncertain: requesting new music at the last minute, hinting that they might or might not be employed in the future. Nanu seemed not to mind.

"And *blue fever*. It's such an unromantic disease. How am I supposed to sing about that?"

Nanu took Athba's hands and brushed her thumbs against the singer's palms. Though Nanu was the younger of the two, there was something motherly in her smile. "You'll think of something, and I'll help with the arrangement. Keloth's always enjoyed what you do. I'd trust him."

In her quarters, Athba started with lyrics. She gnawed nervously at an apple with her left hand while she scribbled with her right, and crumpled page after page. She knew the signs of blue fever: discolored skin, boils, slow suffocation. It was not pretty like *glass*, nor pleasurable like *grapes*. With a dramatic framing story, it might have pleased Keloth. But not a squeamish woman who kept her death under lock and key.

"One day in an infirmary..."

No. What would Irathi be doing in an infirmary, when she knew the risks?

"When Irathi's father..."

That went into the wastebasket straightaway. Bad enough to have to do this for a squeamish Irathi; even worse to threaten her family.

"Without warning, without sign..."

She worked on that one for a little while, leaving her apple to go brown at the side of the desk. It almost worked. Irathi contracted the fever for no reason, through no fault of her own, and everyone clucked over the tragedy while...

While what? While she resigned herself to a senseless and pointless death? While she learned there was some cosmic reason she *had* to die? No. If Athba had learned one thing during her patronage, it was not to bring philosophy into it. No one would enjoy the song, and everyone would start to worry about free will or inevitability, whichever happened to scare them more.

Athba's mind wandered to her family. What would they say if she failed and died? She could picture her father's lined, jowly face, though she hadn't had time to go see him in months. *I told her not to take the offer of patronage,* he would say. And her rosy-cheeked mother would nod: *All the money but constant murder. Not a fair trade in my book. Poor dear.*

At last she threw down her notebook and stormed back to Nanu.

"He's going to kill me."

"Hm?" Nanu looked up, pausing in the middle of a scale, and put down her violin carefully, brushing piles of sheet music aside to make room.

Athba collapsed into a wrought iron chair. "I've figured it out. He's too proud to ally with Lady Irathi, but doesn't want to lose face for turning her down. So I sing a deathsong, she storms out, and the blame goes to me. Keloth kills me with grapes, he's rid of Irathi, and no one blames him. Then Lord Ulan rides in, takes over both holdings and impales everyone."

"Oh, sweetie, that doesn't even make sense. For one thing, I think he likes you too much to kill you. For another, if he blames it on you, and Lord Ulan keeps pressing in at Irathi's borders, she'll want an alliance anyway, once you're gone."

"So maybe he keeps me around, or... I don't know. But I can't make blue fever sound nice."

"Who said it has to sound nice? Keloth never liked them nice. Remember the one where he drank ground glass and vomited blood?"

Athba grimaced. She remembered. Keloth had applauded, and then sent a hooded assassin to her quarters in the night. Not to kill her, or even to scare her, but to explain that ground glass didn't work that way.

"And the one with the molten glass and the angry glassblower? That one made me shudder. But he loved it."

"Yes." Athba took a few deep breaths, forcing her shoulders to relax. "But

Irathi's not Keloth."

"That's the point. You don't really know what she likes. It's Keloth who will decide if you live or die. So write it the way he would like. Let him worry about the rest."

"He'll still kill me." Athba slumped, then straightened again, as the wrought iron chair back dug into her shoulders. Keloth did not furnish his servants' quarters with comfort in mind. "I'm sorry. You're right, of course."

She still thought that Keloth planned to drive off Lady Irathi and blame it on her. But what did that matter? If he had plans for her, how could she stop them? Better to stop worrying. Better to be morbid, like everyone, until death ceased to frighten.

Lady Irathi rode in on a horseless carriage, traveling by some obscure magic of its own, and strode into Lord Keloth's banquet hall with her retinue trailing behind. Her courtiers peered at the blood-red tapestries and copper silverware. Lady Irathi was sharp-chinned and bright-eyed, and wore a long, trailing dress in pale green. Cold seemed to follow in her footsteps.

"Eat," Nanu muttered to Athba, before she launched into an instrumental serenade, the kind that dining guests could listen to or ignore as they chose. "You'll feel better with food." But Athba did not feel ready for food. The wine was even worse: looking at it sickened her. She barely heard anything until Keloth called her name.

"Athba." From the impatience in his voice, it might be the second time he'd said it. "Won't you sing for our guest?"

She forced herself upright and strode to the front of the hall. She could not feel her feet touching the floor. Keloth's courtiers whispered to each other; no doubt they knew why she was worried. But Lady Irathi's retinue kept quiet. Athba kept her face as serene as she could, though her heart hammered. She was a trained performer, after all. She could hide fear.

She took a deep breath and began.

"Plague!" This time she did not start low and menacing, but urgent. The violinists cantered to keep up.

"Plague in the towns,
Plague in the fields and the city

Blue skin bringing death swift and sure.
Wails of despair,
But wise women whisper
That there is a cure..."

Athba widened her eyes and waved her hands, letting the anxiety of a blue fever epidemic fill the room — though she could not allow it to influence her lungs or throat. The sound must come up free, full and pleasing. She kept her own anxiety locked up in the back of her mind. Her expression came not from her heart, but from a place she pictured behind and to the right of her, a repository for imaginary emotions.

Only when the prophecy of a cure appeared did the tempo slacken slightly. Nanu brought in a sweet, hopeful countermelody. But the cure could only be delivered by Lady Irathi's hands, and only with the aid of a particular emerald-green flower.

The song became a quest-song, leaping along in hope and fear. Lady Irathi endured magical trials, found the flower, and went from house to house, laying a petal on each fevered brow. When the fevers began to flee, Nanu's melody leapt in outright joy, though the other violinists played short, tense notes underneath. It was not yet over.

There was always a catch.

When the plague had all but run its course, Lady Irathi began to notice blue marks on her skin. And the emerald-green flower could only be used to heal others.

The violins slowed.

The song became a stately, reverent dirge. The whole land praised the dying Lady. She raved, choked, withered before their eyes, and they only loved her more. Irathi, said the people in Athba's Deathsong, was a saint.

That is how it ended: on a soft, high note and a prayerful arpeggio, and in awe.

Athba forced herself not to try to gauge Lady Irathi's reaction, not even in the ringing silence after the last note.

No one applauded. Everyone knew Lady Irathi's dislike of Deathsongs. Everyone but Athba was watching her face.

And in the silence, Lady Irathi chuckled.

"Lord Keloth," she said, clapping slowly. "I heard you were terribly morbid. I see that it's true. But you have given me a wonderful gift: a chance to forget. To escape into someone else's death, brought by a disease entirely unlike the one fated for me."

Athba stared. Everyone stared but Keloth, who perched there, smiling, not surprised in the least. Lady Irathi ascended the steps to him, leaving a chill in her wake.

"Now, then," she said, "I think we have an alliance to discuss."

Athba collapsed against the wall in Nanu's practice room, accidentally scattering a pile of rehearsal pencils. "I can't believe it wasn't her real death. And he didn't tell me. I can't believe he put me through that!"

"I can," Nanu said cheerily. "He loves this kind of thing. Keeping you on your toes, hmm?"

Nanu and her musicians had kept the wine going all night. Even Athba felt good. After the alliance was settled, Keloth had showered the group with gold. Athba especially.

Nanu drained her wineglass. Athba paused for a split second, knowing Nanu had nothing to fear from *grapes*, then recklessly downed her own. "Eat, drink, and be merry, for tomorrow we die."

"Not tomorrow if I can help it," said Nanu. "So what are you spending your gold on?"

"Savings. In case I survive."

They exchanged grins. It was mostly true. But she had set aside a little for her family, too, and a little to spruce up her quarters. A more comfortable chair. Better lamps. And a little piece of art for the wall. A stained glass rendering of a cluster of grapes on the vine, for inspiration.

After all, these were morbid times.

The Pyromancer

(They gather, the boats, in darkness
each with its lonely lantern.
Lit singly, singing, they wait
as you raise your blackened hands
atop the king's tower
to stir a spark in the sky.)

They say the first thing you burned was yourself.
Surely such power must eat from the inside.
They say each conjured flame is agony,
pulling the scars yet deeper to your bones.

But scars grow only
in healing,
and shackles have keys.

(Those flames! Jewel-colored,
timpani-deep, woven in spheres
and spiraling shafts
to silhouette the battlements
before an orange moon.)

You burned yourself, yes. Once.
Young like a smith's boy, incautious,
touching the forge.
What of it?
Nowadays, mornings, you walk calm
to the grocer with the whisperers and the rest:
cool coins in hand, the same plum juice
dripping down your chin.

Tonight you light the sky, not on orders, not in pain,
but because you love the colors

(just as they all do,
breathing the light, clasping hands, clapping hearts,
each tall to the sound of trumpets
in the shadow of a flame.)

The Mermaid at Sea World

Her house is six light-dappled slabs,
flat, silent, portholed:
children like woodpeckers hammer the glass
and men leer.

Once a day, the show: they pick him
from the crowd, a young man, strong
and camera-chained. The kind
who can't tear his eyes from the fins.
Preferably willing.
They toss him in.

The thrashing. The red-mottled water.
The ripple of wave-cuddled light on dead limbs.
The crowd goes wild, every time

yet, with her tail round his thighs
and his throat in her teeth,
for six light-dappled breaths,
she forgets them.

Finding Shadow

You can't outrun light.
Tai knows, while he waits for the blindfold.
Night's fifty years gone and won't look back,
not since Earth choked on its factory-stink.
Back then we built a smaller dome than sky,
and like shamefaced crayon-smudged children
we colored 'til it shone.

Now blue-fire marquees and tangerine girls
play sky-projected; stock updates
news crawls greetings previews special offers
spam up the whole horizon.
Tai walks, when he must, under leering lights
and through thunder-beats sex-moans mail-chimes
karaoke horns brakes shouts and the smell of sugar:
five research papers overdue
while every storefront strobes his name.

But not in Theo's room.
Not.
Here.

Blindfold's the oldest trick. All you need
is cloth (and soft foam
for the ears). Wait. Breathe.

There's nothing to hear,
only soft rope cradling wrists.
Theo's feather-tender fingers at his jaw.
And in the darkness, Tai imagines sky:
sundowned, shadowed, and at peace.

An Operatic Tour of New Jersey, With Raptors

The Apocalypse begins when Diego sings Count Almaviva in *The Barber of Seville* in Dover, New Jersey. He doesn't notice anything wrong until after the curtain call, when he steps out of the Baker Theater onto West Blackwell Street, struggling to balance the three bouquets of roses in his arms, and walks into a horde of running, screaming people, pursued by a Tyrannosaurus.

For four weeks after that, there are no operas anywhere. Early in the first week, velociraptors eat Diego's fiancé, Juan. Apocalypse Plague takes most of the rest of the opera company. Diego is too shocked to mourn. The local funeral directors are already booked up, and anyway their churches and mausoleums have been stomped underfoot by sauropods. Businesses and utilities shut down one by one. In the fourth week, Diego takes a grief-weary walk down East McFarlan Street and sees no humans at all, only feathers and scales.

Diego learns quickly how not to be eaten by raptors. Humans are not their natural prey. Never corner them; never wear red; make no sudden movements; never crouch on all fours. Never take their discarded feathers, especially not the huge emerald-green and violet ones from the tip of the tail, which are used in dominance displays. Diego often thinks of taking one anyway and waving it at them, but he cannot quite bring himself to suicide. Starvation is not a problem: the fresh produce is eaten or rotten now, and the bread stale as bricks, but there is enough canned food at the grocery store to keep him nourished for years.

In the fifth week, Diego sits at home and reads trashy novels until he cannot stand it anymore.

Then he goes back to the Baker Theater.

The roof has been torn off in a fight between two Argentinosaurs, leaving the performance hall raked by wind and rain. The balconies are smashed beyond recognition, and raptors curl in nests of seat stuffing in the Argentinosaurs' huge footprints. But the stage is intact. Diego picks his way down the center aisle. The raptors angle their heads as he passes, very like birds, looking sideways at him through bright slitted eyes. A few hiss soft warnings.

He skirts those ones, makes no sudden movements, and climbs the steps to the deserted wings.

Even with only monsters watching, there's still that hush in his heart when he stands at the edge and looks out.

Diego takes a long breath and begins to sing.

"Bravi, bravissimi, fate silenzio;
piano, pianissimo, senza parlar."

At *fate silenzio*, the raptors fall silent and turn their heads, each fixed on him with one over-bright eye. His voice is scratchy: he hasn't sung since finding Juan's body. If there are music critics among the raptors, they'll kill him. He does not care.

He misses three of the high notes. He does not care. By the end of the first scene he has hit his stride, remembering the way his throat opens up and frees the breath. He struts through the ruined scenery, standing on a pitted and birdshit-stained fountain, addressing fellow singers who are no longer there.

By the end of the first act he is weeping as he sings.

The raptors do not applaud. Diego does not expect them to. After the finale he walks to his apartment, where he packs as much canned food and bottled water as he can stand, a change of clothes, some toiletries, and his dog-eared vocal score to *The Barber of Seville*.

He has always wished he could sing at every opera house in the country. Well, now, he thinks as he puts on his hiking boots, there is no reason not to.

In Morristown, Diego's first real stop after Dover, the Mayo Performing Arts Center has been burned. Diego feels like a grave robber, stealing through the ashes backstage. This time he warms up before singing. The smoky air and fallen I-beams are too desolate to hold any attraction even for dinosaurs, but in a way, this is a comfort: he can pretend that there are no dinosaurs, that he's only rehearsing in an odd place. Any minute now he will leave through the back door and see a beautiful businessman in a hurry to get somewhere.

Any minute.

In Englewood, a triceratops lives under the balconies at the Bergen Performing Arts Center. It opens a wrinkled eye, considers him, then closes it and sleeps through his performance.

From Englewood Diego cannot resist the temptation to nip into New

York City and sing at the Met. He's always dreamed of playing Almaviva on that enormous gilded stage. He has some vague hope for big-city glitz, despite the apocalypse, but NYC has been flooded. Mosasaurs lurk by the Statue of Liberty. Two inches of brackish water cover the Met stage, and Diego sings Almaviva as a merman.

After that, he begins to experiment. Bivouacking on the I-78 on his way out of Newark, he takes out his vocal score and studies the other parts. Soon he's doing both sides of the dialogues between Almaviva and Figaro, even though Figaro is a little too low. By Princeton he has all of "Largo al factotum" worked up. *"Ah, bravo Figaro! Bravo, bravissimo!"* He learns Rosina next, which is a little too high. Heading east to Red Bank, then to the flooded-out Great Auditorium in Ocean Grove, he throws caution to the wind and does Bartolo, transposed up an octave when necessary. He has secretly always wanted a *basso buffo* voice, flinging out words like a blistering cannon—not instead of his flexible tenor, but in addition, every once in a while, to see what it was like.

In Trenton, by some miracle, the water works. Diego discovers it by accident when he leans against a drinking fountain. There's a sudden cold wet burst and he leaps away. Then he laughs with joy and runs to each of the bathrooms, turning on all the taps. After performing his perfect one-man *Barber of Seville* (he even has Basilio, the servants, and the chorus by now), he finds a miraculously intact motel. Roofs, walls, water, mattresses: everything's in its place. He strips off his road-filthy clothes and has a sinfully hot shower. He even shampoos his beard. He sings "Largo al factotum" into the showerhead. He hums to himself as he plugs and fills the bathtub to soak his clothes. Then, naked and shining like a sex god from a magazine, he collapses into the musty sheets.

When he wakes up, there is a raptor curled up on his legs like a large, feathered lapdog.

Diego stares, frozen.

The raptor raises its head, fixes an eye on him, and chirrups.

"Yes," says Diego, "hi. Nice raptor. Would you mind getting off my legs?"

The raptor clicks its fearsome toe-claws against the comforter.

"Nice raptor. It's just that I have things to do, you see. I have to get across the country and sing *The Barber of Seville* in every opera house. Maybe we could just... Um..."

The raptor rises to its feet, concentrating its weight on two small, talon-shaped spots just below Diego's knees. It picks its way up him until it stands on his chest and peers at him with that sideways raptor glare.

Diego stares back. At last the raptor chitters again and hops to the floor.

"Thank you," says Diego. "Nice raptor. Now, I'm just going to go over here and put my clothes on."

He fishes his clothes from the blackened water. They don't look much cleaner than before, and now they're soggy, too.

"Or maybe," he says, "I'll go to the store." It feels important to keep this creature apprised of his situation. "I'm sure I saw a store on the way in."

He takes his pack and walks to the shop in only his hiking boots. He browses for a rugged and highway-ready outfit to replace his fragile city clothes. Then he strikes out onto the I-95. The raptor walks implacably behind him.

After Trenton, Diego isn't sure where to go. The East Coast is sinking, so they head inland along the Delaware River, which has overrun its banks. Wet sand and crab tracks encroach on the side of the highway. He figures he'll tour Pennsylvania for a while, then venture into Maryland.

The Academy of Music in Philadelphia looms over him, grand with shadows, though cracks in the ceiling let shafts of light in. The raptor follows him onto the stage.

Diego's performance in Philadelphia is one of his worst. He can't concentrate. He screws up even the simplest Italian. Afterwards, he sits in a beam of light and leafs through his vocal score, drilling every difficult phrase. "*Sconsolata, disperata, in sua camera serrata*, dammit. *In sua camera serrata. Serrata. Serrata.*" The raptor tries to poke its nose into the book. Diego slams it shut.

All the way north to Montgomeryville, the raptor makes noises like it wants something.

"Where's your pack?" says Diego. "Where's your family? Why are you obsessed with me?"

The raptor makes a sound remarkably like a reptilian giggle.

"Juan," Diego says without thinking, "stop it."

In Montgomeryville, there's construction. The stage is littered with fallen ladders, plastic sheeting, and sawdust. A can of paint has been overturned, and colorful dinosaur tracks, big and small, litter the floor beside it. Juan-the-raptor scurries around Diego as he gets his bearings for the opening. Almaviva enters from *here,* he imagines, and meets Fiorello *here...*

It suddenly occurs to Diego that Juan-the-raptor is exactly where Fiorello ought to be. He's even holding up a forelimb in a vague impression of a lantern-bearer.

It's hard to remember that *The Barber of Seville* wasn't always a one-man show.

"All right," says Diego, and then he sings: *"Fiorello...Olà!"*

Juan chirrups. It sounds nothing like *"Signor, son qua."*

"No, that's wrong," says Diego. He motions to the vocal score. "Your line is *'Signor, son qua.'* Say it with me. *'Signor, son qua. "*

Juan snaps at the pages as if trying to grab them.

Diego is suddenly enraged with this creature for existing, for mocking him, for taking his dead lover's name. He hugs the page to his chest and backs away. "You can't have this music. It's mine! You don't understand anything about it."

Juan lowers his head like a bull, and for a moment Diego thinks the raptor brain has finally filed him under *prey.* But then Juan scampers away.

Diego sings *The Barber of Seville* in Montgomeryville alone, apart from a single Corythosaurus browsing in the audience. But as soon as he's out on the I-76, there's Juan trotting behind him again.

In Lancaster, the Apocalypse seems to have come during a travelling production of *The Phantom of the Opera,* which Diego finds vaguely offensive. The huge staircase from the Masquerade scene lurks backstage next to the disassembled chandelier. Some set designer has attached statues of revelers to the staircase to supplement the chorus, and some of the statues near the top harbor nests. Not dinosaur nests, but the small nests of spotted brown wood thrushes—though Diego once read that all birds are dinosaurs. Whatever they are, they cuddle together in happy pairs. Diego has a flash of rage seeing them like that, though he can't remember why.

Juan is at his heels even before he can take out the vocal score. Since Montgomeryville, Diego has been forgetting things—even Almaviva's own arias. More and more, he has to pause and peer through this book. He has a feeling of pointlessness, as though he has become too small for any opera.

"I am Count Almaviva," he says. "I am Rosina, Fiorello, and Figaro, Figaro,

Figaro! If there is no audience, I still hear myself."

At the foot of the ridiculous staircase, he digs out the vocal score. Juan rushes in, snapping at it.

"You can't have it," he barks, and Juan hops so close that Diego has to scramble backwards. Juan advances, growling.

He's hungry. He must be. He thinks the score is food.

"It's just paper," Diego says, crawling backwards up the steps. "You won't like it. Eat a thrush. They're sitting right there." But Juan swivels his head at the birds, and they fly away in a fluttering cloud.

Diego crouches at the top of the stairs, hiding the score behind him. He is ashamed of himself. Offering up the life of an innocent creature to preserve his worthless paper. That is not what an honorable man, the kind they write operas about, would do. He watches the thrushes as they find perches higher in the rafters, out of Juan's reach, and lean close to each other.

Juan eyes him. He knows he should put the score down, before Juan kills him for it, but he can't let go. Then Juan turns and scampers back down the stairs, edges to the far side of the stage, and watches.

Diego takes a while to get his breath back. He sings the beginning of *The Barber of Seville* in Lancaster, but his heart isn't in it. He wanders offstage before the first act is halfway done.

Somewhere between Lancaster and Mt. Gretna, Juan and Diego sit in a ditch by an overgrown country road and stare into the campfire.

Going on to Mt. Gretna is pointless. Whatever Diego does on that stage, it will not be opera. Opera is about passion: hunger like Juan's, fear and love like the thrushes'. Diego's only passion now is prancing from place to place, listening to his own voice. As if singing could wake the dead.

Gritting his teeth, Diego holds the vocal score out to Juan. There are parts he can no longer imagine at all. What is that aria Figaro sings, again?

"Here, boy," he says. "Here, Juan-the-raptor. Take it."

Juan considers him sideways in the usual way, then delicately takes the score with his teeth.

Diego nods. "It's yours now."

Juan — Diego could swear to this — nods back.

Then he reaches up with his sickle claw and tears it to shreds.

Diego does not see Juan again. He walks to Mt. Gretna in a daze. He hums, but it is tuneless.

In Mt. Gretna, there is no opera house, only a moderately smashed-up wooden pavilion, open to the air. It is full of dinosaurs. Creatures from bluebirds on up to Tyrannosaurs march around the pavilion, roaring, growling, chittering, stomping. If Diego closes his eyes and forgets Rossini, it begins to sound like music.

He opens his eyes. Maybe that strange procession really does have a cast and a crew. Even an orchestra. He watches their movements, tries to find patterns. As he waits, a new contingent of raptors enter, stage left. They drag a helpless Protoceratops into the centre of the procession. A prisoner, Diego thinks, or a sacrifice. There is blood, and all of those sharp teeth.

This is what opera is for. Pain, beauty, passion.

"Bravi!" he calls. *"Bravi!"* He rises to his feet, full of applause and grateful to cede the limelight.

Under the Clear Bright Waters

Author's Note: This story contains explicit sexual content.

There is a world beneath the water's surface.

Past the drifting lily-pads, past the three feet of depth where a pond *ought* to end, there is a brush like the drawing aside of a curtain. A long passage with rough stone sides, and below it, a weedy, wild place the size of a statesman's mansion, lit from within. Bright fish dart among pebbles the color of jewels, surrounded by pale, wild-haired women who swim like seals and laugh like children.

In a sandy pit at the bottom of this place, Charis kneels, her wrists and ankles bound with bulrushes, wondering how it is she can breathe here, with cool slippery water filling her lungs.

She dove into this water expecting to die, after all. She never expected someone was waiting for her underneath.

Sometimes the naiads dance with the fish in a Dionysian whirl, leaving Charis alone on the bottom. The white of the women, the black of their hair, the gold, green, crimson of a thousand sea creatures: colours spin around her until she has to close her eyes or faint. As a child, at her aunt's wedding, Charis once snuck into the kitchen and stole two bottles of wine — far too much for an eight-year-old body. She has that feeling now: pleasure and sickness from the same well. The light down here is not like the sun. It doesn't fade when the day is over, and Charis can only guess how much time has passed.

Sometimes the naiads settle around her, bickering.

"That turtle was my property!" one complains, pulling another's hair. "You stole him. Give him back!"

"Turtle" is hardly a word for the creature, its shell as striped and shining as onyx, its delicate flippers trailing like multicolored sleeves. But stranger than the word "turtle" is the word "property". As if women can have such things, and under the water, no less!

Yet to Korinna, the naiad who caught her sinking body and bound her here at the bottom — perhaps Charis is something like property.

Korinna swims faster than any other naiad. She is short and a little stocky, her weight concentrated in her supple thigh muscles — muscles Charis can see clearly, since no one under the water bothers to put on even a strophion. Charis can see the dark nipples of Korinna's breasts as she swims, and the way her buttocks flex as she kicks through the water. It is obscene, seeing this much, but Charis has always secretly liked obscenity. She keeps looking.

But if Charis belongs to Korinna, then Korinna is like Charis's farmer neighbor who spends months gambling in the city, then returns hardly knowing what his hired workers have done. Korinna swims and swims: now off to one side of the pond, arguing or joking with one of her sisters, now off to the other to play with the crabs. It is probably not so very long, but to Charis it feels like hours. Her legs ache, and she thinks of trying to squirm out of this position. That would spoil the fun of their game, though, and she is not yet desperate.

Korinna comes to rest now at the bottom of Charis's pit. She has a wide face with narrow, supple lips. Her eyes are bright blue under long lashes, and her gaze roves over Charis's body, making her want to squirm with pleasure at the attention. But she stays still. Korinna crawls to her for a kiss.

It's strange kissing underwater. Pond water seeps in through the cracks. The unfamiliarity of it makes Charis shiver — and makes her push closer, hungry for a taste that's fully Korinna's.

"Have you decided if you wish to stay here?" Korinna asks when they part. Charis shakes her head.

Korinna grasps the back of Charis's head. Charis thinks for a moment that Korinna will kiss her again, but the naiad pulls back. "You must ask for something, pet. Do you wish to be untied?"

"N...no," says Charis. "But I would like not to kneel anymore. Please."

Charis's father has always called her demanding. But Charis's father is gone — alive, probably, but impossible to safely reach. Charis's whole world is gone. She feels hollow, cold, and no longer interested in demanding anything. Perhaps that's for the best.

Korinna unwraps her ankles with quick, light touches, her hands barely grazing Charis's legs. Charis floats upwards, her hands still bound, her calves throbbing as the blood courses through them again. Korinna catches her by the waist and rearranges her deftly. She nudges Charis to lie on her back on the sand, spine arching over her tied hands.

Charis's heart beats faster. She wants Korinna to lie full length against her and press her down into the sand, the way one of her old playmates might have done. But she will not ask for that. She ought to be dead, and it is not right, lying in this hedonistic little pool, demanding pleasure.

"Do you want me to touch you?" says Korinna.

Yes.

She bites her tongue.

Korinna extends a hand as if to smooth Charis's floating hair, then withdraws. "You won't get it unless you ask, pet."

Charis doesn't understand why this is so hard. She swallows, the now-familiar cold water coursing through her throat. "Please."

But Korinna does not lie atop Charis the way she wants. Instead she trails a single fingertip down Charis's cheek. She brushes Charis's mouth, and Charis reflexively kisses at her finger. Korinna withdraws it, then trails it along the outside of Charis's small breasts. Delicate spirals travel inward, making Charis's skin tingle, until she reaches the edge of the areola.

Charis shuts her eyes. She cannot identify what is wrong. She knows she could end this at any time, with any of the three words Korinna taught her when she first sank in the water. One to make Korinna pause and withdraw; a heavier one, which will snap any bulrushes holding her and end the encounter. And a third, a long and terrible word. If she speaks the third word, she will float up into the glare of the sun, completely released. Korinna will never trouble her again.

She does not want that. If anything, she wants *more* than Korinna will give. She wants Korinna writhing against her, crushing her mouth until there is no distinction between kissing and drowning. But asking for it feels like a violation, like making the dead speak.

So Korinna plays Charis's body as delicately as an epigonion, with fingertips and tongue. They are not exactly out of sight, but the other naiads seem to pay them no mind. Charis writhes, despite her bound hands, and pants, with that still-unsettling sensation of water eddying in her lungs. Until Korinna's teasing fingers stray down past Charis's belly and brush her clit. Charis sucks in a larger breath, reflexively pushing her hips upward.

And says, "No."

The first of the three terrible words.
Immediately Korinna is no longer touching her. Charis opens her eyes miserably. She wants this. She wants to belong to Korinna like a pet, wants Korinna's fingers to bring her right over the edge of pleasure. But something is broken in Charis, and she cannot love this water-woman until it is healed.

When Charis lived on land, her father betrothed her to an important city man. Old, but distinguished. His name was Athanasios. A union with him would bring astonishing wealth and prestige. The fact that she did not love him never troubled her at all.

"I'm honored, of course," she said to him, the sun leaching sweat from her neck, the day her father promised her. "I will be ever so happy to spin your wool, keep your household, and give you children. But you cannot control me. I will read your best scrolls and have affairs with your servant girls when you aren't looking. If you beat me, I shall run away back to my father's farm and you will never, ever find me."

Her father's knuckles went white in the folds of his cloak. But Athanasios tilted his head, then smiled.

"Of course," he said. "You are a rustic girl. Why would you not?"

Some men might have said it with their chins in the air, plotting to beat respect into her later. Athanasios seemed genuinely charmed.

Charis would take well to being this man's wife.

She did not spend much time with him. He gave her gifts, even brought her to the city once. City women wore such jewels in their hair, such colors on their faces! But most of the time Athanasios was off in foreign places doing politics, or in the wilderness overseeing some military campaign. "I'll marry you soon," he always said, but he never set a date.

Charis did not mind. She liked helping manage her father's estate, with the security of betrothal but none of the duties of marriage. She grew up at leisure, ran about outdoors, and learned what it was to sneak out by the pond with other girls and play at love. Sometimes she told the other girls to slap her a little, to bring ropes. She did not think much of taking orders from men, but from women — from the *right* women — they excited her in ways she scarcely understood.

The years ticked by, and most of Charis's playmates became brides, wreathed in veils and flowers. Charis's father started to argue with Athanasios. "I will not let that noble make a fool of you," he said to Charis repeatedly. "Rich he may be. But I will not let him string you along, then leave you husbandless and too old for any man's taste. It isn't right."

So finally a wedding date was set. It would be in the summer, six weeks before Charis's twentieth birthday. Athanasios gave her a black beaded necklace to seal the deal, and she used it to count down the days.

Most of her old playmates were gone now. The pond was the only thing she would miss. City water was dirty from too many people bathing and shitting and doing their laundry close together. The pond was pure like a lilied mirror. More than once Charis watched her reflection and had the strangest feeling that someone else looked out from those eyes, watching her. Daring her to slip under the surface.

She counted down to three beads. Two.

Then Athanasios returned to the farm early, pale: a letter in one hand bearing an important-looking seal, a long dagger in the other.

He and she and her father sat downcast around their small table.

"Leave me my daughter, at least," said Charis's father, his lips tight to his teeth. "For the gods' sake."

"You know that choice isn't mine."

Athanasios was a liar. He had used his position to take bribes, conspire, and do other terrible things. So said the note, but it didn't say what the terrible things *were,* and Athanasios refused to discuss it. Charis imagined him creeping through the city murdering people, robbing houses, torturing his servants. For the first time, she looked at him and her skin crawled. She had never really known this man.

Whatever Athanasios had done, he had been tried and found guilty. The punishment was death — *for you,* said the letter, *your accomplices, and your betrothed.*

As a show of mercy, they could, at least, die by their own hands.

"It's politics, that's all," said Athanasios. "They don't like the things I say in the forum. The rest of the charges are trumped-up. I have done nothing."

"Then run away," said Charis's father. "Find a ship or a caravan. Go far enough and they will never find you."

"My honor will not allow it," said Athanasios.

"For the sake of my daughter then," said Charis's father, choking on the words. "My daughter, whom you *used,* who never even got to be a bride—"

"No."

Her father's voice rose to a shout. "You dare to enter my house and demand –"

"Father." Charis's voice silenced him. He sank into his chair, still fuming. "I'll do it."

Honor was not only a thing for men. Charis had many dishonorable options: she could refuse the letter's order and wait for soldiers to come for her, or for some dishonorable little man to decide she was still worth courting. She could run far away — she was clever enough to manage on the roads. Clever enough to steal away on a ship and become a servant or a whore in some other country where no one knew Athanasios's name. She could live a long time and know herself always as a coward.

Good men did not do such things. Why should she?

"I'll do it," she repeated, "but I will choose the means."

She would not die in this shabby house. She would not open her veins and mingle her blood with that of Athanasios the liar. She would die by drowning, in her favorite pond, where the water knew her.

After Korinna swims away, Charis waits, her wrists still bound underneath her, until she is bored. Then she squirms. She arches her head until her neck aches, but she cannot see the whole pond from where she is lying, and she cannot see Korinna.

This is stupid. Charis is as good as dead, and there should be solemnity in death. She should not be lounging in a watery coffin full of nude women, teased and delighted like some city hedonist.

Charis thinks about that for a while, then squirms out of her bindings. It is not difficult. Bulrushes are not nearly as firm as rope. A stretch, a twist, a tear, and she is free.

She suspects that Korinna bound her loosely on purpose.

There is no point in looking for Korinna when Charis still cannot speak to her. Instead, she strikes out for a pebbly, weed-choked rise which becomes a cliff like a wall, encircling everything Charis can see. She has always assumed that this wall is impassible.

But there is a crack in it.

When Charis swims close she can see a dark passage, wide as a hall. She swims inside, trailing a hand along the rough rocks at the side. It feels good to stretch out her body and *do* something.

The passage opens out into another pond. That is the only word Charis has for it, but it's bigger than Korinna's pond, and the light is harsher. The pebbles shine black and silver, and the naiads swim in formation like a school of fish, waving long, barbed spears. Aquatic Amazons, training for war.

Charis creeps across the wall. A stade's length from her passage, there is another. She slips into this one quietly. This time the walls vibrate with sound: an aimless song on something like a flute, squealing and growling.

This time when Charis emerges she cannot see the other side of the pond, only water growing bluer and thicker into infinity. This might as well be the ocean, though there is no taste of brine. There are sharks and even bigger things in the distance, and the weedy bottom grows in stripes like a human farmstead.

A tall naiad with muscles like a soldier seizes her arm.

"Spy," the naiad hisses. "You can't just drift into our territory like a..." Charis gapes, and the naiad suddenly checks herself, surprised. "Like a human. You are, aren't you?"

"What _is_ this place?" says Charis. "How many rooms can there be in one pond?"

The soldier chuckles. "This is not one pond, girl. The earth is like a pumice stone, every crack and hollow full of water. See how our father Poseidon provides! Ask about anything — the sharks, for instance — and I will tell you, if you like. I would show you much more than this, if not for my duty. But I must stay at this post; my honor demands no less."

Honor.

The word hits Charis like a blast of wind. Honor. This place is no watery coffin: it is as full and real as the world above, where courage means as much as it does anywhere.

"Tell me," says the soldier, "where are you from? You look as though you have drowned."

"No," says Charis, "I didn't..." And then, slower, surprised. "I didn't die."

She didn't die. But sudden loneliness threatens to squeeze her inside out. If she is not dead, she can mourn — for the father she will never see again, the husband-to-be she thought she could trust. She can tear her clothes — but she no longer has any. She can wail — but do they wail down here in the water? Even more than wailing, she wants to be held. To dig with teeth and nails into the body of someone who loves her. To feel something stronger than pain. She wants to live. And she wants Korinna.

"I want to live," she says when Korinna finds her at last, crawling back out of the crack in the rocks. Now she sees plenty of other passages like it. This watery world extends in all directions.

"Where have you been?" says Korinna with a half-amused smile, as if Charis is a runaway kitten.

"I want to live," Charis repeats, "and..."

And I want you to touch me? No. Something is still wrong with that line. Charis is tired of lying still like the dead.

"I want to live and I want to touch you."

Yes.

Korinna raises her eyebrows. "Then you've been going about it very oddly. Though I don't object."

Charis silences her with a kiss. She pushes Korinna back against the rough rocks, the way she has always wanted Korinna to push her. She presses the full length of her body against Korinna's, thigh to thigh, chin to chin. Korinna arches her back, and when Charis lets go of her lips, she's smiling, delighted. Charis nips across her jaw and down the midline of her body.

Korinna's pleasure-noises are strange like every sound here, but the motion and the excitement mounting in Charis's core, these she remembers from the girls she loved in the surface world. Grief for that world still fills her, like someone's hollowed her out and poured all the pain in, but in pain she can still feel affection.

She pauses at Korinna's pelvic bone and teases her a moment, lipping the hollows above her thighs and the edges of the outer folds, but going no further. Korinna makes a short, impatient sound, then grasps the back of Charis's head to pull her closer.

Charis pushes her head back, and Korinna lets go. With a wicked grin, Charis takes hold of both wrists and pulls them behind the small of Korinna's back, crossed over each other. She has no bulrushes, but her hands can perform the same service.

"Don't move," she says. "This time, *I* am the captor."

Korinna only grins.

Then Charis does dart in with her tongue. Korinna says nothing because Korinna is too busy crying out with pleasure. Finally Charis is really sure she tastes Korinna: briny, slightly sweet, and entirely unlike pond water. It is not so different from the taste of human girls. Another thing she can keep, after all.

The echo of Korinna's pleasure rushes through both of them, building like a wave until it breaks. Korinna shrieks and shivers, four times, five, and then her body unclenches, relaxing until she drifts freely on the current.

Charis lets go of Korinna's wrists and kicks upwards to kiss her again, deeply, the taste of Korinna's pleasure still on her tongue.

"That was good," says Korinna. "I'm glad you decided to."

"I want to stay," says Charis. "I've decided. It's just that I don't only want to stay *here*, you see? We have a whole world. You didn't tell me about it because I didn't know how to ask, but the world was what I needed. I want to see everything in it, even the wars. With you."

"Of course. I want that, too. I just didn't think you were ready."

"Well, I'm ready now. And," says Charis, "right now I want you to swim me to that pit, tie me up again, and do everything to me that I just did to you."

Korinna grins her biggest grin yet. "I thought you would."

She grabs Charis's wrist just roughly enough to be exciting and tugs her along. When they reach the pit, Charis puts her hands behind her back, obedient, grinning. Korinna ties her wrists, then pushes her down and kisses her roughly.

This time it isn't light and delicate. It's Korinna's whole hands. She squeezes one of Charis's breasts, releases it, pushes her way lower to the ribs and the waist. All this time they're still kissing. Their lips and tongues tangle.

Charis moans far louder and faster than she expected. She knew she wanted Korinna, but she only now understands that it's a *need*, like falling on a roast hare when she's hungry. She wants to push her hips up against Korinna, demanding that she hurry. Then she thinks about that, and the luxury of asking for what she wants, and does. The action itself is a pleasure, an abrupt thing making her more aware of Korinna's weight and of the water swirling over her skin.

Korinna breaks the kiss, grins wickedly, and shoves Charis back down against the sand, which is its own pleasure. She squeezes Charis's hip, then slips her hand across between her thighs. Unexpectedly her fingers are dancing there, sliding between and across Charis's labia, and Charis cries out.

The rest is a blur. Korinna licks and bites her way down until her mouth joins her hands. Charis is deliciously helpless. She can't move her hands to return any of this. She can only writhe and groan as her body demands. She can't tell the difference any longer between Korinna's fingers and tongue. She only knows that Korinna is down there, moving quickly and intricately, and every brush against her skin is bliss. She needs all of this, needs-

There.

The orgasm takes her by surprise, jolting her from toes to scalp. Her hands convusively clench and unclench in their bulrush binding. Again. And again.

Then Korinna slides back up her body as the glow of arousal starts to fade, undoes the bulrushes, and holds her.

Charis wraps her now-free arms around the naiad's waist and pillows her head on her arm. They're pressed as close together as ever, heads and limbs draped carelessly over each other, half-floating. Yes, she reflects, she needed that. And a little of the grief has really lifted now.

"You told me," says Korinna, "that you want to stay. Tell me again an hour from now. With your head clear. Hmm?"

"Yes," says Charis.

She kisses Korinna gently on the lips and lies back. Sleep beckons, and the fish dart around them, here in the world below the water.

Space Pops

It's not true what they say. Humans don't explode in the vacuum of space: it's the sense of wonder that does it. Once they notice real limitlessness, all they can do is grow to match it. Sooner or later — pop!

That's handy on days like today, when Captain Kerner shoves me against the ship's hull.

"You soulless, wire-headed bitch," he snarls, his red face distorted through the space helmet. "What did you do with the telescopes?"

They survive, if they close their minds to the beauty around them. But it makes them grumpy.

I smile, showing white plastic teeth. "Oh, I borrowed them for the day. I'm making a painting of the galaxy."

"Why would you paint..."

But he glances out at the blackness and it catches him. He gasps, like he's never seen it before. His eyes bug out. I start counting.

One, two, three... Pop!

And then I'm floating there alone.

I'm glad I'm an android. Plastic and wires don't swell up the same way. Kerner's ilk can call me what they like, but I'm already limitless. I'm the one who can stare at the stars and live.

Zori Server

You think you know a guy, hanging out with him in the Vee. And I think I did know Jaime Ortiz back then. But some things just never come up. I didn't learn the truth about him and the dancers until I read his obit in the paper. I had a husband and kids by then. Hadn't thought about him for years.

Ortiz grew up in Glendale, Arizona, the obit said. Nine miles from downtown Phoenix, where they spawned me. *He studied electrical engineering at ASU.* Same as me, but ten years earlier. *Headed the folklore club and the dance team. Then moved to Cleveland and rose to a high position in Lily Technologies Corporation. Ortiz was a recreational user of the Vee from its infancy, eventually founding his own VC (Vee Community) on the notoriously bug-prone Zori Server.* Et cetera. Not exactly my life story, but close.

I scanned down to the cause of death. *Heart attack.* Common enough. A morbid bit of my brain pictured my own heart, ten years hence. I tried to ignore it.

The obit didn't mention the dancers. But it mentioned something close enough to take my breath away.

The Vee was born about the same time as me. I'd wanted in since preschool, really, but my parents forbade any kind of neural contact until I hit fourteen. On my fourteenth birthday, I blew my paltry savings on the necessary hardware and jacked right in.

I liked Zori Server best. It had personality. Not the ironically gritty industrial style of the hipster servers, or the faux-fantasy-adventure motifs of the mainstream machines. On Zori Server you could ride a candy-colored Cadillac down a cloud into a forest of razor-leafed steel trees, then climb down a ladder into a cozy wood-paneled reading room and have your nails done by a wide-eyed robot. And on Zori Server I met Jaime Ortiz. Or *Valparaiso,* his Vee name. Back then I called him Val.

I thought Ortiz was the coolest guy ever. He had his own underground lair with tables that played music when you ran your hands across them. One time

I asked him what he would wish for if he found a genie in a bottle.

"Beautiful things for my VC," Ortiz said right away. Like he'd already decided. "But really that's the wrong thing to ask for. Know why?"

"Why?"

"Because a genie takes it literally. Goes right for beauty, just like you asked, without remembering it's more complicated than that. The most beautiful thing is a human life, but you don't want a beautiful dead body, right?"

"Eww," I said.

Ortiz grinned. "So now that I've figured that out, I'm getting beautiful things the hard way. What would you wish for?"

"I don't know. A billion dollars. Or a private jet. Or a fashion-model boyfriend."

"I've got the next best thing," said Ortiz. "A virtual robot tiger. New today. Want to see?"

That's how cool Jaime Ortiz was.

When I met the dancers I was seventeen, itching for the day I could finally drop my legally mandated MINOR tag. I'd driven my candy-colored Cadillac all the way to the top of a cliff. I sat on the grass tossing daffodils off the edge, watching them float down into the mist. New flowers poked their heads out as soon as the old ones died.

I mistook the dancers for a typical Zori effect at first. Vaguely humanoid shapes, but only vaguely. More like stick figures, giant-sized, glowing in the air above me. They didn't move so much as grow and shrink. A stick leg shrank and shortened until it disappeared into a stick body, and another one grew on the other side. They spindled all over the sky that way, tossing beautiful blue ribbons back and forth. I flopped down on my back and watched them.

Eventually one of the dancers, yellow-white and featureless like a bundle of glowing sticks, spindled down to me.

"Saturnina," it said. That was my Vee name. "Do you have a wish?"

That surprised me. I thought they'd been part of the scenery, not a group of non-player characters you could actually interact with. I called up a tag overlay. It's important to know an NPC's specs before you talk to them. Mistake a simple gateway script for a high-def character and you get a long, circular, frustrating conversation. Mistake a high-def character for a gateway script and you miss out on hours of fun. It's a classic newbie mistake both ways, because they're all equally gorgeous.

Tags sprang up all over the place. Every single daffodil said *Item*. But hovering over the dancers, the tags didn't say *NPC*. They said *Player*. My virtual mouth went dry.

"That's impossible."

Your movement in the Vee is keyed into your real-life motor cortex. I don't care how good you are or how long you've practiced: if you're human, you can't move like that.

"Nothing is impossible," the dancer said.

I ran a whois.

Username: Dancer. Hostname: Unknown. Server info: Unknown or blocked. Specs: Unknown. Tags: None.

Well, that was a big fat load of help.

"I gotta go," I said. "I'm late."

I climbed into my candy-colored Cadillac and drove away. They didn't follow. I watched them in my rearview mirror, shrinking, growing, and dancing, until I'd turned out of sight.

I had tea with Jaime Ortiz in his underground lair that night. I knew his real name by then, though I didn't use it much. He didn't know mine: my parents would've killed me if I'd told. "You don't know who you're talking to in there," they said. "Not really."

"Hi, Val," I said, dropping into a plush chair. Giant snapdragons grew out the back, mutely opening and shutting their soft flower mouths, and sometimes one of them leaned over to sip flowing water from the decorative cascade on the wall.

"Hey." Ortiz was using a female avatar that day, a tall woman with flowing dark hair. He was pacing around with a bit of blue ribbon, calling up rulers and magnifying glasses, trying to look at it closely.

"What's that?" I said.

"Found it lying on the ground," said Ortiz. He seemed a little upset.

"What are you doing with it?"

"Trying to figure out where it came from."

"Why? So you can get another?"

"So I can put it back."

I shrugged. "Whatever. The system can just call up another, right?"

"I suppose."

He wasn't listening, so I dropped it and got to the bit I'd really wanted to say. "Hey, you know anyone with the username *Dancer*?

Ortiz looked up at me then. "Where did you hear that name?"

I told him about the dancers. Their spindly movements and the problem with the tags. I mentioned the ribbons, too. "That's probably where it came from." I was pleased with myself, knowing something Ortiz didn't.

"But that's impossible," one of the other guys said. His avatar was about as out there as they get — a fox-man with whiskers, movable ears, and a tail. It takes *years* to learn to control a tail, and he was damn proud of it. Even something simpler, like Ortiz's gender switch, takes hundreds of hours to really get used to. Folks on Zori did that kind of thing to show their status. *Look at me. Look how virtual I am.*

"I know." I raised my eyebrows at Ortiz. "You think maybe Zori got confused? Put a player tag on them when it really meant NPC?" I'd never heard of that happening, but Zori *was* buggy.

Ortiz shook his head. "If it was just the tags, maybe. But the whois would've cleared it up, or you would've got an error message."

"So they're real."

Ortiz looked away. "Did they say anything to you?"

"Yeah. Wanted me to dance with them."

"Don't."

It wasn't like him to be so abrupt. I liked Ortiz partly because he was cool and had an underground lair, but mainly because he never told me what to do. He never lectured. Resentment built in my chest.

"Whatever. I couldn't move like that anyway."

Ortiz took a sip of tea and adjusted his kimono. He looked over at me with an I'm-a-grownup-and-I-know-better look. The kind I couldn't stand.

"Saturnina," he said, "some things shouldn't be looked at too closely. On Zori as much as the real world. Those things are dangerous. I want you to stay away from them."

I pushed my chair back and stood up. "You can't tell me what to do."

"I can't, I know. But we're friends."

"Friends, maybe."

"And I don't want you to get hurt."

"You could at least tell me what they are. Why they're dangerous."

Ortiz sighed. He put down the ribbon and came to sit across from me, scratching one of the snapdragons affectionately on the back of its head. I sat back down, and the fox-man leaned in with academic interest.

"Do you believe," Ortiz said, "that there are things in the real world we can't explain?"

"Sure." It wasn't something I thought about much, but I'd heard stories, same as everyone. The cousins who dreamed things and saw them come true. The friends of friends who swore they'd talked to ghosts.

Ortiz brushed a finger across the table. A few aimless pentatonic notes drifted out. He only did that when he was tense. "Then there's nothing stopping those things from using the Vee, right? Along with us."

I stared at him.

"So they're what? Fairies? Demons? Ghosts?"

"I don't know," Ortiz said. "But I know they're dangerous. They could hurt you in ways the Vee can't fix."

Fox-man looked satisfied, but I sure wasn't. "That's not even an explanation."

"Saturnina, please just listen to me."

But he was still doing the I'm-a-grownup-and-I-know-better thing.

"Whatevs," I said, rolling my eyes. "I gotta go to dinner anyway."

I logged out. Then I jacked right back in and appeared on the hilltop.

I would have been scared, if I hadn't been so mad. Instead, the whirling lines thrilled me. So Ortiz thought he could stop me from figuring this out, huh?

"Saturnina," the dancers whispered. "Do you have a wish?"

I shook my head. I still hadn't decided between the billion dollars and the fashion-model boyfriend. I wanted to learn, but I had a feeling I didn't need to waste wishes for that.

"Then will you come and dance with us?"

I looked up at them and grinned. "In a heartbeat."

They taught me. They whispered in my ears. They wafted me up in the air, tugged at my limbs and spun them. I matched their rhythms in a clumsy human way. I arched my limbs like a human dancer and they spindled gracefully around me. The whole dance, all of us, one coherent picture. I felt glorious with them. Free and at ease. No one would tell me what to do. Not here.

I was exhausted when they lowered me gently to the ground. We were now at the bottom of the cliff, on grassy ground littered with daisy petals.

"Saturnina. Eat with us."

"What do you have to eat?"

One of them reached for my mouth, bright lines extending smoothly, and offered a little red berry.

I gobbled the berry. Sweet, tart and warm, fresh-picked. They offered me other berries, red, blue, pink, and purple, bits of cheese, tiny biscuits. Vee food: all of the taste, none of the calories. It's all in your head. I ate until I was sated and sleepy, with beautiful tastes lingering on my virtual tongue, and I followed them.

They led me through a doorway in the base of the cliff, into spare stone rooms with berry-colored carpets. They laid me down on blood-red pillows.

"Saturnina. Die with us."

I raised my head. "Wait. What?"

The dancers leapt up together in the air and dived, in their spindly straight-line way, straight for my left hand. My fingers unraveled at their touch. Virtual skin spilled to the ground like so much thread. It hurt a *lot*. I don't think anything I ever did had hurt so much.

"No!" I shrieked. "That's not what I came for!" But they spindled to my wrist and up my forearm. My whole virtual hand came apart.

Emergency logout. Where was that command? I called up the main menu, but I could hardly remember which button was which. *Logout, dammit. Log OUT!* I took way too long to find the button. The big red one. Yeah, go on and laugh, but *you* try finding a button while your brain shorts out with panic.

I sat in my Vee chair in my living room, in real life, catching my breath. My left arm still hurt like hell, but that's not unusual when something gets you real bad. Pain neurons can take a while to calm down.

I reached up to take off the electrodes. Only one of my hands connected.

I looked down. The pit of my stomach went cold.

My left arm was still there. Sort of. But from the elbow down it was only withered skin wrapped around bone.

That's supposed to be impossible.

"No." I jerked back in my chair, patted my left arm frantically with my right, tugged on the tips of the numb, limp fingers. "No, no, no, no, no, no, no!" But my arm was gone. There was nothing I could do.

When my parents found out, they shouted and panicked and cried. When I tried to explain, they told me not to make up stories. I didn't try to explain to the doctors. Acute flesh-eating infection not otherwise specified, they said, after glancing at each other in confusion. I grimaced and nodded.

I never really went back to the Vee. I tried once or twice. I reverted my avatar to its last good state, and after that, both my virtual arms worked. The motor neurons were still there, after all. But I couldn't go in without getting twitchy. Looking over my shoulder for dancers. After a few weeks, I gave up and sold the hardware.

"It was just a phase anyway," I said.

I never told Ortiz what happened. Knew I couldn't look him in the eye. He'd warned me, hadn't he? He'd tried his best. I imagined him going into lecture mode, just like my parents. *Now see here, Saturnina, I told you to stay away from those things, and what kind of respect do I get...* I didn't know whether to be angry or guilty. I felt both. Either way, I didn't want to see him.

And I didn't want to admit to myself what I'd seen back then, when my hand was coming apart. It could have been a trick my eyes played. But the pile of thread they'd made out of my arm had been blue, just like the blue ribbons they threw to each other. Just like the one Ortiz had told me he was trying to put back.

Now, decades later, the obit stared me in the face.

At the age of twenty-five, it said, *Ortiz lost all function in one of his legs due to an acute flesh-eating infection. Despite this, he maintained a full life both in and out of the Vee.*

Ortiz's wife, Dania, says that despite Ortiz's long pedigree in the Vee, he was ambivalent about the technology.

"I made some mistakes going in," Ortiz once said to her. "When you're first setting up, anything seems possible. I asked for some things I shouldn't have asked for."

I sucked in my breath and stared at the page, remembering what Ortiz had told me once. *The most beautiful thing is a human life.* I covered my face with my good hand and started to laugh, wondering why I hadn't figured it out.

"Dammit, Val, you knew. You *knew*."

He'd known about them long before I did. He'd been *hurt* by them long before I had. If I was remembering his words right, he'd set them in place himself before they got to me — wishing for beauty, and learning too late what that word meant to them.

For the first time I thought of this from Ortiz's point of view. I had kids of my own now; I understood protectiveness, though I hadn't back then. How did he feel when he realized what he'd really wished for? What guilt when they left him one ribbon after another, each as beautiful as death? And what love of his VC made him stay, trying to fix it?

How long did he torment himself, after I left? Wondering if his words got me made into ribbon. If only he'd been firmer. If only he'd told me more.

If he hadn't been dead, I would have run to the library–these days, you can jack in from anywhere–and found him. Comforted him. *See, Val? I turned out all right.*

I laughed until tears pricked my eyes, and then I stood, shrugging on my coat and heading for the door.

Ortiz had been working to stop the dancers. To protect his VC. According to the obit, he'd stayed active on Zori right to the end.

Maybe he'd found some new protege to keep the work going. Maybe not. It had been a sudden death, after all, and he'd been tight-lipped about the dancers. Maybe there was no one left who'd learned what he'd learned. Maybe, as often happened in the Vee, they didn't even know he was dead.

Either way, it was high time I did my part.

I walked all the way to the library. I found myself a terminal. Took a deep, deep breath. And then, for the first time in decades, I jacked in.

Baku

aches upon waking
dismembered incubus
claws in its gullet

Sage and Coco

It's been a long day, and now Sage's teddy bear is missing.

"Coco," she says, dragging her blue blanket behind her with chubby little fists. "Coco bye-bye." It's maybe the twentieth time she's said it. I've looked and looked around her room, but all I've really accomplished is a bit of tidying. The bear isn't here. "Mommy find."

"Mommy can't find," I say. "Hikari might find." Hikari, my girlfriend, volunteered several minutes ago to hunt through the rest of the house. With all of Sage's other toys and crayons strewn about, it could be a big job. "If you could remember where you last saw him..."

Sage shakes her head, and her lip quivers. "Bye-bye." And it's not her fault she can't say more, even if my neck is cramping up with frustration. She's not old enough to understand the work I do, and how tired I get. How I've spent the day funneling my energy into healing charms and calming talismans for Hikari to sell in our shop. How I've washed the dishes, paid the bills, taken out the trash, checked all the house's wards. And how, every evening, I take what's left and pour it into the pentacle I keep at my throat, a thick sturdy shape with a crystal in the center, the kind that can store things. I replace the power that's trickled out during the day and shape it into a powerful defensive burst, locked up tight, just in case. On nights like these I put Sage to bed exhausted, with nothing left in me.

But looking at her, even at her worst, gives me this sharp assurance, stronger than any magic I've ever done. Whatever good I can give her, I will.

Patience, for one thing.

"It'll be a while till we find him," I say. "Probably he'll turn up someplace when you don't expect it. I want you to stop asking now."

"'Kay," she says, though her fists are still tugging on the blanket. She toddles up to me and nearly falls as she stops, catching herself on my leg. "Story?"

"Story, then bedtime. Want to cuddle?"

"Yeah," she says, holding up her little arms, and I scoop her up and balance her on my knee. I pick up a storybook off the dresser.

Once upon a time, in a magical queendom,

a little dark girl from a little green den
set off to seek her fortune.

It's Sage's favorite, because it has pigs and a pirate ship. She claps her hands and snorts when it gets to the part with the pigs, and for a minute or so we just oink and giggle together.

Hikari saunters in near the end, just when the girl in the story is coming home laden with pirate treasure and wisdom. She sits on the floor by my side and listens with a smile, as though she hasn't heard this dozens of times before. Hikari is an elegant beauty, her black hair brushing the small of her back as her head moves. She's loved me since long before Sage, and she still makes my heart flutter just by walking in.

And there she lived with all her friends,
happily ever after. The end.

I'm proud of Sage. She's patient enough to do the concluding cheer — "Eee-end!" — before she turns her bright eyes to Hikari.

"Coco?"

Hikari shakes her head. "I looked everywhere. Can't find him."

"Coco," says Sage, starting to whine. She's never slept without him.

Hikari gives me a meaningful look, and I sigh and take her hand in mine. I'm low on energy, but hers is as warm and reassuring as ever, and though she doesn't sense these things, she knows how to offer it up to me. I squeeze my eyes shut, thinking hard about Coco and his little brown feet.

I now invoke the rule of three.
What once was lost returns to me.

I can work magic without the silly rhymes, but they're what I learned first, and they help me focus. Into my mind's eye springs a picture of our little house, extending down from Sage's dormer room to the basement. All the cluttered floors and crayon drawings. All the protective wards and charms I've put up over the years. There's no Coco anywhere. I try to push my consciousness further, and I get as far as the porch, but outside, past the wards, is fuzzier. Slower going.

I don't like it outside the wards at all, actually. I must be too tired for this. I drop the spell and open my eyes to slits. "He's not in the house."

Hikari gives me a little kiss, then plucks Sage up off my lap, setting her down in her crib. "I know you were playing with him today. I took you out to the yard to play, remember? I know you had him then."

"You think she dropped him out there?"

"I don't remember if she had him coming back in. But I looked around to make sure she hadn't dropped anything. I would have seen him, unless she hid him real good." She smiles and turns back to Sage. "Is that what you did? Did you hide him real good?"

Sage doesn't answer. She's pawing through her other stuffed animals for a suitable replacement. She holds up a plush kitty and considers it critically.

Hikari turns to me. "I bet she stuck him in a bush in the back yard when I was looking the other way. I went through a phase like that, at her age. Picking things up and moving them everywhere..."

She's still talking, but I don't hear a word. Something thumps loudly against the wards, drowning her out. I freeze.

The sound's not in my ears. I wish it was, but I can tell the difference. It's a mind-sound. Magic.

"Hikari."

"What?"

But I don't have to answer. She sees the expression on my face now. My skin prickles, and she goes as pale as I feel.

The thumping happens again. Like someone rapping on the biggest door.

"It could be nothing," she says, uncertainly.

I shake my head. "Hikari. Nothing else is this *loud*."

She knows me well enough to know what I mean. Maybe there are lots of super-powerful beings in the world who'd want to get my attention by smashing into the wards. But I've only ever known one.

And I was hoping he was gone for good.

I look at Sage sulking in her crib. "Stay with her. Don't let her out of your sight. Yell for me if she does anything strange."

Hikari's hand goes up to grasp mine, her eyes wide. "Be safe, won't you?"

"Yeah."

She moves in, but pauses before the kiss this time, waiting for my nod. Then she presses her lips hard against mine and squeezes her arms around my waist. I linger in the doorway when she's done, trying to calm my heart. Hikari's already gone back to Sage, and she smiles like nothing's wrong, cool as honeydew. "I'll be staying in here a little while. Want a goodnight kiss?"

"Kiss!" says Sage, throwing out her arms eagerly. Hikari picks her up and kisses her cheek. I feel a little burst of pride, under the panic. Some people just can't get that rule in their heads, but I think Hikari always knew it. *Ask first. Teach her that her body is hers.*

Before Sage has time to return the kiss, I'm gone.

My stomach is doing flips already, and I'm only in the kitchen. My head spins. Why did it have to be now? Why at night, when there's hardly anything left of me? Maybe it's part of his plan. Maybe he's watched me long enough to see how I overextend myself. And how he can use that against me.

I pick up the green glass jar I keep in the window, shaking it gently. I can smell the protective herbs. The house swims into my mind's eye again, covered in shimmering blankets of magic. No disturbances. That means he's outside. Good. Well, better than inside, at least.

I take a moment to breathe deeply. To try to recharge. I run a fingertip down my blue crystal pentacle. I've spent countless afternoons charging the spell inside, but I've never actually used it. I hope I don't have to find out if it works.

I look across at the fridge, at the swirly crayon drawings, the alphabet magnets, the grocery list, and my *MUST DO* list.

Clean bathroom.

Laundry.

Take boxes to recycling.

I add *Find Coco* with a black pen. Not because I need the reminder, but so I can pretend this is still mundane, like taking out the trash. There's another crashing sound as I finish, making me jump. The last *o* comes out as a leaping scribble.

"Give me a minute," I say to the air, though I know he won't. I do a quick check of my personal wards. My shield is weak, but I've got nothing much to build it back up with. I'll have to make do. I unlock the back door and step out onto the porch.

He's waiting for me out in the yard, beyond the house's wards, floating ten feet above the ground, so when I stand on the elevated porch we're face to face. He's a formless thing today, a man-sized column of smoke and mist, broad hazy wings wafting out on either side. But he can't disguise his eyes. Big bright circles, orange, like flames. His familiar deep voice makes my fists clench. "How nice to see you, dear."

I think of him as *Goetia*. It's not his name, but it's a word that stuck, back when I was still reeling from that first summoning. *Secret spirit, come to me. Unseen knowledge let me see...* Back then I was just coming into my power, and I didn't know a single other witch. I was insatiable for knowledge, any knowledge, even his.

But when I finally saw him back then, when I asked for his wisdom from the other worlds, he laughed at me. "Not until I'm done with you, dear."

Remembering used to make me sick. Little things used to remind me, and Hikari would come home from work and find me crying. But nowadays, since Sage, it only makes me angry.

Anger is what stops me, now, from collapsing in a nervous pile. "Stay away from me. And stay the hell away from Sage."

Goetia chuckles. I've heard his voice do all kinds of things, but today he's made it cultured and authoritative, like a voice-over. "But I *have*. The shields on that girl! You've done vexingly impressive work. I wanted very much to speak with her. I'll simply have to settle for making her miserable, hmm?"

One corner of the mist coalesces, taking the shape of a hazy hand, and it tosses Coco up in the air. Coco's all too solid and all too real, and way too high above the ground.

My stomach does another couple of flips. I feel so stupid. I can't believe I went to all this trouble protecting Sage's body but never gave a thought to her favorite bear. "Give him back."

"I think I'm well within my rights. I didn't touch a single one of your silly spells. She dropped him at one end of the yard and went off to look at birds at the other end. I didn't have to come near her."

"Give him back."

"No." He pulls Coco around behind him, still visible through the mist. "I think it's cute, by the way. How you lie to her. One day she'll find out that there aren't any magical queendoms, and that not everyone asks permission. One day she'll be a big girl, and she'll want to go to summer camp, or college, without you, and the shields will start to fade. What will she do then?" The mist grows into a sharp shape for a moment, a burlesque of a handsome face and a crown. "She'll want to meet a prince."

"I'm not here to speculate." I keep my voice steady, but my heart pounds inside me.

"I'm not speculating." Coco starts to spin in precarious little circles. "And if they don't fade, what then? They keep you away from me as much as they keep me away from you. Ultimately it means you and your cute little make-believe family will spend your lives cowering inside them." He manifests claws and tears a methodical line down the tip of Coco's paw, baring stuffing. "While I wait just outside, destroying everything you—"

"Like hell."

Before I can tell myself to think it over for a minute, to just use the goddamn stairs, I swing myself up to crouch on the porch railing and push off, launching myself into the air. I drop my shields, so they won't keep me away from him. I scrabble at empty mist for a second. Then my hand connects with Coco. I grab him away, heedless of the claws that are already there, slicing through my fist.

After that there's only half a second of *Ohshit*— before I hit the ground.

Pain blasts up my leg from my ankle and I land in a heap. I spit out grass. Goetia laughs and whirls towards me, all mist again. "I was hoping you'd—"

"Get *away*!"

I'm outside the wards now, unshielded. I've never done this before, rushing out to fight him instead of waiting it out. I have no plan. I push myself up to run back to the house, but my ankle goes sideways and gives out underneath me and I fall again, pain shooting through me like sparks.

Goetia chuckles a fatherly chuckle, the kind you'd trust if you didn't know better. "Do you remember, dear? How it feels to stop fighting? Or is fighting all that's left in your little mind?"

I can't believe I let him goad me into dropping my shields. I don't have power left to rebuild them at full strength. Even if I did, I don't have the time.

But I do have a plan for this, sort of.

My hand finds the pentacle at my throat. Power pulses there, barely contained. I've never tried to let it out before. It might not work.

Goetia reaches for me, and a fingerlike tendril strokes my cheek, burning like acid.

Then the pentacle springs to life, and blue, crystalline light blazes out in a bright beam, straight through him, dispersing the mist and dissolving him. It's all I can do, with the anger and fear left inside me, to keep the beam focused. I visualize it tearing him apart.

"Do you think I only have one trick?" I shout. "Do you think I haven't learned anything all this time? Do you think, by the time she's old enough, I won't know *more?*"

"Yes, dear," he says in a fading, withering voice, though there's hardly any of him left now. "Yes, I—" And then he's gone.

I sit there panting on the grass for a moment, watching the air where he used to be, half-expecting it's a trick and he'll show up behind me. I don't see him — not with my eyes, not with my mind's eye. He could be under a glamor, invisible. I could do a spell to scan for him, if I had the power, but all I have now is eyes. I count to ten before I let myself think of anything else. Watching. He doesn't return.

Then the adrenaline wears off and the exhaustion hits and I just want to curl up and die. I crumple to the ground, pulling my knees to my chest. It's over now. He's gone. It's okay.

I don't think he's dead. I don't know a witch in this world who could kill him. But I've bought another few months, at least.

At last, I hobble to my feet and test my ankle. Not broken. Just a bad twist. The skin on my hand isn't broken where I felt the claws slicing through, but my fingers on that side won't move, and my face is cold and numb where he touched it. Coco's got a bad gash down his woolen leg, but he's salvageable. The pentacle hangs drained around my neck, the crystal cracked and useless now. It's okay. I can make another. Now that I've seen how the blast works, I think I can do it better next time.

When I make it through the door, I sit Coco on the kitchen counter and limp up the cluttered stairs to make sure Sage and Hikari are okay. When Sage, restless and wakeful, asks after Coco, I put a finger to my lips. "He had to go to the doctor. He'll come back soon. Be patient, sweetie."

Working with Hikari, it's only five minutes' stitching. The suture is visible on his leg, rough against grasping fingertips, but he still looks like a bear, and his stuffing is safe inside him where it belongs. It's my idea to work simple shielding knots into the fabric. In a few days, when I have enough power to finish them, they'll stop him from getting lost again. It's Hikari's idea to wrap a miniature Tensor bandage around the site like it's a sports sprain. Sage has seen those in books. I get the real thing for my ankle.

She's only half asleep when I sneak back in, carrying Coco clumsily with still-frozen fingers. Even on the muffly carpet, my steps wake her up. I planned to nestle him next to her as a surprise for the morning, but instead she pulls herself upright and holds out her arms through the bars of the crib, smiling bigger than her little face should let her. "Coco!"

"Coco fell and got hurt," I tell her, handing over the bear. "But he's all fixed up now. Mommy won't let him get hurt again."

Sage grabs him and hugs him tight to her chest, swinging from side to side with joy. "Coco, Coco!"

My breath catches in my throat as I look at her, at that big smile and those chubby fists, and at her eyes, the ones I fell in love with in the delivery room, back then, against all odds. Those big, trusting, orange eyes.

"Coco owie," says Sage, looking down at him and inspecting the bandage. "Coco fix." She looks down at my bandaged ankle, but then her eyes stray to my useless hand, and up to my face. It's my cold, numb face she reaches out for, with a bewildered look. "Mommy owie?"

I don't know quite why, but that pushes me over the edge into tears.

"Yes. It's okay," I say, wiping my eyes. "I can fix it in a couple days. Do you want a hug?"

"Hug," Sage agrees, holding out one arm for me and clutching Coco with the other. I pick them both up and I hold her as long as I can, while I cry, like she's only so much stuffing. Like she'll come all apart in my hands when I let go.

When she starts yawning, I tuck her in, and then I shuffle into the kitchen, being careful of my ankle. Under *MUST DO,* I cross out *Find Coco.* I add:

New pentacle.

Extend wards across back yard.

I'll protect her. I'll teach her everything I know. And I know it won't be enough. But one day, with those eyes, she'll be stronger than me. She'll have other witches around, as she grows, to help answer her questions. If I do it right, if I'm the mother I try to be, then when she's grown and slips out of my hands, she won't need me.

For now, she's my Sage, with Mommy and Hikari to help her, and she sleeps warded, safe and sound

Centipede Girl

Says one Centipede Girl to another: *Are you real?*

Fleeting, that moment. Must be her reflection at the other end of the sewer, maybe in some metal, but she watches it just in case. Holding her breath, she gazes down the long dark tunnel. Wills her 'pedes to stay still a minute, though they never do. Splish goes the stinking water, up to her ankles, as the 'pedes scuttle up and down her legs. And at that tiny noise, her faraway reflection starts and darts away.

Breath rises in her chest, a smile splitting her invisible face. *Moved when I didn't. Means she's real.* Not really a reflection, but someone looking like her, taking up space. Someone that can be touched. And Centipede Girl wants so bad to touch.

She dashes forward, splashing, panting. The 'pedes squat, cling and sting, holding on for the ride. Splash goes the water as two or three of them lose their balance and fall, and they disappear with a fizz, becoming nothing.

Centipede Girl has hands, feet, teeth, a tummy, just like a real girl. Forgets they are there, sometimes. She is invisible, not through magic, but through layers and layers of 'pedes. Scrambling, writhing, waiting. Human skin never shows through.

In her memories, at five, she still has a face, but even then, the 'pedes crawl all over her. She drinks poison, when big looming parents say *Now, listen to the nice exterminator man,* and vomits blood for a week, but the 'pedes remain. Doctors shake their heads. Big looming parents slowly give up hope. And the 'pedes breed.

Lives in the sewers now, in their comfortable, dark stench. Tries going up in the light sometimes and is greeted with screams.

A horrible uproar of water, and a run that burns her lungs and sides, before she catches up to the reflection that is not a reflection.

Don't go! says Centipede Girl. *Wait! Wait!*

It turns to look at her, 'pedes shifting and squirming in the vaguest semblance of a head. It speaks hissing, as though layers on layers of hisses have to be put together just right to make the words.

Why wait?

Because you are like me, says Centipede Girl. *Because you could be a friend.*

An infested silence, as the other girl looks her up and down. Not exactly like Centipede Girl, after all. Bigger. Taller. A grown-up Centipede Woman.

Friend, Centipede Woman says, as though tasting the word.

Friend.

You hunt?

I hunt, says Centipede Girl. More often she scavenges, faceted 'pede eyes spotting some half-rotten thing. But fresh meat pleases her more. She's learned to send one or two 'pedes out a short ways, keeping her mind on them so they don't disappear, luring in some hungry rat or lizard, then pouncing with strong human limbs.

Centipede Woman nods. Barely perceptible under the writhe of her face.

We hunt.

So long since anyone touched Centipede Girl. Maybe not since she was born. She has thought of it in her sweetest daydreams, the ones that hurt the most. Hands holding hers. Arms around her. Warm sides to lean against.

One time she climbs all the way out of the sewer. Tells herself the screams won't stop her. She'll hold him down, the first unlucky passerby, and grasp his hands in hers, just for a while, just long enough to remember she's real. But the screams turn to gags and prayers and bestial howls as she chases him, and she can't do it. Not brave enough. Lets him get away.

She watches now as Centipede Woman hunts. Centipede Woman gives gruff instructions. *Stand like this. Watch more careful. Never get full if not watch more careful.*

Centipede Girl half-listens. Other half longs for Centipede Woman's hands. Centipede Woman won't scream. Nothing to scream about. Nothing on her that isn't on both of them already.

She asks Centipede Woman every evening when the hunt is done. *Will you let me hold your*
hands? Please?

You don't want that.

Makes herself pitiful in the asking. Lets the tears creep into her voice, if they like. *I do. Please,*

I do. I want it so bad.

No.

And the nights are silent. They sleep, on opposite sides of the tunnel, every day.

She is good a long time. Ignores the ache inside and keeps her hands to herself. Hunts and hunts. Does everything Centipede Woman says, till at last, after months, Centipede Woman hunts all silent by her side. Still moving, same as before, but out of words.

Two days. Three. No words. And the ache is a pounding raging thing inside her head.

Think we go two ways now, says Centipede Woman, after three days silent. *Think this done. Taught everything. Done.*

No, says Centipede Girl. *No.*

Yes. Sleep day, then in evening, go two ways.

And Centipede Woman falls asleep.

The thing in Centipede Girl's head pounds and rages, and though she knows it's a bad, bad thing, she creeps to Centipede Woman's side. Watches the rise and fall of the 'pedes on her chest. Looks up at Centipede Woman's writhing skittering face, down to the hills of her shoulders, down the throughways of 'pedes up and down her arm, over and under each other, down to the squirming brown mass that is her hand.

Takes a breath, and then she reaches down and plunges her hand into the 'pedes.

Centipede Woman's 'pedes skitter across the skin of her hand, probing it, tasting it. Shuddery, that feeling, even though Centipede Girl has 'pedes too. These ones aren't hers and she can't see through their eyes. But she brings her hand down anyway, right through the mass that should be Centipede Woman's fist, right down to the ground.

There is no fist. No wrist, no forearm. Just 'pedes and 'pedes and 'pedes.

And Centipede Woman screams. *What is this? What is this you do?*

Centipede Girl backs away. Doesn't know what to say, so just babbles. *I'm*

sorry. I only wanted to hold your hand. I wanted it so bad. I'm sorry. Please.
You want my touch? says Centipede Woman, only half the 'pedes hissing. Other half screaming, eerie and shrill. *Have my touch.*

And just like hunting, Centipede Woman lunges.

Centipede Girl reels, bracing for the great slamming limbs of a woman, even though she knows better now. All that hits her are light little 'pedes, 'pedes upon 'pedes, until she staggers under the weight of such light little things. Centipede Girl screams, and the 'pedes scream, and blood billows in the filthy water.

Last she remembers, she is falling, collapsing, her limbs folding up into each other, and the bloody, mucky water rushing at her face.

Centipede Woman is gone now. Gone for a long time. Centipede Girl hunts alone.

Runs away now from mirrors, still water, anything to reflect her. Afraid of what she'll see. Once she does see herself, distorted, in a shiny metal panel. Looks the same as before. Just 'pedes. Feels different, though.

In her memories, she has hands, feet, teeth, a tummy, just like a real girl. But all she can see now are facets. All she can feel now is hunger. Sometimes she reaches through the 'pedes and paws at herself. Tries to remember her shape. *Be real. Please. Be like a real girl.*

But her hands go right through herself, and there are no bones anywhere. No more girl. Just 'pedes and 'pedes and 'pedes.

The Changeling's Escape

A child, night-creeping
far from the whitewashed porch.
A winding aisle through pillar-trees
to lie in hallowed darkness
as the summer creatures hum.
Something floats in these trees,
viewless, mind-visible,
sharp-limbed and laughing,
not luring.

The child grasps wind-thin hands,
laughing along, not thinking
of a screaming mother miles behind
and the dark of an empty cradle.
She rolls in the crackling leaves
and sings, and says, "home" —

borne away in viewless arms
to a tree-tangled, night-quiet land
without the piercing flicker-flare of the sun.
Without the smack-handed women calling her "fey."
She carries the word in her pocket,
not stolen but wild,
as she climbs.

What Great Darkness

"I'm going to get you!"

Wolf's voice rings through the cottage. Red ducks into a cupboard, suppressing a grin. It's an old game, but it keeps her mind off what's outside in the woods. A hunting howl makes the kitchen rumble.

He opens and slams one cupboard door after another. Her toes curl, nestled in with the pots and pans and rosemary. Finally he bursts in on her. She ducks her head to let him drag her out, giggling.

"I've got you."

"You've got me."

He pins her against the kitchen wall. Kisses her. His wolf breath is hot in her throat. She curls her fingers into his soft fur.

"Oh. Oh, what big teeth you have."

"The better to bite you with, love."

She can hardly suppress her smile. "What big—"

There's a knock at the door.

Both freeze. Red's cottage — once Grandmother's — lies deep in the darkest woods. No one comes by unannounced. Not since the last argument with Red's mother, back before the Plague. The last slammed door, the parting shout— "Fine! Throw away your life!"

Since then, nothing but the creatures. But creatures don't knock like this — a smart, hesitant, well-timed rat-a-tat-tat. Creatures scratch at the door and hiss.

The knock repeats itself, louder. A man's voice outside. "Red. It's Evander. Please."

Red meets Wolf's eyes — already wide, fixed on hers.

"You don't owe him anything," Wolf says. "You don't have to."

"They'll eat him if he carries on like that."

Evander never understood her, but he wasn't an evil man. She won't have his death on her conscience.

She scrambles to the door. Peeks through the keyhole to make sure it's really him. Not some other woodcutter wanting a wolf's head to mount on his wall. Not one of the creatures, learning a new trick.

It's him. Bedraggled, panicked, sweat greasing his once-tidy hair. He's got the same broad shoulders. The same blue eyes. The body Red ought to have loved.

"Red," he calls again.

She grits her teeth.

She opens the door.

Evander can barely speak, the panic is so strong. "Red," he makes his mouth say, and "please", but it will do little else. Red scurries around him, offers chairs and blankets. Doesn't seem to know what to do.

At last she forces a cup of bitter tea down his throat, and things start to realign in his head.

"They've got my father. And the kids."

Red looks stricken. He thinks of Red's own mother, threadbare and mean from months of barricading her house. The curses that woman calls up against her daughter. Blaming the Plague on Red, though Evander never put that thought in her head.

He thinks of his father, the once-strong hands too palsied to hold an axe. The children. God, the children.

"I didn't mean to," he babbles. "I swear. I thought they weren't on my trail. Thought I'd finally lost them. I just wanted to visit them at the cottage for a little while. Make sure they were alive. But the creatures followed. Red, they're surrounded in there. They've got the windows boarded up but I don't know how long it'll last."

It's strange begging her, the girl he always tried to be strong for.

"You want our help."

Our. He glances at Wolf's silent bulk in the corner. His skin crawls. What choice does he have? "Yes. Yours and Wolf's. Please."

"I don't owe you anything." She stands. "We could die doing this. Do you understand?"

But she's already going to the mantel, getting her axe. Evander clenches and unclenches a fist. One day she'll understand what she owes him.

Red met Wolf on her way through the forest, years ago, long before the Plague. He looked at her. Smiled, and there were fangs in the smile. Her heart beat wildly, and not with fear. She had never seen anything like him before.

If she hadn't followed him off the path, that day, maybe she would be another woman. She would live in the city with Evander, who courted her since childhood. She would have boarded up her windows in the Plague and hid from the creatures, same as anyone, waited for them to pick her friends and neighbors off. But she would have neighbors. She would remember making them shawls and petticoats, baking them cookies. Maybe, in the wreckage, they would love her.

Maybe she would be happier. Maybe not.

Maybe she would turn restlessly in her sleep when things howled in the distance. Dream of tiny curled shapes, half-human, half-wolf, in her womb.

Evander crouches next to Red in the underbrush, gripping his axe. Tries not to listen to her breathing. Or Wolf's, heavier, on the other side.

He thought he was used to the creatures. Used to the guilt. But nothing will get him used to what he sees through the branches. His father's cottage, once clean and solid with his father's sturdy carpentry. Now moldy on the edges, black in streaks with acidic spit.

The creatures always make him feel like there's a hole in his eye. Like the fabric of the world has to be bent back just to let them in. Faces full of tentacles, insectile limbs, spines, mouths where there shouldn't be mouths — they make no sense no matter how long he looks. You could go mad looking at creatures like that.

They make a hissing noise like oil in a skillet, and they scratch at the door. Already half through.

His father and his little cousins are in there.

"Too many," Wolf whispers. "We can't take them all. Not in a fair fight."

"We've got to try," Evander whispers back.

"We can distract them. Long enough for the kids to get away, at least. Trap them."

"Bait," whispers Red.

She looks at Evander, like she thinks it should be him.

"You ever fought anything with an axe?"

"I'm learning." She blushes as bright as her hood. Evander can just imagine. Wolf guiding her through the woods, picking the weak creatures, the easy prey. Finishing them off himself and patting her on the head. Like a cat with her kittens. Like anybody has the luxury of learning slowly anymore.

"You're the weakest. And you're easy to spot."

Her glare back at him could boil milk.

Red stands in the middle of the clearing, thirty feet from the woodcutter's house. Thirty feet from the creatures. She throws back her hood with shaking fingers, waves it beside her head. A matador.

"Me!" she shouts. "It's me you want!"

The creatures turn, their tentacles looping as if tasting the air.

She can't move until they come closer. That is the plan.

The creatures creep toward her.

She watches the cottage's windows. Waits until she sees a clear path. Something moves behind the curtains — a child, she hopes, ready to run for it — as the creatures leave the cottage behind.

The foremost of them reaches out and touches her hair with a single antenna, and she feels a fizzing, like part of her has slipped out of the universe.

She turns and bolts. South.

Red is light on her feet, but these creatures are fast. She keeps an eye out behind her, slashes with her small handaxe. Zigzags. Turn too far forward, give them too much of a blind spot, and it's over.

Wolf and Evander move in behind her, blocking the creatures' retreat. A few at the back turn, try to creep back to the cottage, and Wolf and Evander cut them down.

The cottage door opens a crack. Four children and an old man creep out and run north, to the village, unpursued.

Red looks down at her feet, hops lightly over a wooden board. The creatures follow, hot at her heels, and a skittering leg nudges wood. There's a *shing*. Spare axes, ropes, splintered logs, whatever was on hand — all of it falls in a deafening chaos. Pounds, slices, buries them.

But only some of them.

A slimy tentacle wraps around Red's wrist. Her hand goes numb. Too slow

— too much time watching. She hacks at it with the axe in her other hand, until it comes off with a sucking sound, and she backs away, rubbing her hand on her thigh to try to find the circulation.

It's not over yet.

Evander courted Red before the Plague. She was fickle, strawberry kisses and blushing retreats. The more he chased, the less she gave in.

But her fling with Wolf was permanent. Months passed, nearly a year, while he waited for her to come to her senses. No girl could love a Wolf. Not with those teeth...

He wanted to save her. He came by, at last, wielding his axe and saying a hero's words. He remembers the heat in his face as he stormed away, realizing she did not want to be saved.

Before the Plague.

He sulked in the darkest heart of the forest, swinging his axe, breaking saplings left and right. Into a thicket, barely looking where he was going. He cut wood until nothing was left but soil, then knelt in the soil and began to dig.

Manly work. To take his mind off the frailty of women.

What deep roots you have.

He had told her to choose for herself. But he hadn't meant *this* choice.

The hole grew so deep that he had to step inside.

What long shadows you have.

It was not his fault. He loved her. He had done nothing wrong. Yet there was this shame, this anger, so deep it seemed to be leading him down.

Something seemed to be leading him down.

His hand caught on something like a root.

A tentacle snaked past his wrist, or something like a tentacle — something the world had to be bent to allow.

Bent, or dug through.

What great darkness you have...

They pushed out around his hand, more and more of them.

He has never told anyone. The townsfolk would kill Red if they knew. It's her fault, after all — if she had stayed on the path that day, he would not have had to come here, and there would be no Plague. But they hate Red enough already. She already bears the shame of loving a Wolf. He is a good man; he will not tell.

He doesn't know why the creatures let him live.

Red ducks deeper behind the trees and circles back. The surviving creatures close in on Wolf and Evander. Both of them shouting, Evander in his good-boy baritone, Wolf in a howl.

The children are far enough gone now. Out of sight. The creatures left over can't follow. The question now is getting away from them.

Wolf backs up, cornered by two of the creatures. Evander's busy with his own. The creatures hiss, undulating. They lunge in and wrap his limbs with their tentacles. He shivers. Drops his axe.

Red breaks into a run.

She hears herself shouting. The creatures flatten Wolf against a tree. They drive their tentacles into his eyes.

There's no blood. Only howling and hissing.

She gets to them and swings. Wildly. Hacks at them until one falls in a shower of slime and the other one pulls itself out of Wolf's face, turns towards her. Hacks at that one too. And hacks.

Still learning. She doesn't know the best footwork. She knows enough for this.

She hacks until she finds herself swinging, breathing hard, next to Evander, and there are no creatures left. She's dizzy.

Evander's eyes are wide. He's got his share of slime, too. "Red, are you..."

She drops to her knees next to Wolf.

No blood. Still breathing. But where his eyes used to be, there is darkness. A hole in the world.

She touches his hairy cheek, not wanting to believe.

"Wolf."

"Red."

"Are you..."

"I don't know."

He can hear her, at least, and that's something.

She starts to shiver. She has seen the wounds the creatures make before. She has never seen someone survive them, not even this long.

The place where Wolf's eyes used to be is dark beyond dark, a nothingness that creeps inside her.

She spares a brief glance for Evander. "Can they heal this? If I bring him back to the village."

"No." He shifts behind her as she turns her attention back to Wolf. "They wouldn't let a wolf in the village anyway. Least of all these days. But you..." His voice catches. "You could come back with me."

"No."

She doesn't know what will happen. Maybe Wolf will live. Maybe he'll die. Maybe he'll be a creature himself, when next she wakes beside him, and kill her. But they already warned her he'd kill her, back before the Plague, when she left home to live with a wolf. She will not let him languish alone with those eyes. She will not leave him.

"Red, I..." Evander hesitates. "I want you to know I..."

But she is no longer listening.

"You're going to live," she tells Wolf when she gets him back to Grandmother's cottage. She tucks him up under blankets and feeds him the salted meat they were saving.

"I think so," says Wolf. "Everything looks funny."

"What big eyes you have," she teases. No one laughs.

There are other cuts on his body, bruises, streaks on his side where the creatures bit, all dark. A small tentacle snakes out of one and curls around her hand. Gently. This one doesn't numb her.

"I know what you're giving up," he says. "I know what you're risking. You could go back to the village with him. I would mourn, but I wouldn't stop you."

Red grits her teeth. "Don't say that! I know I have a choice." The choice is what Evander keeps throwing in her face. She likes it better when she can pretend she doesn't have one, when it's the Wolf dragging her out of cupboards and having his way with her. Having to choose him, again and again, exhausts her. "Don't tell me I have a choice. Tell me I made the right one."

Wolf reaches up blind. Misses her face by a handspan.

"You always did all right by me," he says.

Red lies atop the covers, curls against him. Tentacles or not, she knows she'd never trade him for Evander.

"I know," she says, and closes her eyes.

The townsfolk tell stories. Red the witch who lies with wolves, and worse than wolves. Red the victim, carried off by a monster. They cast pitying looks at her mother. They argue over the end of the story: she is dead, she was eaten, the thing that was Wolf wears her clothes and tries to go among people.

Maybe not. Maybe both of them live. Maybe Red is as happy as she can be, hiding with him while the world falls apart. The townsfolk, who do not dream of wolves, will never know.

Daphne Without Apollo

Not running away. Not pleading
for a hiding-place — vain boy of a god,
did you think you would blot me
from the world? — but running *to*

the earth I craved. The strength I sprawled against
in summer and winter, mourning my pink little hands
which could only trace roots in the rocks.
Only sing love-sick in watery notes
till the broad earth laughed her earthquake laugh
at last:
Yes, love. Come.

You saw me then, running to tangle
my feet at her heart. My face grown tall,
upturned. The wind ashiver in my thousand arms,
grown solid, heartwood-thick
and riddled with birds.

Vain boy, did you mean to chase me? Yet I
have forgotten you.

Miss Sprocket Tinkers

Miss Sprocket gaped over Terence's shoulder as he carried her into the the New Chautauqua tent. All of Muskogee County seemed to have assembled under that canvas, and every corner housed a different attraction — hollering lecturers hyping the universe's secrets, stern priests pacing to and fro, even a miniature opera company. But those weren't what caught Sprocket's attention. She'd seen things like them every time New Chautauqua's educational attractions came to town. What she twisted to look at, beating her tail on Terence's chest, were the mice.

Dozens of them! White, gray, brown, fat and sleek, scurrying fast as you please around the biggest cage Sprocket had ever seen. Round and round they went on the big brass wheel, up and down the ladders, in and out of little hidey holes. Sprocket wanted those mice.

She squirmed to be let down, but Terence, mean old thing, held tighter. He'd seen the mice too.

"Meow," said Sprocket.

"Oh, the poor dear," said a woman in a linen shirtwaist, laughing. "Does you want to chase the mousies? Does you?"

"Sorry," said Terence. "I plum forgot there'd be mice. Here, I'll take her back home."

Sprocket growled low in her throat. Terence brought her to the New Chautauqua meetings every time. Mean of him to change his mind today, just when something interesting happened.

"I don't think as you'd need to," said the woman. She turned and hollered to a big man in a second cage, connected to the first by a little tunnel. "Bobby? You mind if a cat runs 'round in here?"

"Ha! You shoulda seen Kennewick," Bobby called back. "Whole herd of strays up there. These cages is solid enough for anything. You go ahead."

The woman smiled daintily.

"You know him?" said Terence.

"My cousin."

"You work here?"

She shook her head. "Thought I'd drop by for this one, just to see what Bobby does. I'm Miss Barbara."

"Terence."

"Meow," said Sprocket. Terence let her down.

"You be good now," he said. But soon as her paws hit ground, she was off.

Those mice ran around in the cage like mice possessed. The smarter ones ran away to little hidey holes when Sprocket batted at them. The dumber ones just kept running and spinning the wheels, and the dumbest ones — Sprocket could not believe it — came *closer*, sniffing her, like they'd never seen a cat before. But for all she batted and swatted, she couldn't get more than a solitary claw through the wire mesh around the cage. She chittered and sighed, biting into the air the same way she'd bite a mouse. It did no good. She got to wondering if the ones that ran and hid were the dumb ones.

"Ladies and gentlemen!" Bobby bellowed. His country cant was gone, replaced by a slick educated voice. "Fair citizens of Muskogee, be amazed at the Secrets of the All-American Super-Mousetrap! This is no ordinary nipper. It usurps the neurological processes of the common house mouse and uses their simple animal psyches to any end you desire! Ladies and gentlemen, I am about to demonstrate cutting-edge science!"

Sprocket didn't like Bobby's big, low voice, but it was hard to ignore. Her ears swiveled toward him, even while they flattened a little. He went on and on about the All-American Super-Mousetrap. Sprocket didn't see the point. New Chautauqua was all about bringing cutting-edge learning to ordinary folks, so usually the lecturers talked about something exotic. Like the shiny-feathered birds that lived in jungle parts, far away. But Sprocket had seen plenty of mousetraps.

Bobby opened a little gate, and a brown mouse scurried through the tunnel onto a table in the second cage with him. There was a solid steel wall between the two cages, so the rest of the mice couldn't see. Sprocket sauntered over so it didn't block her view. The wire mesh of the second cage still blocked her way.

"First, the traditional function of the mousetrap."

He got the pistons pumping on a little steam-powered apparatus. Magnets whirled. Little lights blinked at the top.

The little brown mouse fell down dead.

Bobby picked it up by its tail. Sprocket salivated. She pawed so high up the wall of wire that she balanced on her hind paws for a second, meowing. But big, mean Bobby tossed the mouse in a wastebasket, inaccessible behind the wires.

Sprocket growled.

"Now, of course," said Bobby, "you're thinking, 'why go to all that trouble for a mousetrap? Why not use our Mr. Hooker's spring-loaded design? Better yet, why not leave it to this enthusiastic little moggie here?'" There was a smattering of laughter. "The secret, ladies and gentlemen, is in the All-American Super-Mousetrap's flexibility."

And he showed them. He talked about mesmeric neurology and vital fluid, and he brought up mouse after mouse. A mouse tapdanced. A mouse squeaked a verse of "Yankee Doodle". A mouse carried a pen twice the length of its tail. And then Bobby got to taking requests. A scuff-shoed gentleman requested a double somersault, and a little white mouse did one. A parasoled lady asked if a mouse could hurl itself down from the top of the cage, breaking its neck. A little black mouse did it quick as you please. Bobby, to Sprocket's irritation, dropped it in the wastebasket with the other one.

"You see, ladies and gentlemen, these mice are untrained. I have not used our Mr. Thorndike's law of effect, offering rewards and punishments. Mesmerism does the job for me. Do you wish to kill mice? Then kill them with a thought. Do you wish to remove them humanely? Then make them sincerely desire to leave. You are limited only by your own imagination."

The audience applauded. Sprocket kept her eyes on the mice. She thought the Super-Mousetrap was wasted on Bobby. Why, if *she* had one, she wouldn't waste time making mice sing. She'd have them run to her paws, then run out again, so she'd always have something to play with. Better yet, she'd farm them. Make a whole colony in Terence's basement and pick them off as she pleased.

"And now," said Bobby in his slick city voice, "I will show you how to make an All-American Super-Mousetrap of your own."

Twitching the tip of her tail, Sprocket sat and listened.

After Bobby's lecture, the miniature opera troupe sang loud and long. A populist minister strode up and down the stage in his black cassock, hyping temperance, and a thin-fingered doctor talked about diseases. Sprocket didn't listen too closely to those. Terence picked her up at the end of the day. Miss Barbara in her linen shirtwaist was still at his side.

"You been a good kitty?" he asked. "You got any mice?"

"Meow."

"Oh, ain't you a precious little thing," said Miss Barbara, reaching to scratch Sprocket's ears. Sprocket squirmed away.

"I had a real wonderful time," said Terence.

"I liked it too," said Miss Barbara. "We should come again tomorrow."

And Terence hardly paid attention to Sprocket all the way home.

Sprocket had used to hate New Chautauqua meetings. Stuffy air, shuffling feet, and long loud lectures on things she didn't care for. But Terence loved them, and he always brought Sprocket.

"Ain't nothing so American as learning," he would say to her as she fussed on his shoulder. "And we're all Americans here, even the cats."

Sprocket was pretty sure that Terence only took her there because he took her everywhere. To the pub, to the doctor, to Fourth of July picnics. If he'd been allowed, he would even have brought her to work: the kitchens where he washed dishes and the shops where he swept, on account of he couldn't sell enough of his steam-powered gadgets to make ends meet that way. Terence didn't have lots of friends. When other poor, disheveled tinkerers came through town — for there were no rich tinkerers down south — then he had folks to really talk to. Those days he let Sprocket roam free. The rest of the time, snubbed by beautiful women, rich men, and even other sweepers, he hugged Sprocket extra-close.

Terence specially loved tinkering. He'd hear about some new invention and rush home to try it, cobbling together the ratchets and gears in his cluttered basement until he had one of his own. Sprocket liked the ratchets and gears. Gears made neat sounds when she chased them across the floor. But with no thumbs, she couldn't do more. So plans for machines only frustrated her.

Then one day, a couple months before he met Miss Barbara, Terence dragged Sprocket to a lecture by one Mr. Lundgren, both a doctor and a tinker.

"In my work," said Mr. Lundgren, "I have often come across men and women missing hands, fingers, even whole limbs. Men and women who are blind, through birth or misfortune, who are deaf or palsied or cannot speak. What a tragedy if these men and women cannot reach their full potential!

"At my institute I have been developing assistive technologies. Books in Mr. Braille's raised alphabet for the blind. Systems to transcribe speech quickly for the deaf. But what I will show you today, ladies and gentlemen, is a device you have never imagined. A means of manipulating objects, with astonishing precision, for those without hands."

Terence liked the idea. He went home and made one himself. He put slippers on over his hands and moved the device's handles clumsily. It wasn't as easy as using his thumbs, but he stuck with it and made a whole doll-sized dirigible that way.

"Innit funny, Sprocket?" he mused as it puttered by. "I never even thought of them folks without hands. But there must be some, come back from the Philippines, their fingers blown clean off. Ain't nothing braver'n that. I'm glad them folks can still tinker."

"Meow," said Sprocket.

While Terence was asleep, Sprocket slipped into his workshop and picked up the device herself. It was slow going. They'd designed the thing for the movements humans made, not the batting and biting that came naturally to Sprocket. But Sprocket worked hard. After a night's worth of clatter and clank, she had a simple little gear-box. Not a useful one. Just one to show she could do it.

She picked up the gear-box in her teeth and dropped it on Terence's pillow.

"Tarnation, Sprocket," said Terence sleepily. "Was that you making that infernal racket all night? What you bringing me this little toy for, huh?"

Then he took a closer look at the gear-box. All at once his eyes went wide. He smiled a funny little smile.

"Well, ain't you the cleverest moggie in all of Muskogee," he said. And he got up and gave her tuna flakes for breakfast, the very best. From then on, she paid extra close attention to tinkering lectures. Whenever she finished a bit of clockwork, Terence gave her tuna flakes and a thrilled smile. Like it was their little secret.

The other thing Terence especially loved was tales of the world. He and Sprocket would sit rapt while lecturers hyped the Wonders of Africa, the

Orient, or the Amazon. Sometimes the lecturers brought little birds and mammals in bright colors, and Sprocket squirmed and thumped her tail, wanting to chase them.

"Someday, Sprocket," Terence said those evenings, while he and Sprocket sat in his workshop, making some engine or music box. "Someday I'll strike it rich and we'll see the world. Won't that be nice?"

Sprocket thought of the strange, bright creatures and purred.

That was how things were until the night Bobby hyped the All-American Super-Mousetrap. That night, Terence didn't talk about seeing the world. He didn't go in his workshop to tinker. He got out a bit of chicken for Sprocket, and then he sat in his worn-out armchair, smiling all unfocused, like someone was scratching under his chin.

"Meow," said Sprocket. She jumped up and pushed her head under his hands. She wanted to go tinker.

Terence petted her a little, but he stayed rooted down. "Ain't she something, that Miss
Barbara?"

"Meow," said Sprocket. She did not agree.

"I know you didn't spend much time with her. You with your mice."

"Meow."

"But you'll like her in time." His voice got vague and soft. "She's something special, she is."

"Meow."

She nudged him towards the workshop, but he wouldn't listen. So Sprocket jumped off his lap, shook each one of her paws in disgust, and headed down to build an All-American Super-Mousetrap of her own.

Terence took her to New Chautauqua every day that week, before the lectures ran out and the big tent folded up. Sprocket ran free. She listened to lessons on flight, women's suffrage, fiddle music, the Lobes of the Human Brain. Terence hardly listened. He spent all his time sitting in that funny daze next to Miss Barbara. They laughed at the same little jokes.

After the big tent folded up, Terence took to staying out. He remembered to feed Sprocket, but that was about all. Sprocket worked on the All-American

Super-Mousetrap by herself.

It took three whole weeks to get the thing done. And a beautiful mousetrap it was, all gears, pistons, valves and flashing lights. She waited with childlike pride until Terence came down to the workshop. As he set foot at the bottom of the stairs, she nosed the "ON" button.

The steam engine shuddered to life, smoke rose up, and little lights began to flash on and off. Sprocket rubbed up against Terence's ankles.

He sat down and petted her. "Clever moggie," he said. But it was faint, vague praise. Sprocket's ears went flat against her head.

It was a minute or two before a little brown mouse scurried out of the woodwork and ran right up to her. She pounced and caught it, holding it up proudly.

"Clever girl," said Terence again. He wandered back upstairs. She didn't even hear him getting tuna flakes. Just his light steps as he walked to his armchair and sat down again.

Sprocket bit through the mouse's spinal cord.

She tried setting the All-American Super-Mousetrap to mesmerize Terence instead of the mice. She punched in programs for compliments. Mice scampered up with adoring expressions on their faces. She coded orders for tuna flakes. Mice raided the pantry. Terence barely even noticed. He was out all the time now.

Sprocket killed the mice in specially vicious ways. She left them, dismembered, on Terence's pillow. Terence scolded her, cleaned them up, and went back to not paying attention. She coughed up hairballs into his shoes. He washed them and went back out to see Miss Barbara without her. At last she turned the mousetrap back off.

She'd paid enough attention to the lecture on Lobes of the Human Brain to know humans and mice were different up there. Maybe the mousetrap only worked on mouse brains. She took to sitting hopelessly in the workshop, flicking the tip of her tail.

One day, Miss Barbara came to visit Terence's smoky little home. She and Terence sighed and giggled all through dinner, with Miss Barbara's uncle standing chaperone. Sprocket hid in the workshop.

She heard Miss Barbara's voice upstairs. "Oh, Terence, I got to see that moggie of yours afore I go. I haven't hardly seen her at all." And the two of them trooped down, hand in hand.

Miss Barbara dug through a pile of gears. "Lordy, Terence. When will you get to cleaning up all this junk? You know there ain't money in tinkering. Even Bobby can't hardly get by, and he's a trailblazer. Sells the patents to Yankee robber barons for hardly nothing. I don't want that for you. And your lungs'll rot from the coal."

"I know," said Terence, his voice wavering. He sounded like he'd heard that before.

Sprocket raised her hackles, puffed out her tail, and hissed.

"Oh, ain't you the cutest," said Miss Barbara. She reached out a hand and Sprocket scratched it, drawing blood. "Oh! Oh, what a vicious little thing!"

Terence and the nameless uncle both rushed to her. "You all right?"

"I'm fine," said Miss Barbara, dabbing at her hand with a handkerchief. "Don't know why she was so angry."

Terence grinned. "Suppose you can stanch your own wound, at that."

Miss Barbara grinned back. "Physician, heal thyself. I'm fine, long as she ain't rabid. I'll go get some peroxide."

"Meow," said Sprocket. *Physician?* she thought. All the doctors who lectured on anatomy at New Chautauqua meetings were old men, and Miss Barbara was a slim young woman. But she might be a medical student, or a doctor's helper.

And doctors knew how brains worked.

While Miss Barbara looked for peroxide, Sprocket searched out Miss Barbara's handbag in the anteroom. Sure enough, piled in the bag were a stack of books with pictures of skeletons, muscles and eyes. Sprocket never learned to read, but she knew a skeleton when she saw one.

When Miss Barbara returned, Sprocket was sitting on the handbag.

"Oh, ain't you a sassy little thing," said Miss Barbara. "Is you gonna 'tack me again? Is you?"

Sprocket dearly wanted to. Instead she stood up with a chittered greeting and rubbed against Miss Barbara's ankles.

"Well, ain't that the funniest thing. She likes me now."

"Looks like."

It took a long and determined campaign. First it took hours of nosing in the book bag and meowing until Miss Barbara got the hint. Then it took months of purring in her lap while she read from her medical texts. Sprocket even saw fit to lick Miss Barbara's forearm once or twice. Somewhere in that book it explained about brains, and she was getting there if it killed her.

"You know," said Miss Barbara to Terence. "If I didn't know better, I'd almost think she understands me." She ruffled Sprocket's fur. "Doesn't you?"

Sprocket waited for Terence to explain that Sprocket was an inventor, the cleverest moggie in all of Muskogee. He never got round to it. At first, his silence miffed her something awful. After a few weeks, though, she reconsidered. If Miss Barbara knew how clever Sprocket was, she might catch on. And that might end everything.

Finally one day Miss Barbara got to the good part. She explained in a sing-song voice about the frontal lobe, the neocortex, Mr. Broca's lobe, the hippocampus. The bits that were simple in mice but folded all up on themselves in humans. Sprocket listened with her ears perked.

When that chapter got done, she forgot to nuzzle Miss Barbara's hand. She hopped off to the workshop straightaway.

Miss Barbara's voice floated after her. "Oh, ain't you a fickle moggie? Ain't you? I wonder what I did."

Sprocket wasn't working from New Chautauqua instructions anymore. This stuff might never have been done before, even at the universities.

The first test, a month in, did nothing. Miss Barbara came down and Sprocket pushed "ON". Steam engines hissed, gears turned, lights blinked. Miss Barbara blinked too.

"Terence," she called, "you left this thing on. Why'd you build an All-American Super-Mousetrap when you got a mouser already?"

"Oh, that was for fun," said Terence. He hurried down and pressed "OFF".

"No money in it," said Miss Barbara, "'specially not for building something someone already made. If you was an original, like Bobby, you might scrape by."

Sprocket cuddled up to Terence that night. She dropped a couple feathers on his pillow, not feathers from a bird she'd killed, but red and green parrot plumes from the New Chautauqua tent. "Someday, Sprocket," she wanted him to say. "Someday we'll see the world." But she expected he wouldn't say that. She expected he'd be mad about the All-American Super-Mousetrap turning on, wasting coal.

But Terence just scratched her ears and lay down to sleep. He didn't say a thing.

Sprocket had to wait longer and longer every test, because Terence and Miss Barbara went to the workshop less and less. Every time they did, she turned on the All-American Super-Mousetrap. Every time they paused a little longer. One step closer to doing what she wanted.

A few months in, Terence came down and got to picking up gears, pistons and whatnot, shoving them in a big sack. Cleaning the place out.

Sprocket pawed up his leg, trying to stop him. "Meow."

He scratched her behind the ears. "Don't you worry. I ain't takin' all of it. Just enough to sell at the junk shop" He sighed and got that dreamy look again. "Ain't it nice, Sprocket? Knowing what you want?"

"Meow." She'd always known what she wanted.

Her ears stayed back against her head, but she followed Terence and only complained a little. Just every few minutes. Enough so he wouldn't forget she was there.

He turned to the All-American Super-Mousetrap. "Might get a pretty penny for this one. You don't mind, do you, Sprocket? I know it's yours, technicalwise, but I need the money for something'll make me real happy. I'll buy you tuna flakes for a week, how's that?"

Sprocket yowled so loud he put his hands over his ears. She stood in front of the Super-Mousetrap, puffed out her fur, and hissed.

Terence laughed and backed off. "All right. Didn't know it were so important to you. You sure is a funny thing, but I'll leave it be."

She stood in front of the All-American Super-Mousetrap the rest of the day, her ears back and her whiskers puffed, in case he forgot. When he left, the workshop was cleaner, but sparser and sadder. Not a place where anyone worked anymore, just a place where they'd strewn a few odds and ends. A couple of lonesome gadgets lay in the corners.

The week after that, Sprocket walked in on Terence and Miss Barbara. Terence was down on one knee. Miss Barbara had a new ring, a shiny one with a little white stone.

"Oh, Terence," she said. He stood up again and they hugged hard. Miss Barbara's uncle, in the corner, wiped a tear from his eye.

Sprocket didn't see what the fuss was about. Little white stones didn't flutter like birds, nor scurry like mice. She sure was unimpressed if he'd traded in all his machines just for this.

"Oh, look," said Miss Barbara. "It's Sprocket. Now it's all of us together."

"Looks like."

Miss Barbara scooped Sprocket up. Sprocket was too baffled to resist. Miss Barbara sat down in Terence's armchair and petted Sprocket's fur smooth for once, scratching behind her ears. She didn't even baby-talk.

"Oh, Sprocket," she whispered, "if you knew how happy I am. Soon we'll all be together in a big clean house, not a coaly little one like this. We'll stay there forever and ever. Won't we, Sprocket?"

The next time Miss Barbara came down to the workshop, she looked around and tsked, like it was hers now. "He said he'd cleaned it up. Poor dear. Well, Miss Barbara, you want a thing done, you do it yourself, now, don't you?"

Sprocket nosed the "ON" button. She couldn't help letting her tail slap back and forth real quick. No telling how many more tests she could do before Miss Barbara took everything away.

Miss Barbara stopped and stood still where she was. She tilted her head and whistled a tune. "Yankee Doodle".

Sprocket purred.

It was only a test program, but programming the behavior would be easy. Latching it on to human neurology was the hard part. "Yankee Doodle" repeated like a stuck phonograph until Sprocket nosed the All-American Super-Mousetrap back off.

Miss Barbara shook her head a little. "Now, why was I in here?"

Sprocket had thought of making Miss Barbara cut her own throat or pitch herself off the top of the house. But a funny kind of loyalty had stopped her. She didn't really want Miss Barbara dead. She only wanted Terence back. Him and his gadgets and tuna flakes. His plans to see the world.

She'd take only what she needed.

When Terence came down the stairs, Sprocket was waiting. Steam engines hissed, pistons pumped, gears turned, lights blinked. Terence paused, and then he smiled bigger than Sprocket had ever seen.

"What a damn fool I been, Sprocket!" he said, sweeping her up in his arms.

"Meow," said Sprocket. She groomed his forearm.

"What a damn fool," said Terence again. "Here's what I'll do. I'll ask Miss Barbara for the ring back. Then I'll sell it. It's near good as new." He held up Sprocket and looked in her eyes. "Can you guess what I'll do with that money?"

"Meow."

"Ship's passage all the way to Africa. We'll see the world, Sprocket! At long last."

He held her tight and sank to the floor, grinning fit to burst.

"'Course, we'll take that, too," he added, nodding to the Super-Mousetrap. "Wouldn't want to be without a mousetrap, would we?"

Sprocket purred.

The Tooth Fairy Throws In the Towel

So it's quarter to fairy rush hour and this kid's got
a booby-trap in his pillow. He thinks it's so funny,
fairy-baiting, right,
and I ain't even the kind with wings and glitter
but I got string and chocolate syrup all over me now
and it's all I can do to throw the dollar at the laughing brat's
head 'stead of strangling him.

Which is when I get this text from Rob.
"Drop what you're doing, grandma. Get us undersea:
I got the biggest fucking job of your life."

Now listen, you little potty-mouth,
I'm the best at what I do. I was dragging
tusks out of mammoth graveyards before anyone
in the whole sorry human species
could talk. I used to work for tyrannosaurs—
you know those six-inch steak-knife premaxillaries
in the dinosaur museum? Those are nothing.
I was there when a fish *invented* teeth,
that was a real ornery fish believe you me and there ain't no
    reason,
ain't *no* job big enough, for you to use that language with me.

"No," he says. "I mean really fucking big. Listen."

You know how hard it is to flag down a submarine at rush hour?

So anyway it ain't no island cruise:
we're down there in the coldest black,

the abyssal plain they call it, and Rob points.
Smug.
There's this tentacle lying there, wide as a jet liner,
and even I gotta squint a little to see the rest of the guy—
wings and tail and squid-head,
potbelly like a whole slimy continent and he's on his face
groaning
over two fallen-out fangs the size of mountains.
Yeah, have your little laugh, Rob: I admit it,
all the things I seen and done,
and no one told me Great Cthulhu had teeth.

I won't talk 'til he quits smirking.
"Well?"
(Says Rob.)
"You got a tugboat? Aircraft carrier?"
We both know the carrying-off's not the problem.
See, we ain't looters in my line of work. We take,
but we pay. Every time. Cash on the humans' pillows, right?
The fish wanted fish food. Tyrannosaurs traded
sparkly flints, real small ones, so they could fit
in one tyrannosaurus hand, and the mammoths had
these fancy carved branches. But the Great Old One,
well, nowadays everyone knows what he wants.
And I don't know if you understand this, Rob,
but just by coming,
just by standing here being what we are,
I think we've already sealed the deal.

And far as I'm concerned, if the world's fit to end,
I know just where to start. You see this? I still got
a chocolate-sticky string stuck in my hair. Rob's a brat
but he ain't dumb or lazy: he makes the thoroughest lists
on the continent. Every cavity, every tartarous muckhole
and ungrateful child, we've got it all written down,

so let me tell you, and listen close,
'cause this time tomorrow every one of you will be gone:
mad, wretched, and sacrificed,
nothing left of you all
but a penny on the pillow.

The Wives of Miu Fum

We found a cave in the side of the mountain and built Miu Fum a death-house as large and well-furnished as any living man's.

Rui, who read to him by candlelight, brought handmade books with golden covers. Sae, who managed his household, brought a platter pulled by four strong deer, stacked with honeyed meat, shining fruit, and fluffy powdered-sugar confections, never to be eaten.

I, who was nothing until he pulled me from the riverside huts — I brought a single flower.

Sae choked us with incense. Rui repeated the death litany until her voice cracked. I sang, though not well. He had loved to sing with me.

The tomb would not be sealed until the fourth day. When Rui and Sae rode back to the palace weeping, I stayed, running my fingers along the lacquered wood.

I could almost believe that his spirit would walk down the hall to me. But I never heard his voice no matter how long I listened, fooling myself with incense and gold.

A Toast to the Hero Upon Her
Defeat of the Wyrm of L'Incertain

CHLOE

Dawn makes brass of the air and I raise my cup:
I, to whom you whispered first of glass-scorched earth
and the burning beast: I who calmed your lips with mine
murmuring to you that you were strong enough:
I who bore your shield through silver peaks at last:
I have earned this first address.
May you ring on smiling tongues forever:
Fear-scorning, scale-splitting, all-freeing — Hail!

CHORUS

Hail! She holds the dragon's heart in hand,
Ruby-hard, unmoving — and her own beats strong.
Hail! And let the hero's lovers sing.

NADIA

Joy-music breaks like the sea and I raise my cup:
I who worship the knife of your eyes:
I who wore your collar on the burning crags,
for you taught me to give my body to courage:
I who craved your orders and your hands:
My turn, now, to order the world.
May you live long past the crumbling hills,
Victorious and strong as ramparts — Hail!

CHORUS

Hail! Her corded arms, her shining mail,
The panther swiftness of her flashing hand!
Hail! Let those who love her best give praise.

AMBROISE

Wyrm's teeth sharpen the wine and I raise my cup:
I who counted breaths in hushed night, homebound,
praying for your footfalls: I who fell upon you three,
my loves, flame-braving, loud with life and pain
and closed your blackened wounds with kisses.
Now I shout to wake the world.
May you live — we live — whole with this joy,
Through every coming rain of arrows — Hail!

CHORUS

Hail! She holds them all around her now,
Fourfold laurels, earned, and shared with all.
Hail! For love that ends in victory.

The Chartreuse Monster

Light filled the convention centre. It poured in through multicolored glass, dodged the latticed rafters, and shone down on the Chartreuse Monster. Rough fins jutted down at strange angles from the Monster's body. Bristly ridges shadowed its inanimate eyes and profuse antennae stuck out over the bulging, fang-filled mouth. Indrani tried to ignore it, but willpower and attention span shrank as her sleep debt grew, and the monster's presence nagged at her.

The artist's alley smelled like ink and metal and soap-deprived bodies, but it looked like a fairyland, she thought. A very loud, bright, crowded fairyland with sketches and digital paintings in every nook. A few yards away, a scruffy cartoonist sat signing things, and his devotees lined up filling half the room. Indrani was hanging out here with Quinn, trying to catch her breath between panels on astrobiology and military ethics so she'd have energy left for the dance in the evening. But Quinn wasn't helping, and neither was the monster.

"What is it, anyway?" she kept asking.

"A chartreuse monster," said Quinn, absorbed in someone else's art book. He flipped through a series of demonesses and harpies, paused on a mermaid. "That's what. Why are you so annoying?"

Quinn's aura was thick and chunky and nervous. Worry streamed out of his skin and made dark, ugly clouds all around him. Quinn was worried no one would buy his art, and he'd be out several hundred dollars for admission and transportation — dollars he couldn't really afford. Indrani had liked his art when she saw it online. It was full of swooshy, dynamic lines and deep colors, and she liked those. In real life, though, it was all covered with his aura. When she touched it, she could feel faint, spongy remnants of him on her fingertips, and she got queasy.

There was no way to explain all that in words Quinn would understand.

"You're just tense," said Indrani.

"*I'm* tense?" said Quinn. "You're freaking out all the way here because of Laska, and then you have a nervous breakdown when we get here because of

Laska, and now you're freaking out because of a stupid paper-maché gimmick, and *I'm* the one who's tense?"

"I'm going over here," said Indrani.

"Here" was a more or less random direction. Almost everyone in the building was getting chunky or wavy by now. To one side, four girls in superhero outfits sat chatting, sipping coffee, but their auras strobed painfully bright with nervous tension. In another direction, three bearded fanboys with stuffed shoulder dragons argued with each other. Their auras spun, bobbed, and swung like drunkards. There was an oddly strong current of happiness under it all, for most of them, but no peace. Indrani was hungry for peace.

She checked her bag and wandered into the main art show, though it wasn't that much less chaotic than the alley. She found the least objectionable corner and fixed her eyes on a lunar landscape. The bidsheet was filled for this one, and the artist was doing well. There was pride here, mixed with relief. That might be enough for now. She pictured her feet in the lunar sand and the quiet, the absolute stillness. She took a deep breath.

Just above the moon painting hung a print of a spaceport bustling with life, in all the colors, textures, and energies Indrani was trying to avoid. She didn't want to look at the spaceport, but the bright characters drew her in. They looked familiar.

"You like it?" said a woman behind her.

Indrani turned around. Pride and relief shone out of the woman's pockmarked skin, along with gentleness.

"It's nice," she said. She was relieved to realize this was the truth, for once. She pointed to the spaceport. "It reminds me of the station in *Matuta's Truth.*"

The artist crossed her arms. "Freakin' Laska. But yeah, that's what I was going for, too, more or less."

"That book saved my life," said Indrani.

She said it half to spite Quinn, who'd warned her in no uncertain terms not to talk about Laska anymore. She also said it because of the artist's aura, because she looked like she'd get it, like she wanted the connection.

"Yeah?" said the artist.

Her aura gave a warm little pulse. Empathy. Good. A relief, saying this to someone who got it.

"Laska understood how everything is. How crazy it gets. But he never lost hope. He wrote about bookworms and misfits and magical people, and I felt like if they could get through all that shit that happened in his books and still turn out okay, then maybe I..." She looked down, rubbed her wrists. "I wanted to tell him that. While he was here. I thought he deserved to know."

The artist shook her head. "I feel bad for the guy. All that money, but no family, no kids, no wife. I just hope he has a good priest. And someone to read him his fan mail."

"Yeah," said Indrani. And that thought made her stomach do a lonely little flip, so she slunk away. She sat next to Quinn and thought about death, and how it made even less sense than a chartreuse monster. The monster still stared at her, implacable and inanimate, and she couldn't tear her mind away.

Abraham Z. N. Laska was the whole reason Indrani had gone to this stupid convention. There was Quinn, too, but honestly she hadn't liked Quinn enough to drive across the country just to meet him. The whole way, she thought about Laska to keep herself sane, while her brother Swaran's aura jangled impatiently in the driver's seat. Swaran's best friend's aura kept shifting from green to white and back, fighting off nausea, and the three strangers who took up the rest of the van got progressively grumpier as the trip went on. Indrani repeated her plans in her head like a mantra, trying to block out everything else. She was going to meet Laska. She'd get him to sign her books. She'd get her picture taken with him. She'd tell him how much he had meant to her all these years. He'd smile and nod and sign things and not even notice, because he probably got people telling him that all the time, but hell, at least she'd have said it to him. At least she'd have seen his face.

She wondered what color Laska's aura would be. She figured probably blue. A gentle blue, but a deep blue, a wise blue.

"Not a word about Laska," said Quinn when he joined the caravan, six hours in. "Seriously. I have heard all of your rants about him before."

Quinn was already getting lumpy at the edges. Indrani decided she had liked him a lot better online, as an elfin avatar with a bow and arrow.

"Whatever," said Indrani. "You're a fan, too, you know."

"I'm in the actual fan club," said Quinn. Indrani was not. They had been over this, online, many times.

Indrani hunched her shoulders against the seat of the car. She'd never written him a letter, either. She'd been too shy. But that hardly mattered now. This time would make up for everything.

Quinn wouldn't leave her alone, though. "You could have joined if you cared so much."

"I just never really saw the point of a club," said Indrani.

"Point?" said Quinn. "Does there need to be a point? I'll show you the point of my arrows. That's a point!"

"Not as pointy as a sword."

"Know what's pointier? A *shatter* spell!"

"That's not pointy," said Indrani. "The shards left over after are pointy, maybe."

As long as she could keep him in game speak, Quinn was okay.

The real problem started when they got to the convention centre. Early-arriving fans milled in a crowd around the registration desk, and their auras were dark, disappointed, angry.

"What's going on?" said Indrani.

Quinn blinked at her. "What's what? That's the registration desk." He didn't have auras to go by, and he hadn't got close enough yet to see their faces.

"They're upset," said Indrani.

"They look fine to me," said Quinn. "Ugh, you're so weird. Look, I'll just go up and hold everyone's place, but you better be there when I need your ID."

"Okay," said Indrani.

Quinn went up, stood in line, chatted with the people next to him. Indrani watched his aura. It flickered and dimmed, and he abruptly broke out of the line, stumbling back to her.

"Laska's not here," he said.

"What?" said Indrani.

"He's not coming," said Quinn.

"What?" said Indrani.

Quinn explained. His aura didn't grate the way most people's auras did when they lied. Still, Indrani had to check with the desk herself before she believed him.

"But he was in remission," she reminded Quinn. "Getting better. All the press releases said so. All your stupid fan club bulletins said so."

He had apparently failed to get better.

Laska had lied, it seemed, about how serious it was. He hadn't wanted to worry the public. He had been hoping to make his guest of honor speech and talk at panels and sign autographs and get pictures taken and make everyone happy, and lie, and pretend things were fine. A hard thing to do when you can't sit unsupported anymore.

He was in a hospice somewhere, fixing loose ends. And not, as promised, at the convention.

"Oh, don't give me that look," said Quinn. "It's not my fault. I'm upset, too."

"I paid all this money," Indrani mumbled. It was a stupid, selfish thing to say, but she was feeling stupid with shock. "I sat in a car for two days."

"I know, I know," said Quinn. "Look, Gaiman and Czerneda and Stross and all those other guys will still be there. I'll still be selling art. We'll still have fun. Just don't cry on me, okay?" Quinn's aura wavered and lumped up. "Seriously, don't. I don't know what to do. Oh, god." He looked over at Swaran. "She's crying. Do something."

"I'm not," said Indrani. "I'm not crying."

"Come on," said Swaran, putting an arm around her shoulder. "We're gonna go check out the hotel rooms and get you some quiet time."

"I'm not crying," said Indrani.

It was the last night. Indrani had the free books, the action figures, the silly pinback buttons, the photographs of cosplayers, the autographs from people she liked only slightly less than Laska. She had flirted unnecessarily, asked insightful questions at science and worldbuilding panels, danced until she felt sick, watched prestigious awards handed out like candy. She was still not satisfied.

The Chartreuse Monster still bothered her. If everything else had been okay, she might have shrugged and let the mystery stay a mystery. But she was exhausted and bombarded and she had missed her last chance to see Laska. She wasn't going to let another last chance go past.

She waited, looking at the ceiling in the darkness, until Swaran and the other people in the hotel room were asleep. Then she slipped out of bed, took a key, went to the door, closed it carefully behind her, and padded in her pajamas down the curling stairs.

The door to the artist's alley was shut tight, with a "Closed" sign, but it wasn't locked. Indrani pushed the door open as quietly as she could. She shuffled forwards through the darkness, reaching forward until her hands met the monster's rough carapace. She leaned her head against it. She imagined she could almost hear some indefinable hum from inside, like machinery. Or like breathing. She pulled back a little so she could see the thing, moving her hands across it. Its hide was coarse and papery.

It was, she realized, easier to see than it ought to be. It almost had an aura. Not quite. Not the chaotic splashes of aura she found in art shows. The monster was dim and diffuse. It had been built by many hands. But it had been built with love. Love and fear.

One of her hands abruptly slipped across a panel. A recessed one, invisible from a distance.

She snuck around the side of the monster, peered at the thing. It was an alphabetical keypad. Like you'd use to put in a password.

That was insane. What would they need a password for? But she was too tired and too crazy and too curious to leave it alone. She tried *abcdefg*. That didn't work. She tried *password* and *pass123*. Those didn't work either.

And then it hit her.

There were monsters in Laska's books, in places. There had been one, a *chartreuse* one, in one of his very first. *Plasticity*. An obscure book from before he was famous, one it was hard to find these days. She couldn't believe she hadn't remembered. She'd never pictured the monster looking remotely like this. But it had been a good monster. Strange and maddening and alien and dangerous, but ultimately a sweet thing, a hopeful one. Like everything Laska did.

That was what the monster was. A tribute. Someone in love the way fans fell in love had built the thing at the last minute, as a distant second best to having Laska there himself. A coded message to those who knew enough to care.

Plasticity swung open a hidden door in the monster's side. Too tired and too crazy and too curious to leave it alone, she stepped through.

The moment she opened the door, a small fluorescent light sprang to life, illuminating the inside of the monster. Art hung laundrylike all over, fluttering slightly in the breeze from hidden ventilation slats in the ceiling. Good art and terrible art dangled in front of her, all styles of art, with no rhyme or reason to it at all. Even Quinn's swooshy, dynamic lines and deep colors had found their way into a corner. Fan club submissions, she supposed.

The rest of the monster was a mess of wires, lights, tubes, monitors, and IV lines. And on a small, neat mattress, plugged in to way too many wires for any one person, lay a wizened little man. A man with a blue aura, a wise kind of blue. He was propped half-upright, gazing sleepily at a tilted viewscreen in front of him. A night nurse sat on a stool at the other side, reading a paperback novel; a curtain to her side half-obscured a chemical toilet and a dispenser of hand sanitizer.

Indrani's hand went to her mouth. "I'm sorry." She backed away. "I'll go. I... I shouldn't have... I'm sorry."

"No, it's okay," said the night nurse. She put a bookmark in her novel and set it down. "He said he wouldn't mind if someone figured it out. You're not the first."

Indrani shook her head. She wondered if she was too tired, if she'd fallen asleep back in her room after all. "But how—"

The night nurse shrugged. "No family. Nothing tying him down. But lots of money. He wanted to be here, whatever way he could. I think it's a little silly, as last requests go, but it's what he wanted, so he made it happen." She gestured to the viewscreen, which was black — but an odd kind of black. Not a turned-off black. A black that said it looked out into the darkened convention center, even now.

"He sees everything," said the night nurse.

Indrani looked at the viewscreen, and she looked down at the man. He turned his head ever so slightly in her direction and met her eyes. Opened his mouth, then shut it. Couldn't speak anymore. But he put out a hand and beckoned weakly.

Indrani dropped to her knees next to the mattress.

"I want you to know," she said, "that *Matuta's Truth* saved my life."

Abraham Z. N. Laska died that weekend, surrounded by his family: the misfits and bookworms and magical people. His friends and those who had known him held a service the following week, after Indrani's brother had already dragged her home. She held a secret minute of silence for him, alone in her room. Through the grief, she was strangely content. She'd done what she needed to.

Laska's books survived him, as the best books do. And so, in a way, did the Chartreuse Monster. Hollowed out and cleaned, with the cameras removed, it reappeared in corners at that convention for years. Every once in a while, as someone passed, they would look at it and pause, and smile to themselves. Sadly. Fondly. Knowingly.

CPSIA information can be obtained
at www.ICGtesting.com
Printed in the USA
FSHW010027130319
56269FS